GARY L. STUART

MY BROTHER
MYSELF

BOOK 2

A DR. LISBETH SOCORRO NOVEL

My Brother, Myself: A Dr. Lisbeth Socorro Novel, Book 2

Copyright © 2023 by Gary L. Stuart. All Rights Reserved.

For information about this title or to order other books and/or electronic media, contact the publisher:
Gleason & Wall Publishers
2039 East Glenn Dr., Phoenix, AZ 85020
www.garylstuart.com
gary@garylstuart.com

ISBNs: 978-1-7368946-8-2 (print)
        978-1-7368946-9-9 (eBook)

Printed in the United States of America

Cover and Interior design: 1106 Design, Phoenix, AZ

To Kathleen and Kara

OTHER BOOKS BY GARY L. STUART

The Ethical Trial Lawyer

Ethical Litigation

The Gallup 14

Miranda—The Story of America's Right to Remain Silent

Aim For The Mayor—Echoes From Wounded Knee

Innocent Until Interrogated—The True Story of the Buddhist Temple Massacre and the Tucson Four

Angus Riding the Rio Chama

Ten Shoes Up

The Valles Caldera

Anatomy Of A Confession—The Debra Milke Case

The Last Stage to Bosque Redondo

Let's Disappear

Call Him Mac—Ernest W. McFarland— The Arizona Years

Emergence

Tracking Tom Horn's Confession

Shared Memories

Nobody Did Anything Wrong But Me— The Northern Arizona University Mass Shooting

The Sandra Day O'Connor College of Law at Arizona State University—1965 to 2020

CONTENTS

BRICKSTONE CATO-
SPECIAL AGENT—FBI

Brickstone Cato got his nick name, "Brick," in high school on the football field. He played fullback and led his Class 5 high school team to two consecutive state titles. In his senior year he stood six foot three, weighed 210 pounds, and boasted an eight pack. His high school annual described him as sure-footed, rock hard, and most likely to crash through life just like he crashed through the front line at football games, math classes, and half the girls in the senior class. But no one predicted his upward spiral through the chains of command and influence in the Federal Bureau of Investigation.

He was a consummate cop who hated the limelight and media interviews about his job. To his dismay, he was ordered by FBI HQ to give an interview to a cheeky CNN reporter named Sal Durango.

"So, Agent Cato, thanks again for agreeing to this interview and giving CNN an inside look at . . ."

"Nah, Mr. Durango, this is not an *inside look*. That's not what I'm doing here," Brick said. "This is a background interview only, not on the record, and not for publication on CNN news, or otherwise. I only agreed to a brief overview of what the FBI's FREST unit does in a small number of American cases."

"Hey, man, that's not how I got it from my editor in Atlanta. I flew here to Quantico planning on a great story. Ya know I'm totally on the FBI's side and you guys really smoke if you want my opinion . . ."

"Smoke what?" Brick asked.

"I mean CNN respects the FBI and all, that's smoke, isn't it?"

"Mr. Durango, I'm just going over the ground rules here—the standard news media rules apply to all information given by FBI units to the media. This is background only, not on the record, and not for playback on TV. Got it?"

"Whatever you say, man, but I gotta record what you say. There was a time when reporters just took notes. Now we record interviews. My editors want a short, typed summary by me, about my digital conversation. We want to support the FBI. I'm here for basic information about your unit. I shoot it to my editor, and he then decides whether to go on air, or not."

Brick smiled. "Sounds totally fair to me. But if you run on TV what I say, and spin it as a hot news item, I'll have to open a file on you. You don't want to be on file with the FBI, do you?"

"Okay," the twenty-something reporter gushed. "Now you said something about a fresh unit or something? What is that?"

"I said FREST, not fresh. We are a highly specialized unit here at Quantico. FREST is the acronym for *Forensics Research Evidentiary Suspect Team*."

"Okay, that raises two questions. What do you research? Are you just researchers or do you guys make arrests and carry guns and wear black jackets with giant yellow letters on the back saying you're FBI?"

"We carry guns when necessary and we occasionally make arrests, but always in concert with field agents and sometimes local law enforcement. Our primary mission is researching and evaluating stalled cases sent to us by law enforcement agencies all over the country."

"Wadda ya mean 'stalled'?"

"We review cases that are still open but stalled because the local agency has no clues, insufficient forensic evidence, no suspects, no new places to look, and most importantly, likely to experience a fourth case sometime soon."

"Fourth case? What's that mean?"

"Most of our work is on serial murder cases. Mind if I ask how old you are?"

The reporter narrowed his gray eyes clenched his jaw. "How old? Wadda you care how old I am?"

"Because I don't know how much historical context you need to understand serial murder cases. If you were born in the seventies, then you might already know something about serial murder cases."

"I was born in the eighties, late eighties. What does my age have to do with serial murderers?"

"Nothing, except that the FBI noted an increase in the frequency of serial killers in the seventies. Before that there was no name for it—the media started calling those early cases 'serial.' About ten years ago, the FBI adopted a definition of a serial killer as 'the unlawful killing of two or more victims by the same offender in separate events.' The rise in serial murder cases back then caused the FBI to create units and departments to study and analyze the psychological science and data points of serial killers. One example you're probably heard of is the Behavioral Science Unit, later identified as the FBI Behavioral Analysis Unit."

"Yeah, I remember that, like that guy in *Silence of the Lambs*, based on a real case I heard."

"No, that was a movie, pure fiction, not a real case."

"Well, you're the FBI. So, I'll take your word on it. But you know, I'm unclear on the science here. Do you mean, like, only crazy people kill multiple times or multiple people?"

Brick and Mr. Durango had been sitting in his office for under ten minutes when Brick's eyes starting to bristle. He began finger-tapping the steel topped desk and rubbing his brow as if to ward off a headache.

"Well, that's a fine question, Mr. Durango. Glad you asked. You're interested in the connection between psychopathy and serial murders. Let me give you a brief overview. The academic and science communities we've used over the years have some answers to your very interesting question. Fact is, serial killers are not all the same, they don't kill for the same reasons, and are caught sometimes almost by accident. But the best of them, by best I mean most prolific, and those who get big media coverage are often identified by the same certain traits. Here are a few we see quite often. Sensation seeking, a lack of remorse or guilt, impulsivity, a need to be in charge, and most often, predatory behavior. Do you know what psychiatrists think when they see these traits in a patient?"

"No sir. I've never interviewed a psychiatrist. No crazies in my family, either."

"Good for you. But 'crazy' is not a diagnosis. When a psychiatrist sees these traits, they have to rule out *psychopathic personality disorder.* Serial killers are not just sociopaths; they are psychopaths. The FBI is actively on the hunt for psychopaths, but we mostly ignore sociopaths—state agencies handle those just fine. We look for those particular traits in men identified as psychopathic by all US cases sent to us, as well as other sources. We focus on serial murderers afflicted with serious mental disorders. That's why we take courses in and read reviews within the criminal justice system to understand, as lay observers, psychopathy, and its relationship to serial murder."

"Like, how do you do that?" Mr. Durango asked, even though he looked like he wanted to be someplace else.

"We know as law enforcement officers that psychopathy is a personality disorder manifested in people who use false charm, hidden manipulation, overt intimidation, and violence to control others. They do this to satisfy their own selfish needs. So, Mr. Durango, do you have a sufficient sense of what FREST does here at Quantico?"

"Yeah, I get it. When you run out of normal people to arrest you go to the funny farm and see if any of the psychos there did the crime."

When CNN left his office, Brick took a deep breath. He had never tried to explain that serial killers rarely leave clues, kill without known motives, or connections to their victims, and often cross state lines. The simple fact was that, once local law enforcement excludes local sources and suspects, and they have no viable investigative leads, their cases land in his office.

The thin file on his desk, FBI-FREST #00104-2018, matched their profile. Here, a fourth murder was only a matter of time. Three cases were stalled, stymied by a serial killer who chooses victims sharing five unique elements. One—all victims were male identical twins. Two—they were shot on their birthdays. Three—in different states. Four—all died from head wounds inflicted by the same .22 caliber pistol. Five—the only forensic evidence at each scene was hair follicles.

The hair follicles always ruled out the survivor twins. Given the known similarities, Brick was sure there would be a fourth twin murder and it would not happen in New Hampshire, Massachusetts, or Vermont. It would probably happen in some other New England state. He surmised the serial killer knew better than to kill twice in the same state.

The New Hampshire case was first—two and a half years ago. The victim, Emiliano Estancia, was a twenty-four-year-old

Hispanic man who lived with his wife and an adopted child. The City of Manchester employed him in their water services department. He was well liked, quiet, with no police record, and had one year of community college. Someone murdered him on his birthday, December 14, 2014, by shooting him twice in the base of his skull as he sat in his City of Manchester water services truck on a job in a lightly populated part of town at 6:15 in the morning. His autopsy confirmed the bullets were .22 caliber shorts. He had no known enemies, addictions, bad habits, or tattoos. There were no witnesses, no plausible explanations, limited crime scene forensic evidence, and no viable clues as to the identity of the killer.

Six months later, another male identical twin was murdered in Salem, Massachusetts, on his birthday, June 5, 2015, by shooting him in the forehead with the same .22 caliber pistol loaded with .22 shorts. Caleb Lawrence was black, single, gay, unemployed, and living in his parent's home. At the time of his murder, he was confined to a wheelchair because of a spinal fracture three years earlier, which had rendered him paraplegic.

The third stalled murder case happened six months ago. Harington Schwartz was celebrating his twenty-nineth birthday on September 4, 2015, when he was shot in the back of his head while sitting on his front porch in Burlington, Vermont. Same gun. He had been listening to an Audible book on his iPhone. He had no known enemies, no serious criminal record, except for one DUI and a half-dozen speeding tickets in two states. And like the first two cases, the only forensic evidence found was hair follicles that cleared his survivor twin in all three states. There were no witnesses, no suspects, and no arrests.

ALL HANDS ON DECK

The mandatory Monday morning AHOD meeting started like every other Monday morning did at FREST. Brick sat side by side with his lead analyst, Lee Hyori Cheong. While accidental, seeing them sitting next to one another at the head of the five-foot wide table was a contrast in body types *and* personality. Brick, at six foot four, weighing over 220, liked to crack wise at meetings. Lee, at five foot two, weighed barely over a hundred pounds and never told jokes or laughed at his. He smiled at the slightest sense of anything funny and she frowned when he did. But they shared a common trait that made them very good at this job—they worked furiously to catch the worst of the worst the criminal world offered—serial killers. They were worse than mass murderers because they are rarely caught at a crime scene. Conversely, mass murderers mostly died at the scene of their crimes—gun in hand. Serial murderers were experts at evasion and existed off all criminal justice radars.

"Okay, are we A.H.O.D., Lee?" Brick asked without looking at her.

"All hands on deck," she answered, leaning forward to the middle of their space at the end of the table to fish out a file folder.

"Take note everybody," Lee said. "Write the file number down because Brick will be keeping the print copy on his desk for a while. It's double zero 104-2018. He is taking lead himself on this one because he thinks it's hotter than my mother's Kimchi."

The swarthy, overweight guy on the far end looked up from his yellow pad. "Kimchi hot? Christ Almighty, yawl know I'm from San by God Antonio, home of the Alamo and the Texas Chiltepin, which I'm proud to say registers 100,000 to 265,000 in Scoville heat units. For you upper East Coast elites, that's triple what Korean Kimchi registers."

Brick held up both hands, palms motioning downward.

"Cut the bypassing, guys, we need to jump on this today. Law enforcement in three states have no clues on three definite serial murder cases that are clearly connected by means or persons unknown. One unique Unsub exists, and he or she puts a shiny gloss on the term *unidentified*. Got it? We are the only agency on the planet that might get in close enough to spook this particular unidentified subject—hell's fire—he may be not just unidentified—he may be unidentifiable."

"Okay, boss," said Agent Abentito Spontani, fondly known as Abe. "What exactly makes this guy unidentifiable?"

"Because suspects like him are virtually unknown in CODIS, or inside any other active serial murder investigation. We have a new clinical assistant here, guys. Welcome Cynthia Myers, from Nebraska, right Cynthia?"

The newest member of Brick's team nodded in his direction.

"Yes, Agent Cato, I'm a psychiatric nurse practitioner. My work at the Cleveland Clinic evolved over a three-year period and ranged from assessing psychosis in adolescent patients to using forensic tools. The goal there was to try and anticipate psychotic breakdown so treatment centers will better understand both etiology and treatment choices."

"Alright, thank you, Cynthia. Now, the agencies investigating three connected murders over the last two years connect the cases both forensically and methodologically. Crime scene forensics at all three crime scenes captured hair follicles that served two purposes: they ruled out prime suspects—family members. And they partially identified the racial makeup of our Unsub."

Abe, almost always the most inquisitive member of the group, interrupted.

"Brick, can hair follicles rule out race or ethnicity?"

"Maybe, Abe. We know human hair can be associated with a particular racial group based on established models for each group. Forensic examiners differentiate between hairs of Caucasoid, meaning European ancestry, or Mongoloid, meaning Asian ancestry, and Negroid, meaning African ancestry, all of which exhibit microscopic characteristics that distinguish one racial group from another. Head hairs are generally considered best for determining race, although hairs from other body areas can be useful. And the hair at all three scenes was head hair and is suspected by local examiners at each crime scene as coming from the same head. They think all three sets of hair follicles are from an adult head. And they caution that head hairs from people of mixed racial ancestry might indicate, under the microscope, characteristics attributed to more than one racial group."

"Sounds shaky to me," Lee said.

"Right," Brick agreed, "but shaky evidence is at least some evidence. What the three agencies all say is that the hair follicles are consistent with one another—so they think we're looking for the same guy as the Unsub in all three cases. Not sure, of course, but there is another forensic clue that tightens that loop. All three Vics died from gunshots to the head from a .22 caliber bullet, a .22 short. All bullets were fired from the same gun—that's what three different crime labs say. One's for sure, the other shaky.

Taken together it looks like the same guy. And there's one more thing that is connected—the victims were all identical twins."

"Hold on," Lee said. "I don't see the twins' connection."

Brick pushed back in his swivel chair and rubbed his temples. "Maybe connection is too strong a term. But the same person killed all three Vics, because all three were shot by the same gun. The fact that they were all twins ties the knot fairly tight. Our Unsub *is* a serial twin killer. Well, maybe. I've been connecting these dots for two days and I'm typing up an allocation sheet. You'll get it later this morning. Log all assessments in the digital file—double zero 104-2018. I'll respond individually to each of you. Plan on giving me strong leads or a major change of focus next Monday, same time, same place, AHOD meeting number two on the twins' case. Read all three complete agency files. There's a lot there I haven't mentioned here."

ELEVEN MONTHS AGO.
MANCHESTER, NEW HAMPSHIRE

Before even realizing the driver's door was opening, Emiliano felt the metal stick or pole or whatever was against his left ear.

"What the . . . ?" he said, before being cut off.

"Emiliano, do what I say," the voice behind him said. "Slide over or you're dead where you sit."

Emiliano turned his head toward the voice. The man pushed him, growling. "You have a twin, and you don't love him, right?"

The man moved from his back to his side and Emiliano was stunned to see a man wearing the same style hard-hat he was wearing. It was milk white with a red and gold seal on front identifying him as an employee of the City of Manchester. He wore the same uniform; jeans and a lightweight sweatshirt, with a red and chartreuse safety vest and a tool belt the same as those issued to all water services workers. Once settled on the passenger side of his old two-door Chevrolet Silverado, he dared a look at the man holding the gun against the side of his face.

"I have money," Emiliano said, choking back a sudden need to spit or throw up.

"Your money won't save you. Your twin won't save you because you don't really love him, do you?"

"My brother? You mean Ernie? What are you talking about . . . ?"

The man's voice was halting, and his forehead looked sweaty. "His adult name is Ernesto, not Ernie. I know you don't love him even though today is your birthday. And his. But you might as well be a bastard because he is not here, is he? Where is he and why are you having a party tonight without him? Tell me the truth and you can go to the party. Lie to me and I'll kill you right now."

Emiliano felt a burning urge to urinate in his pants. He could feel sweat building up under his armpits and felt like he might pass out. He'd never been brave, didn't like camping, and never engaged in contact sports in high school, not even baseball. He was afraid to bat and could not imagine sliding into home plate. He liked chess. Ernie was the brave one— played football in the fall, rugby in the summer, and was into rock climbing in good weather. Actually, that's why he wasn't coming to their birthday party tonight—he was rock climbing in Vermont somewhere.

"I don't understand. You are not robbing me, but you know about my birthday? What is going on?"

"Look at me, you ungrateful assy fucker. I've seen your pictures—you mostly by yourself—your brother sometimes in a picture, but Facebook makes it clear. You and Ernesto live separate lives. Right?"

"I don't know what you want, but I'll do whatever you say. Just take the gun away from my face, please."

The man with the gun moved it from his left cheek to behind his left ear. "Can you feel the muzzle of my gun? It says you know exactly why I'm here and what I want from you, you dirty piece of cow shit. I might kill you anyhow, but I'm here because you don't love him and somehow think you can celebrate his birthday without him. Don't you fucking know that's wrong! You are all he has in the world! I read his page too. He climbs rocks to hide his shame at the way you treat him. I been watching both of you on Facebook all year. Living separate lives like you weren't even brothers, not to mention products of a single egg in a mother who doesn't seem to exist. You didn't invite her either, did you?"

"My mother? If you know so much about me and Ernie, how come you don't know that I *did* invite her?"

Emiliano never felt the first blast. The man in the driver's seat of his truck pushed the muzzle of the gun hard into the skin and bone behind Emiliano's ear and fired twice in rapid succession. He reached in his shirt pocket and pulled out a Kleenex, opening its folds, and shook loose hair follicles onto the now bent forward dead man's body. He put his sunglasses back on, got out of Emiliano's truck, and walked back into the rear parking lot where he'd parked his 2010 Honda Fury motorcycle. He put his helmet on and pulled out onto Highway 101, headed north, never gunning it over sixty.

It was 6:20 and he knew the other truck with Emiliano's three co-workers would not get here until 6:30. He'd watched this parking lot for three consecutive days. The routine was always the same: first, Emiliano shows up a little after six, opens his coffee thermos, and stuffs down two Dunkin' donuts and an apple fritter while waiting for his crew. They'd find his body in the truck. No one else around.

Over the next week, the City of Manchester's water services division would mourn his loss. The county would insist on a quick autopsy, and the city police would begin an unfruitful investigation. The hair follicles and the two bullets lodged inside

Emiliano Estancia's brain cavity would be the only forensic evidence.

In seven months, the Estancia murder case will be transferred to FREST, 511 miles away in Quantico, Virginia.

PRESENT DAY. QUANTICO, VIRGINIA.
FREST CONFERENCE ROOM

Brick smiled his CNN smile. "Good morning, Jacks and Jills of the FBI. Happy to see well-scrubbed faces amid the donuts and coffee mugs. How about we start with individual gut reactions to our newest and most challenging case? It's a serial three-murder case in New England. Victim number one in the series was Emiliano Estancia—Lee, what's your first take on this one?"

Lee, biting her lip, started her assessment as though it were a mathematics problem she couldn't solve.

"I'm betwixt and between on this one. The killing was brutal—gun barrel on the Vic's skin and two shots fired? Wow, not sure I've ever seen that. Crime scene photos show blood spatter all over the truck and must have been all over the Unsub too. Not sure what that tells us about him. Was he enraged? Or just stupid? Did the Vic start at him, raising a fist maybe? There's lots to puzzle on the forensics, but the actual shooting from arm's length says something; I just can't read it."

Brick pointed his finger at Asot. "I know you did a stint in ballistics analysis. Lee's focus on the double bullets directly on the skin is insightful. What do you think?"

Asot was rarely at a loss for words, and this was no exception.

"Does everyone in the room get the significance of what happened in this case? Let me give you the ballistics. Fact is, almost the only time you see death by gun directly on the skin is in suicide cases. That's because anyone committing suicide with a gun does not want to take the risk of missing. So, you put the gun in your mouth, or stick the muzzle on your forehead. But in homicide, it's different. The shooter almost never gets this close—that is, gun barrel on skin—because of the risk of the Vic turning away, getting your gun, or you shooting the bed, or wall or lounge chair, whatever. Let me chill you a bit about how bullets work at the muzzle-end of the barrel. Milliseconds after the hammer strikes the firing pin at the back end of the shell casing, a hot cloud of gas bursts inside the shell and screams its way down the barrel before the bullet gets to the business end of the barrel. If the shooter's gun muzzle is in touch with the Vic, the flame from burning gas burns his skin in a star-like pattern. This shows up as a burn-ring around the bullet hole. Then, the bullet shoots out of the barrel. Behind the bullet is more skull and cavity. Projectile particles of gunpowder follow the bullet's trajectory. They cause *tattooing* on the skin that even morticians have trouble washing off. That's because those tiny but angry particles are actually embedded in the Vic's skin. And here's the thing, that soot on the head of the Vic is also on the hand of the shooter. Gruesome enough for yawl?"

Looking like she might faint, Cynthia clasped her hand over her mouth and raised her eyebrows to max height.

"My God, I've been involved with a few suicides and counseled family members, but never on the brutal mechanics of gunshot wounds. I can't imagine what would command the most depraved killer to shoot this way. Was he, the shooter, covered with blood, did you say that? I think that's important. It may say something about the Unsub none of us want to think about."

"Like what?" Brick asked.

"Like maybe the shooter wanted to feel his victim's hot blood. In the most bizarre cases, blood is crucial to feelings at the time of death and for years afterward, like vampires drinking blood and eating flesh."

Asot chimed back in.

"It's worse than I said. When the barrel of the gun is pushed onto the skin on your head, directly on the skull, the gases shoot under the skin, expand it, and then rip it apart in the explosion. You see, there's no space for the expanding gases to go except into the cranial cavity through the skull. Depending on the shape of the bullet, the entrance wound can look like an exit wound because there's an abrasion collar and a muzzle stamp in the same small place on the skin."

The room went quiet again, some sipped their coffee, and Cynthia blew her nose into the already-used Kleenex still in her bunched fist. Brick let silence settle for a minute before upping the trauma ante.

"Well, guys, that's where the choice of bullet shape makes a big difference. Our Unsub was using .22 caliber shorts with hollow point bullets. Asot, you're more up on gun science and technology than I am. Remind us about why some shooters use hollow point bullets."

"Sure," he said, putting his beat-up Starbucks travel container down on the table.

"Hollow points, sometimes called dum dums, or expanding points, are engineered to expand or mushroom after hitting their target. That makes them more lethal and more effective when defending yourself, and less likely to over-penetrate and injure innocent bystanders. They stay inside their body. What happens is the front of a hollow point flattens out—causing a lot more damage inside your skull and not exiting out in most cases. It rips up brain tissue like a piece of wood slammed down into a chipper shredder."

Lee jumped in.

"What's the technical difference between .22 caliber shorts and .22 long rifle bullets?"

Asot loved questions that turned him into an expert on anything.

"Well, Lee, that's a good question for this case. The .22 short was the first original .22 rimfire metallic cartridge in America. It's more than a hundred years old. The first revolver fired a .22 short. The .22 long is the second oldest .22 rimfire cartridge, invented years later at about the same weight but had 25 percent more black powder than the .22 short. But you know, you don't need more black powder if you're sticking the muzzle against the skull with the intent to kill, not wound. And you can do it with one shot—you don't need to pull the trigger twice."

"But," Brick interrupted, "our shooter in this case, in fact in all three cases, fired twice. What's that tell us?"

Cynthia raised her hand and got Brick's attention.

"It tells me the Unsub was in a psychotic state at the exact moment he fired the gun. He might not have known about the difference in black powder. All that mattered to him was to be sure to kill, and he might have thought the best way to make sure was to shoot twice."

Lee answered, "You might be right, but the hollow point already does that for him, right?"

Asot waived and pointed back to Brick.

"Brick, you're lead on this and if memory serves, you been in the FBI for nearly thirty-five years. How come our Unsub used hollow points and fired twice?"

"That's why these group sessions are absolutely necessary when we're trying to find a serial killer. Maybe our Unsub didn't know much about guns. Maybe he had a .22 pistol just for plinking or maybe shooting varmits somewhere. Maybe he only bought shorts because they're cheaper. Or, maybe there's a much more sinister reason layered over the other possibilities. Maybe we need to hear more from Cynthia about connecting the Unsub's choice of weapons with a deeper reality. Maybe in addition to mental illness and psychotic breakdown, he was really enraged by something his victim did, something no one else would notice because motive is so variable and so hard to pin down. Cynthia, can you enlighten us a little more?"

"I can guess, but without a social history and more insight into the Unsub's mental status, this is just speculation. Mental status is important. Emotional wounds are always something to look for when a mentally unstable person commits an act of violence. Sometimes they try to cure their own emotional trauma, or wounds, by traumatizing or hurting someone else. Everyone has emotional wounds—not getting picked on sports teams—getting a third-place ribbon when you thought you'd get a blue first-place ribbon—losing out to a sibling member for parental affection and hating them both for it. Emotional wounds are negative experiences that cause deep psychological trauma. If it felt brutal at the time you experience it, lasting repercussions can follow for decades. In many cases, emotional trauma creates a domino effect for other hurts that follow, or other people that don't appreciate how their conduct affects emotionally trauma-tized people. Maybe our Unsub is one on those—wounded and feeling the hateful need to wound others."

"Or maybe," Lee said, pursing her lips, "our Unsub knows little or nothing about guns. Maybe the gun is a relic that's been sitting in a metal box in his garage for years. Maybe he doesn't know shorts from long johns. He's new at this killing stuff, you think?"

Brick closed his folder and put down his ballpoint.

"Maybe you're both right. He could be emotionally wounded and gun ignorant. So, let's take up case number two in a shorter session the day after tomorrow. I moved these three cases to the top of our stack, but we've all got things to do on our existing case load."

SALEM, MASSACHUSETTS.
A MONTH EARLIER

Caleb Lawrence liked getting up early in the morning in summer because he had always been an outside kid—at the beach with his twin brother Chaim. His family and close friends could always tell them apart even though they were identical twins. Caleb was adventurous and loved the ocean and its power over beaches, houses, and towns during storms. Chaim was cautious and engaged the ocean only when Caleb was close by. They liked the same music, girls, and food, and both loved Salem. But Chaim was smarter, read more, talked less, and was the introvert to Caleb's outgoing personality. Caleb went to community college and Chaim went to the University of Vermont. After college Chaim stayed in Burlington and became a bank teller. Caleb did his two years, got an associate's degree, and went to work on Pickering Wharf, holding two half-time jobs for a harbor cruise company and a sporting goods store.

His carefree lifestyle ended two years earlier when he walked against the light on Congress Street and was run over by a laundry truck. He got disability coverage through Social Security but hadn't found wheelchair work yet. The car wreck put him in the hospital for three weeks, then in rehab for five months, and now in a wheelchair for the rest of his life. He was paraplegic; they said something about a T-12 spinal cord injury. As best he understood it, he had no motor or sensory function in his legs or pelvic area. His twin brother, Chaim, blew up and almost got arrested in the hospital for slugging one of the rehab therapists. The therapist had just told both twins and their mother that the word paraplegia came from Ionic Greek and translated to "half-stricken." Chaim took it as an insult.

Caleb got up before dark on his birthday, June 5, 2015, hoping for an early call from Chaim up in Vermont. Their house had a planked back porch with an overhang, a picnic table, a grill, and a cooler box. He made coffee in the kitchen, poured himself a cup, set it in the cup holder strapped to the side bar on his wheelchair, and wheeled himself out to the end of the backyard deck to wait for sunrise.

He had taken two sips when he saw a shadow at the end of the deck. Then he saw a man step out of the shadow and walk toward him.

"Hey," Caleb said, "what are you doing here in our back yard, don't you know . . . ?"

"Shut your face, Caleb. Why are you up so early on your birthday, Caleb? Waiting for your twin brother Chaim? Well, he isn't coming. I saw your Facebook posting. Pathetic, I'd say, you unloving shitface. You and he live what, hundreds of miles apart? He lives his life. You live yours. You owe him but here you are sitting on the porch in your fucking wheelchair drinking coffee not giving a fuck what he's doing on the best day of your twin years! Goddamn you to hell. You don't deserve to live because you forced him away, didn't you, and . . ."

Caleb was frozen by the look on the man's face and by the ice cold feel of what felt like a gun barrel pressing hard on the right said of his head, behind his ear. The man was pushing so hard on the gun that Caleb's neck twisted sideways over the side rail of his wheelchair. He tried to think of something to say, but words froze in his mouth. He never knew what hit him.

His mother, still in bed upstairs, heard two loud bursts from the back porch. She later told the police she didn't recognize them as gunshots. They asked if she'd ever heard gunshots before. No, she said, except in the movies. She had seen no one near the porch when she came downstairs ten minutes later. All she saw was the coffee machine on and the porch door open with the screen closed. She called out to Caleb, thinking he was enjoying his morning coffee on the porch, like always. She walked out, discovered his body on the deck, and nearly fainted herself. His face was full of blood, he was splayed out on the wood planks and his wheelchair was down the two wooden steps in the dirt at the far end of the porch. There were no guns anywhere. She assured the officers they had no guns in the house and her son had never fired one. He was confined to his wheelchair but had a positive outlook on life and had been looking forward to his birthday party later that day.

Mrs. Lawrence told the Salem 911 dispatcher that Caleb had been shot a few minutes ago. The dispatcher had the address on her screen when she asked for the son's name. The transcript revealed how small Salem was and how well known the Lawrence family was.

"The victim is your son, Mrs. Lawrence?"

"Yes, please hurry. We think he's dead, and . . ."

"What's your son's name, Ma'am?"

"Caleb. That's my son's name."

"Ma'am, I've dispatched the police and an ambulance. You should be hearing the siren in a minute or so. You're not far from the station. Ma'am, I know your other son, Chaim Lawrence. He's not at home right now, is he? I think I remember he moved to Vermont, right?"

"Yes, Chaim lives in Vermont. It's Caleb. He was sitting on the rear porch in his wheelchair and please send someone and, oh wait, I hear them coming."

The transcript says the caller hung up. The autopsy report called it a homicide. Massive brain damage caused by two hollow point bullets to the right side of decedent's head.

PRESENT-DAY QUANTICO, VIRGINIA— THIRD MEETING ON TWINS SERIAL MURDER CASES

Before the AHOD meeting started, Lee's phone rang. It was Brick asking her for a few minutes before the meeting. She walked down the hall, knocked on his door, and smoothed out her skirt.

"What's up, boss?" she asked, knowing he was not fond of that moniker.

"Lee, why is that you're the only one in our group to call me boss?"

"Dunno about that. Could be I'm the only one that wants your job when you hit the big R and move to Florida."

"Well, that may come before you're ready. This triple murder of twins is singularly bewitching."

"Wow, Brick. You've been reading the file on case number two—the one from witch haven, the unvarnished tourist trap known as Salem, Mass. Did you see the pics of the squad cars at the crime scene with their cute little witch symbols?"

"Yeah, I saw that, but I hope you also caught the alliteration in my description of that case."

"I minored in English, Brick. Remember? I even read some poetry to you back when you and I were an item."

"Yeah, I remember your poetic muse and other non-FBI traits. Then you ruined it by meeting your tall, dark, and hand-some husband and ruined our dalliance. So, what's up—ready to parse the Salem murder?"

Sure, she said with a shallow sigh. Brick didn't seem to notice.

"So, Lee, I came in early this morning and made a short list of factual similarities I see in all three cases. I thought I'd run it by you first."

"Read them to me."

He turned his laptop screen sidewise so he could see her and the screen simultaneously.

"Okay, I found ten things that show up in all three files. One, all Vics are identical male twins, with no known enemies, psychiatric, or criminal histories. Two, they're all in their twen-ties. Three, these cases all occur on the victim's birthdays. Four, all of the surviving Vics were close, but not like mirror twins, and they have all moved out of the family home. Five, each surviving twin is cleared as a suspect by hair follicle evidence and uncontested alibis. Six, all three Vics were shot in the head by the same .22 caliber pistol. Seven, every murder occurred in a New England state. And eight, the most interesting similarity of all, every family member and their close friends have alibis and no suspicious history. Nine, none of the victims were especially close to their twin or could be called *inseparable*. Ten, all sur-viving twins grieved, but managed to go on with their separate lives, at least on the surface."

"Print that out for me, Brick. I'll run through the whole list for the meeting, but I have two instant reactions. I forget which number it was, but you mentioned that all of the surviving twins were cleared as suspects by hair follicles found at the crime scene. That's astounding."

Brick tilted his head back and smiled.

"Astounding, yes, and vital to our chances of catching the Unsub. I think it can be explained by how close the shooter was to the Vics—within arms-length. There might also have been physical contact in addition to sticking the muzzle of the barrel on each Vic's head. And shooting that close up may have caused head shaking by the Unsub, so he lost a few hairs right there on the crime scene."

Lee interrupted.

"That's exactly why I think it's astounding. Could it be that the Unsub wanted the cops to find those hair follicles?"

"Don't get your point, Lee? Why would a murderer want the forensic team to find his hair follicles?"

"Could be he wanted to clear the surviving twins. Maybe he hated the twin he killed but did not want to expose the surviving twin to a murder investigation."

"Wouldn't your supposition mean that he actually knew each set of twins somehow? Why else would he want to take suspicion off the survivors?"

"No, nothing I've read signals our Unsub knew these families. But he is a very smart man. We know that from the lack of any other forensic evidence."

"Ah, but we do have other forensic evidence—the bullets," Brick said, grinning.

"He had to leave those behind. And you're right—he is very smart. So, he must be worried about both kinds of forensics he left behind."

"Ah, maybe not. Maybe he sends a message to all three surviving twins with hair follicles and bullets. Maybe he even wants us to know his signature—double bullets where one by itself would do the job."

"Lee, you got me there. Maybe our Unsub's a maniac and having a psychotic breakdown when he pulls the trigger. Maybe it's not a conscious choice—it's just rage. Okay, give me five to visit the men's and I'll see you in the conference room."

As is the reality in almost every class and conference room in the world, when the four gathered in the conference room, everyone took their usual seat. Brick and Lee at the top, side by side, Abe on the side facing the door, and Cynthia facing him. The other end of the table was cluttered with file baskets, pen and pencil holders, Sharpies, and orange, red, and yellow highlighters. And, to prove the cliché of a government office, the room reeked of stale air, empty waste baskets, thanks to the nightly cleaning crew, and the obligatory photo of President Obama on one wall.

"Good morning, everyone," Brick said, befitting the last member of the team to arrive. "Sorry to keep you waiting. We have a short list of ten similarities spanning across all three cases. I see you all have it, thanks to Lee. Let's start there. Any disagreements about the list?"

Abe frowned.

"Yeah, it's too short. I can think of at least two other similarities. One, the police forces in each venue are your typical underpaid, short-staffed detectives that often miss valuable evidence. And they did here. I didn't find the full autopsy report in any of the files. There were references to the report, but the whole deal is missing. We need that autopsy and a detailed list of all forensic evidence secured at the crime scene. Second similarity is that none of the detectives in these venues ordered any scale drawings of anything. Scale is important in crime scene evidence, and we don't have it here."

"Okay, Abe, good catch. Why don't you take the lead and see if those police shops can get that scaling done? And a deeper look at the autopsies and medical examiner opinions. That will add to our paperwork."

Cynthia raised her hand, still tentative in her new setting.

"Well, so I'm new to serial killings but the third point on the list is very surprising to me—all three victims died on their birthday. That demands close planning by the killer and a tip to what you said, Brick, about a fourth killing coming from the same man. It could not have been coincidence, the birthdate, I mean."

Brick answered. "Yeah, there's a plan here which we can't see. The case files are short on how the surviving twin felt and reacted to losing his twin to a murderer, but there's no suggestion in the files that the survivors anticipated any kind of trouble on their own, not mention their twin's birthday."

"What I was wondering," Cynthia said softly, "was whether the killer picked his victims by knowing their birthdays."

"How could anyone know that in three different cities, unless the Unsub knew each of his victims and had lots of information about them, including their birthdays?"

"No," Cynthia said, shaking her head from side to side. "That's not what I mean. I'm wondering if that might be the *only* thing he knew about his victims—their common birthdays. Maybe they became his targets for that simple reason—they are all having twin birthday celebrations, and he kills one twin before the party, three times in a row."

Lee asked, "These cases happened in three different states. How could the killer know their birthdays?"

Brick jumped in.

"Holy crap! Maybe that's it. Lots of people, maybe millions in that age group, use social media to announce upcoming birthdays. Facebook is the worst, right? They pry into everything, including birthday parties. And its nationwide, right?"

"Not necessarily," Cynthia said sheepishly. "All my friends announce in advance. And these three cases are all in New England. The three cities are just hours apart. Anyone with decent mouse skills could find twins having birthdays close by if he just limited his search to small New England states."

Brick smiled and said, "Okay, Cynthia! Good catch. I'll plug that into our digital AI section and see what they come up with. Now Cynthia, you're in the mental health therapy arena. What does the fact that all three victims were shot by the same gun, and that they all were shot twice, mean to you? Are those two facts connected together?"

Abe jumped in before Cynthia could gather her thoughts.

"One thing the bullets do is tell us one Unsub did the deed three times. He's signaling us. And he's daring us to find him at the same time. I don't mean he wants to get caught—he thinks he's smarter than us and his planning and execution are pitch perfect. But maybe this is not intended for us. Maybe it's intended for his homies, you know, other identical twins. Has anyone done a full media work up on these cases? You know, like following up on social media to see if there's a buzz out there in these particular homicides?"

"Thanks, Abe. Lee, will you push that notion out for us? How do we follow media posts?"

"Yes, I can do that. I'll set up a Google alert on my laptop. I have two sisters at home still and they are social media queens to the max. I'll enlist their aid and let everyone here know what I find."

Brick looked at his watch and gathered his notes into little piles.

"Hey guys, any brainier ideas about what we should to anticipate a fourth twin murder?"

Lee pushed her water bottle aside and reached for her legal pad.

"Yeah, Brick, there is one thing we could do, although I have no idea how to do it. We have already connected the three murders by their twin birthdays. Wouldn't logic say that the fourth case will also happen to a twin on his birthday?"

Abe answered. "Yeah, but I never heard of a list of twins' birthdays, even narrowed down by individual states. What would tell us that?"

Brick scratched his head with the eraser end of his pencil.

"I dunno. I'd bet there is a registry somewhere because twins are so widely studied in scientific circles. But even if we could find a registry, wouldn't it be private—like inside a federal database or maybe a university research lab?"

They kicked that around for a couple minutes until Cynthia raised her hand. As usual she'd immediately turned to her Mac laptop.

"Well, Wikipedia has something on this. I'll read it to you. 'US twin registries cover researchers at academic institutions, such as the Michigan State University Twin Registry, the Washington State Twin Registry, Washington State University, and the Minnesota Twin Registry. The largest twin registry in the United States is the Mid-Atlantic Twin Registry.' Maybe I could dig into that. Maybe I should call somebody to see if they have data on twins' birthdays in New England."

"Yes please, Cynthia," Brick said.

They continued the discussion for another twenty minutes. Brick said he'd make another list—this one identifying the unique elements in the three cases that were different and found only in one of the three cases.

LEBANON, VERMONT, WEEKS EARLIER

In the false dawn on September 4, 2015, on US Highway 4 near Vermont's Killington Peak, sunrise was an hour away. Harrington Schwartz, called Hare by everyone who knew him, pulled into the parking lot farthest away from the two lines. He wasn't there to ski—the 1,100-foot butte facing him was today's target. Getting out of his Ford Ranger, he rolled back the tri-fold tonneau cover on the pickup bed and sorted his climbing gear in the locked metal box into the bright orange backpack. Forty feet away he noticed a man in a heavy coat and a sealskin Bennie taking pictures with what looked like a video camera.

The view of the narrow valley was as good as a rock climber could ever get. On the far side of the two-lane paved road was a snow-covered trail through the brush. The photographer seemed to be slowly moving his lens from Hare's side of the road down and across to the trail leading to the butte on the far wall of the Coolidge State Forest. Mauve and blue cliffs. The cone across the top was dark, as if a rain cloud hovered, but there were no clouds, just a black top on top of the 900-foot climb Hare hoped to make that day.

Hare was on his knees on the flex rubberized bed looping rope when he heard the voice behind him.

"Hello, Harrington Schwartz. It's your birthday today, right? Where's your brother Hector?"

"Ah," Hare said, turning back to see the man across the lot taking videos of the mountain.

"'Ah'? That's all you got to say, you assy fucker?"

"Sorry," Hare said, standing up to face the man. "Do I know you?"

"No, you don't. And from what I see on Facebook about you, you don't know your twin brother very well either. Not even well enough to invite him to your birthday party tonight in town, right? You are a piece of shit, ya know."

The man in the sealskin beanie laid his small video camera down on the pickup's tailgate and reached into his parka. He took out a black revolver and aimed it at Hare's crotch.

"Get down on your knees, and slide over here to the tailgate. I have a question for you, piece of shit."

Hare's otherwise rosy cheeks turned ashen white, his calloused hands were suddenly clammy, and his chin and lips trembled.

"Who are you?" he squeaked out, staring not at the man's face, but the gun in his right hand.

"Get the fuck over here or I'll shoot you in the balls right now!"

Hare turned all the way around and crawled two feet to the tailgate. He leaned backward on his knees and held up his hands.

"Put your hands down and listen carefully to my question. Your life depends on it. Why didn't you invite your twin brother to your party tonight?"

"My brother? You mean Hector? Well, he lives a long way, and besides he has a job and probably could not get off work anyhow—I plan on calling him tonight and . . ."

"See?" said the man with the gun. "That's what I thought. Instead of sharing your birthday party and going to him, you stay hiding up here and act like it's okay because you're going to call him on the fucking telephone. You hate him, don't you!"

"No, I don't understand this and . . ."

Knocking his video camera off the tailgate, the man in the sealskin beanie jumped up onto the tailgate and smashed his gun into Hare's ear. He waited five seconds to catch his breath and then, slowly, he cocked the revolver with his right thumb.

"What's that? What are you doing? Oh God, don't kill . . ."

Hare may have heard the explosion and felt the burn blast of the first shot. He never heard or felt the second shot a half-second later.

Fifteen minutes later, a man in winter coveralls pulled off the road and into the parking lot. He was about fifty feet away when he saw a body lying on the asphalt at the rear of Hare's pickup. His 911 call on his cell phone was almost detached.

"Hello, 911, I'm up at the ski run in the front parking lot. There's a guy here on the ground dead. Can you send somebody?"

QUANTICO, VIRGINIA.
PRESENT DAY

Lee walked into Brick's office two days after their last group meeting with a copy of a research paper in her hand. "Boss, know what this is?" she asked, lifting the paper up and down with the palm of her left hand.

"Don't tell me, it's a freshly printed copy of the FBI's 2018 Crime Data Explorer."

"Yes, it is. How'd you know?"

"I can see the yellow page tags from here. I think those are mine from that case we had last January on data sharing with other law agencies."

"So, it is. I confess I didn't even know it existed. The preamble says the CDE aims to, quote, 'provide transparency, create easier access, and expand awareness of criminal, and noncriminal, law enforcement data sharing; improve accountability for law enforcement; and provide a foundation to help shape public policy with the result of a safer nation. Use the CDE to discover available data through visualizations, download data in .csv format, and other large data files.'"

"Yeah," Brick said, looking over the rims of his cheater glasses.

"I've used it over the last year or six because I have no real sense of how data collection meshes with forensic crime data in paper form stored in cardboard boxes and shelved in the DC office archives."

"Me neither. Do we have someone here who can do that for us? I mean discover data?"

"Yeah, sure. The behavioral health and discovery group has data farmers who can dig up stuff in digital archives that us old luddites never knew existed. What are you thinking we need?"

"Well, for openers," Lee said, pushing one of the leather-back armless chairs closer to his desk, "we have three twin brothers murdered in three New England towns over an eighteen-month period on their birthdays. Do we have data connecting those three things with the other seven factual similarities that we all agree exist in this case?"

"You mean actual data in a digital file somewhere connecting all this?"

"No, that's probably too much to ask, but might we have data, or in-house talent, that could give us a better sense of how these similarities could possibly exist, when we know that all three murders were committed by the same serial killer?"

"Good idea—it's always good when you're land-locked to look upstream and see what kind of help might be coming down river. You know the FBI loves its acronyms. I could call somebody at CIRG, who could call someone at BRIU, who could pass it along to BAU-5, knowing they shift everything up to the bridge deck at NCAVC."

"Refresh me, boss, on converting acronyms to words."

Brick grinned.

"The original team at the Behavioral Analysis shop were usurped by the Critical Incident Response Group. They renamed it the Behavioral Research and Instruction Unit. Now it's called Behavioral Analysis Unit (5). And they are more or less merged within the National Center for Analysis of Violent Crime. Got it?"

"FREST forever," Lee said, grinning like she had a hologram on her face.

Two days later Brick got a phone call from an agent he knew now stationed in San Diego, California. He had been alerted by a call from NCAVC.

"Hey Brick, how they hanging? I don't think we've talked in what, two years, since that Montana thing put us on the same logjam."

"Sammy, it's great to hear from you. To what do I owe the honor of this call?"

"Our data guy got an all-points email saying your Quantico team was interested in connecting crime scene evidence with data storage on a case involving the murder of twins in several cities—original crime scene collection by locals but cases now in your shop at Quantico. Our guy was connected a while back to a psychiatrist out here. She works in the jail services group that covers federal jails and prisons here, up in LA and in San Francisco. I've worked with her—she's great. She probably knows everything there is to know about the sociology and psychology of identical twins. Would that help you?"

"Yes, I'd love to talk her, can you send me her contacts?"

"Sure, I'll send them now. Her name is Dr. Lisbeth Socorro."

Brick got the flash email, picked up his phone, and called her office in San Diego. He didn't realize it was only 5:05 a.m. in California, so he got voice mail and left her a message. She called him back three hours later.

"Agent Cato, I have a voice mail from you this morning. Something about data research on identical twins. How can I help?"

Over the next three days, via email, shared documents, telephone calls, and a Zoom session attended by Brick and the full FREST group, everyone brightened up. Dr. Socorro turned out to be an expert who could give them a close-up view of twinness and psychology.

She briefed the FREST team and highlighted a recent research paper titled, "Twins and Telepathy—The Invisible Cord." She sent them a copy after their Zoom session. It confirmed her expertise and surprised everyone on the team. She emphasized remarkable similarities between identical twins reared together. One particular case discussed twins who behaved synchronously. As she explained it, those twins were unfathomably connected from birth to young adulthood. They did everything together, screamed, or sulked if parted, talked in unison when under stress, used the exact same words in identical voice patterns that created an echo effect. One clinician who treated them described their linkage as telepathy. Talking, working, playing, in public or in private, with friends or strangers, they function in unison. And perhaps most surprisingly, they tested high on IQ tests and suffered no mental illness.

During the Zoom session, Cynthia Myers, the team's only member who had studied both psychology and sociology in college, asked about mirror twins. "Dr. Socorro, I've heard the term mirror twins but I'm not sure that applies to all identical twins. Does it?"

"No, not at all. It is frequent and common, but still limited to between 20 and 30 percent of all identical twins' births. And of course, it only occurs in monozygotic twins, the fertilization of a single egg that splits in two. Identical twins share all of their genes and are always of the same sex. What makes mirror twins physiologically interesting is they are reflections of one another. The mirror notion is a good metaphor. One monozygotic mirror twin will be right-handed, and the other will be left-handed.

Internal organs and skeletal features will be on opposite sides of the body. And hair whorls will turn in opposite directions. Mirroring is just as much of a mystery to medical science as is the etiology of identical twins."

Abe had not asked any questions until Dr. Socorro summed up what she said would be her last point. He held up his hand. She turned to him on her screen as he enunciated his question. "So, doc, am I right in guessing that since only about 25 percent of identical twins are mirror twins, we can assume they are rare. And . . ."

Dr. Socorro held up both hands to the screen.

"So sorry to interrupt your question, but it raises a point I should have covered earlier. There is a further scientific differentiation among twins past mirror twins. They can be monoamniotic-monochorionic twins. This very rare type of monozygotic-mirror twins share a chorion, placenta, and an amniotic sac. It scares the hell out of ob-gyn docs because it means a riskier pregnancy."

"How so?" Lee asked.

"Well, because the babies can get tangled in their own umbilical cords."

"Okay, I didn't mean to get that technical, but we're trying to fathom why someone would kill only identical twins and take pains to make sure their surviving identical twin is not a suspect in the killing. So, we're looking at scientific data to see whether medical issues might play some role in these serial murder cases. Can you give us a short laymen's understanding of chorion, placenta, and the amniotic sac?"

Dr. Socorro explained. "In the uterus, the chorion develops a rich supply of blood vessels and forms an intimate association with the endometrium, that is, the lining of the female's uterus. The placenta is an organ that develops in the mother during pregnancy. It delivers oxygen and nutrients to the baby. And last but not least, you asked about the amniotic sac. It's full of amniotic fluid to protect a developing child; just think of it as a cushion. Amniotic fluid also helps regulate the baby's temperature."

"Yeah," Abe, ever the chauvinist, said, "basically plumbing, right?"

"But," Dr. Socorro continued, "I have a rather large research file on twins. Actually, I did my PhD thesis on twins. I doubt you will find a medical answer to your question, but there are psychological studies on twins and how they interact with one another and the world around them. Tell me a little more about how you've concluded that the serial killer you're after makes sure that the survivor twin is not a suspect."

Brick answered, "Well, it's very weird, but we have hair follicle evidence from each crime scene that does not match the victims, or their twins. We think the hair follicles may have been left at the crime scene by the Unsub on purpose. He seems to take pains to make sure their surviving identical twins are not suspects in these killings."

"Wow," Doctor Socorro said, with a quizzical look on her face. "It's very common for twins, especially identical twins, to protect their brothers and sisters, but I've never thought about someone else going to such extremes to protect a twin. Is it possible that a family member, not the surviving twin, is your Unsub?"

"No, we think not. All members of the three immediate families have been cleared by local authorities based on strong alibis. Of course, we know that hair follicle evidence is never 100 percent reliable, but we're sure the hair follicles at each scene came from the same person. That's why we know this is a serial murder case and not three different killers."

Later that afternoon, Brick texted all FREST members and asked if they could gather in the conference room at four-thirty. When they showed up, note pads in hand, Brick said, "In addition to similarities in each of the three murders, we need a list of dissimilarities too."

"Why, boss? I mean, what can we learn by that? Yeah, they take place in different towns, at different times, and to different people, but what do those dissimilar things tell us about who this bastard is?"

"Well," Brick answered while smiling and nodding at her. "You've just made my point. The different times, people, and places are not really dissimilar, because in each place the same Unsub killed a twin—that's connected, not disconnected. We have already identified ten similarities and now you've identified number eleven. And here's another thing that connects them—New England. Each of these states are geographically connected. All are within two and a half hours' drive from one to the other. And all are relatively small towns with modest law enforcement staffing. What I'm thinking is maybe even dissimilar things might give us some insight into who, why, and how our Unsub picks his victims."

Cynthia flipped through her lab book and held up her hand.

"When Dr. Socorro was lecturing us, I wrote this down. Twins, especially identical twins, protect their brothers and sisters. So, that's very dissimilar. Our three cases all end up with one dead identical twin *and* a live one. The live twin wasn't there to *protect* his twin."

Abe interrupted. "Hell yeah. In all three cases, the killing took place in different venues—first a truck, then the back porch of the Vic's home, then a parking lot. No surviving twin around and no surviving twin is a suspect. But this last point—no survivors are suspected—is protection, right? Protection from investigation, protection from charging or indicting."

Brick was scribbling and held up his hand.

"Guys, shouldn't we be looking at this the way Dr. Socorro does? Psychologically as well as criminally?"

They kept it up until dinner pangs showed up at 7:00 p.m. Brick said he'd order pizza in. Lee begged off, something about her sister waiting for her. But Abe, Lee, and Cynthia chose pizza. By 8:30 they had a list of dissimilarities. One, the victims' ages were different. Two, the families were unknown to one another. Three, the Unsub *picked* different states, presumably for different reasons. These dissimilarities could be important clues. What FREST needed to do now was interview the surviving twins and other family members to test Dr. Socorro's research. Did these twin sets protect one another? And if not, does that fact tell them something about the Unsub?

Brick added a cautionary note.

"You're all right. We need to know more about the Vics than local law enforcement looked at. We need to interview all surviving twins. But before we do that, I think we need to ask Dr. Socorro for a list of questions we should ask. These families are New Englanders, and they will be as independent and probably as stubborn as most New Englanders are."

Brick sent Dr. Socorro a quick email asking for another Zoom session but got an out-of-office notice saying she would return to her office next week but would read email "on the road." He wrote asking her to call as soon as possible. Forty minutes later she was on the phone. It turns out she was at Johns Hopkins in Baltimore and would finish that visit the following day. Since Quantico was only about seventy-five miles from Baltimore, she said she could stop by so they could talk in person. She was happy for the opportunity to have dinner with a close colleague in DC before flying back to San Diego.

Five minutes after he wrote the email to Dr. Socorro, Brick got a soft knock on his door. It was more a tap than a knock. Brick could guess who was outside the door.

"Cynthia, come on in," he said.

Cynthia tentatively pushed open the door and leaned into the room as though she was afraid to take a full step inside.

"You sure I'm not bothering you at all, Mr. Cato, I could come back and . . ."

"No, Cynthia, I'm never too busy to listen to you, what's up?"

"Well, sir, I hope I'm not stepping over a line here, but I just wanted to tell you that I know Dr. Lisabeth Socorro. I don't mean I *know* her, but boy, do I know *about* her. I mean it's all good and all, but she will be amazing to meet and maybe even work with. Do you know who she is, I mean like how psychiatric nurse practitioners like me know who she is?"

"No, I don't. What should I know?"

"Well, I did two out of town rotations in my master's program at UCLA—at a hospital in San Diego and a mental health clinic that did in-patient care in San Diego. In both rotations, her name came up. A lot. That's because her expertise is pretty rare. I mean her job is amazing."

"Amazing how?"

"Because she's a jail psychiatrist. Did you know that prisons have more mental patients that hospitals do? Prisons now have more serious mental illness than the state-run asylums across the country. The number is tenfold. Twenty years ago, mentally ill people in prison would go to state psychiatric hospitals."

"Okay, Cynthia, I see the problem, but how is that relevant to Dr. Socorro?"

"Well, she's a leader in trying to get proper treatment in all settings for mentals, you know. I remember someone saying she's such a big expert because her husband was murdered by a mental case and before her eyes. I think she might of gotten shot, not sure."

"How long ago, do you know?"

"No, I'm not even sure what happened, much less when. But she's written a lot about emotional wounds that afflict people all their lives when they experience that kind of emotional trauma. She knows what it's like to see a loved one die and she knows a great deal about treating and understanding that level of trauma. She teaches solutions, not reactions. She's very professional, I'm sure."

Dr. Lisbeth Socorro was one of those women who never looked her age. At sixteen she looked older, but when she turned thirty, she looked younger. Slim, trim, and on the rim is how everyone saw her. She was a frequent traveler back and forth between both coasts with frequent stops at the Cleveland Clinic, the Mayo Clinic in Rochester, and Johns Hopkins in Baltimore. She had degrees or post-doc affiliations in each city and friends in both San Francisco and Austin—two cities that were young and old in the ways cities mature while keeping their shine. But her looks were not her strong point. Her personality, like her research papers, was affable and engaging.

Brick, twice her age and knowing nothing about psychiatry, was instantly smitten.

"Dr. Socorro, this is a pleasure."

"All mine," she responded without blinking her eyes, as she reached into her brief case and lifted out a three-ring binder bound in leather, not vinyl.

"Is that research on the psychology of twins?" he asked as he motioned to the chair in front of his desk.

"Hardly," she said with a slight sideways shake of her head.

"Academics have been studying identical and fraternal twins for at least a hundred years, especially since genes became known rather than just suspected. Twins are the key to untangling the influences of genes and the impacts of environment and nurturing. Here's an opening line I've used for years in making presentations to colleagues and students. If a human trait is more common among identical twins than fraternal twins, it suggests genetic factors are partly responsible."

"Nature rules while nurture tags along? Is that it, doctor?"

"Please call me Liz, even though I'm Lisbeth as opposed to Lizabeth. My mother thought Liz sounded hip, and Lis was a hiss. Can I call you Brick?"

"Right, as in brick wall dumb when it comes to the psychology of twins."

Over the next hour she coached him on the basics of psychological, psychotic, and pathological issues exhibited by identical twin males, based not on actual events, but large-scale studies. He was surprised when she opened the subject of personality in identical twins reared apart. She referenced a famous study done at the Minnesota Center for Twin and Family Research, almost fifty years ago. That study looked closely at identical and fraternal twins separated in infancy and reared apart. The study concluded that identical twins who had different upbringings often had remarkably similar personalities, interests, and attitudes.

"Can you give me an example?" Brick asked.

"Sure, it's one almost every genetics student knows today. A pair of male identical twins who had been separated from birth were reunited at the age of thirty-nine. Then they became part of a large-scale study on personality traits and personal interests common to long-term separated twins. Both had married women named Linda, then divorced, and married again to women named Betty. One named his son James Allan, the other named his son James Alan, and both separated twins named their pet dogs Toy."

"So, the study proved what? That genetics determines name choices, wives, dogs, what else?"

"No, not anything like that. The study, and thousands of similar examples, is cited not to point out genetic determinism, but rather how we enter the world is not random or blank. All of us have free choice, but for identical twins that free choice is often based on things we like and are good at. It's research proof that there is a dynamic interplay between what we like, what we want, and the environments that we choose."

Brick said he'd take her word for it.

"Don't," she said. "But since your victims are identical twins and the survivor twin is available, you might dig more deeply into how he felt about his twin, what made them different, what made them tick, and what losing their twin did to them emotionally and psychologically. You should look for the role nature played in the survivor's life that will be very different now that they have lost their twin. You know you can't get away from nature, but your natural environment may affect you in different, even harsher ways than genetics."

"Okay, here's another thing one of our team wondered about; you'll meet her in the morning when we hold our weekly case status meeting. She questioned whether the twin sets in our three cases felt guilty, or somehow responsible or maybe implicit in their twin's violent death. Were there incidents of violence before these bullet-to-the brain attacks? Did these twin sets protect one another? And if not, does that fact tell us something about the Unsub?"

Liz bit her lower lip as she leaned back in her chair and pondered the question for a few moments.

"Brick, do you or anyone on your team have any experience interviewing identical twins? Or maybe have twins in their extended families?"

"I sure don't. Come to think of it, over a thirty-year career I don't think I've investigated a murder or a violent crime involving twins. Can't speak for the team, but in the two and a half weeks we've been looking at these cases, no one has volunteered any real familiarity with twins as subjects or relations."

"That's understandable. The chances of having identical twins are low. I think the latest data shows around three or four in every thousand births. What makes identical twins so unusual in the population is how sharing the same set of genes impacts one's sense of self. Twins see themselves as identical to their twin. That is a genetic trait. They identify with one another. Their relationships, when reared together, are intimate and intense."

"How intense?" Brick asked, leaning forward over his desk and staring at her.

"Well, it would vary of course from one twin set to another. But in every case I've studied, highly emotional issues or tragedies are aggravated in identical twins. At the risk of overstating emotionality in twins, I'll put it this way. Emotions are like colors of a rainbow: you need all of them to make up an entire spectrum. For twins, there's often a deeper meaning when scared, sad, or happy. Remember this, an identical twin is born with his best friend. A person your exact age who looks like you, likes what you like, and at least in childhood can't stand to be away from you. One twin is the other twin's built-in best friend. They have a person their size, who looks like them, and with whom they can share their most private feelings and secrets. Twins know one another in ways their parents or singleton siblings can't imagine, much less understand."

"So, doc, what's the downside of that closeness, that dependence on a twin? I'm a detective; I always look for the opposite or the reciprocal of known realities. Your sense of how dependent identical twins are on one another makes me wonder what happens when a twin loses that closeness, like in our three murder cases. I mean all siblings are crushed when we lose a brother or sister. Is that amplified a thousand percent with identical twins? Can you quantify or expand on that?"

"Brick, for starters think about it this way. Siblings are close or distant with one another as a matter of course. Every family is different. That's because siblings see the world through their own eyes, based on their experience, likes, dislikes, and hopes. Each sibling is an individual—they know who they are. But identical twins, especially mirror twins, can live exhilarating lives *because* they always have one another. Think about it; how do you figure out your own identity when you're the identical half of someone else? When you are one and the same? Offline we call it the 'one and the same' syndrome. There's no such technical name in identical twins' research or literature. But we all know it exists because once patients become accustomed to therapy they eventually start talking about identity. What it means and what happens when it's lost."

"You know, Liz, this conversation is telling me something no one on our team knows. We're all handicapped by our dismal understanding of identical twins, their genetic makeup, how they think and react. So, is it possible for the FBI to borrow you? Just temporarily? You know, to stay here and help us in more direct ways? I'm thinking maybe you should take over the interviews we need to set up with the twin survivors and their families."

"Oh my, that sounds exciting as long as I don't have to wear a gun or arrest someone. The Federal Bureau of Prisons is a sister agency to the FBI, isn't it?"

"Great," Brick said, smiling like a high school kid on his first date.

"I'll look into it right away. The Fed Bureau of Prisons is part of the Department of Justice, just like the FBI. I'll leave a message for you at your hotel in DC."

"Sure," Liz said. "My job is to make sure federal offenders serve their prison sentences in safe, humane, and secure facilities. I think my boss in San Diego will let me help you with this case. We have twins in prison, and I've interviewed and treated several over the last four and a half years. Our bosses can work out the details, right?"

It took only one day to clear Liz for a short-term assignment from Jail Services in San Diego to FREST in Quantico. The team met for lunch inside the secure facility in Quantico. Liz spent the morning with the office administrator and a security clearance officer getting her equipped, cleared, and familiar with the databases and logins for her loaner iPad, laptop, and the desktop computer in her cubicle inside the FREST quarter-floor in the central BAU building. By noon she had a decent start on how to engage and use ViCAP, the violent criminal apprehension program database. That tool was available to all law enforcement agencies nationwide, but this was Liz's first time in *enforcement* as opposed to *consulting*.

Lunch was served military style, given that the BAU cafeteria was surrounded by US Marines and dozens of what they called chow halls. To Liz's dismay, the line hosting large round containers, warming tables, and metal bowls, displaying serve-yourself offerings that *looked* like chow, was not the food she was used to in San Diego. Salad was at the end of the line, in a two-foot diameter tub. Lettuce, heavily mayonnaised, was the only choice. The other dishes were meat, potatoes, pizza with meat, and what she suspected was canned spinach. But the dinner rolls were large, fresh, and under a warming light. Iced tea in chilled glasses was available. Steaming hot coffee was also at the end of the line.

She quickly discovered the talk at group lunches was about everything but the business at hand. They didn't talk about cases, crimes, or catching Unsubs; they talked about real food, movies, music, families, the stock market, and politics. Lots of politics. Mostly of the conservative stripe, but Cynthia and Lee were progressive voices, and Abe avoided table conversation that did not involve sports.

Brick's cell phone rang halfway through lunch. He lifted it out of his coat's inside pocket, grumbling about lunch time. He looked at the screen, said hello, and held up his other hand to the table, palm down, with a dampening movement.

"Yes, sir. Right. How long ago? Who's the lead on the scene? Yes, sir. Two of us will be on site at 0800 tomorrow. Yes, sir."

Brick got up and swiped to phone to off.

"Hey folks, let's meet in the conference room in five minutes. Someone just tried to kill one of the surviving twins in the Manchester, New Hampshire, case."

Because they were twenty-first century government, each team member had all relevant documents in all three murder cases on their iPads. But because Brick, at fifty-nine, still had Luddite tendencies, he stopped in his office to retrieve a print version of the New Hampshire twin murder case. He took it into the conference room where Lee, Abe, Cynthia, and Liz were seated, iPads open, waiting for him.

"Okay, guys, here is what the Assistant Director told me. Ernesto Estancia, age twenty-seven, is in a hospital in Manchester, New Hampshire, in a stable condition. Someone tried to kill him last night about midnight when he parked his car at his parents' home, where he is apparently living. The city police force report says Mr. Estancia got only a graze on his shoulder. They have a weapon; in fact, they have two weapons. One carried in a holster by Mr. Estancia and the other apparently dropped at the scene by his assailant—name and description unknown. The assailant escaped on foot. Neighborhood search found nothing—no track or eyewitnesses listed. Because the local police chief knew we were working on the stalled case, he took the liberty to hold off all interrogation of the wounded Vic, family, and other associates.

"Do they have photos, video scans, anything like that?" Abe asked.

"They took crime scene photos. We'll get first crack at the Vic tomorrow morning. The police chief—his name is Weatherford, Chief Weatherford—wants to hold a press conference tomorrow afternoon and hopes we will be there to take the lead on the case from this point forward. But there's at least one unruly reporter in town who's raising hell."

Abe couldn't resist.

"Hey boss, can I go? I'll button up the frickin' reporter."

"We'll talk about assignments in a minute. But first, let's talk about witness protection. That will be managed by the locals, but I'd like comments from everyone on this angle. At first take, seems to me that this family ought to be under FBI protection now. They've lost one twin and the other is in the line of fire. But that assumes the attempt last night was by our Unsub. Let's go around the table on that—opinions, not certainties. Lee, you start."

Lee looked up from her iPad screen.

"I just read the *New Hampshire Union Leader's* e-version of the attack. It's page-three coverage, two paragraphs, but it notes the Vic is a twin and that his brother was tragically murdered in 2014. The reporter, Clayton something, reported the local cops were bobbing and ducking on details, but that word had leaked about a press conference tomorrow. So, boss, this is already a family story about twins, one dead, and one shot. It'll almost certainly go viral. And here's something odd, well, maybe not odd, but interesting. The attempt last night was on his birthday."

Cynthia looked up from her iPad.

"Maybe not viral, but the story's on Twitter and at least a dozen Facebook pages. It'll catch fire long before tomorrow's old fashioned press conference. Is there a race or political issue in this case slash story? That would ramp up the digital count."

Lee, holding her palms down, said, "We ought to hear Brick's telephone conversation that interrupted our lunch conversation, just when we were getting to know Liz."

"Okay, guys," Brick said. "As you know, my conversation was about sixty seconds long. But it was from an Assistant Director. I don't get those calls more than twice a year. He knows nothing about the case. In fact, no other agent, except the four of us, knows anything. We have not conducted the ground investigations into this case or the other two on our plate now. All we know is what's on your iPads. I think we need a US Marshal with us tomorrow. And we need ballistics and an FBI crime scene forensics team too. I'll work on that from here this afternoon. And we need clear focus and a timeline of what preceded the attack and exactly what happened afterward. But all of that is standard FBI protocol stuff. Let's focus one level deeper: the motivation question. Why did someone try to kill Ernesto Estancia last night? More specifically, is this failed attack tied to the killing of Emiliano Estancia? If so, how? Abe, your thoughts on the *why* question?"

"Boss, I read the thin NH investigation file over and over. The local yokels didn't even try to assess the shooter's motivation. They looked for him but had no idea how he got to the house, how he got away, how come he picked a twenty-four-year-old water services worker to kill. There were no witnesses, damn little forensics. Crime took place in a fairly low-rent part of town, early in the morning before anyone got up. I'm not even sure they had detectives—none of the officers filing reports had the title. No one offered a guess as to why this happened."

"Yes, Abe, but you are a detective, and you know everything they knew the day after the killing. And now you know a little more than they did. You know the Vic was an identical mirror twin. You know he had no known enemies and that his family was cleared of all suspicion. What's all that add up to?"

"You want a wild-ass guess, boss? The kind you hate? Okay, here's my take. The guy that killed Emiliano did it because he was a twin—that made him a target. I get that because I know about the other two cases. All three bought the grave by the same gun, in the hand of the same Unsub. So, yeah, the fact he was a twin is the motive for killing him. Wild-ass guess."

"No Abe, I wasn't asking about the motive for the first New Hampshire shooting, I mean last night's shooting attempt on the second twin. Give me your wild-ass guess to that motive."

"Coulda been coincidences, boss, but that's a fifty to one call. The guy last night missed a bullet to the head because he was a twin, a what did you call it, a mirror of his brother? Now, I ain't putting money on it, but if we find the first shooter, I think we gotta shake him down on both cases."

As they went around the table, Liz scribbled in her lab book, and Lee said they ought not to get too deep into the twin weeds. Cynthia thought that both cases reeked of abuse, despair, and psychotic rage. Brick gave everyone a chance to speak their mind before getting back to what for him was the core question—motivation.

"So," he said, "we'll know more tomorrow than we know now, but we need a plan, a target, a box to put these two New Hampshire cases in. We have no motive for the murder, in part because the ground investigation went nowhere. The fact that the Vic was an identical mirror twin was interesting and unusual, but not in any way connected to his death. Now we have an attack on his twin brother, again at night, by gun, and again without an arrest or a suspect list. While I do not make wild-ass guesses, that's why we have Abe on the team, I cannot escape the bells going off in my head—these two cases are *directly connected*. As Abe put it, the odds are fifty to one. It's no coincidence that both Vics are twins. That's not the motive, it's the consequence. So, starting at 0800 hours tomorrow we dig into both cases at the same time. A second look at the first murder to dig for *why* it happened. That's not a plan, but it's a scratch in the right direction. Liz, can you go with me tomorrow to Manchester? You know twins, so work on a set of questions we should ask first responders, the family, and the survivor twin."

"Sure, Brick, I'll have a long list tonight. But I can tell everyone now what I think might be the most important question to answer. Did your Unsub pick the twin's birthday to kill Emiliano? If that turns out to be right, then motivation gets a lot easier to look for. From a psychiatric perspective, some people kill for impersonal reasons—money-hate-rage-revenge. But those that kill because it's personal fall into very different diagnostic categories. So, if the attempt last night was also *personal*, then we are probably looking for the same shooter in both cases."

Lee raised her ballpoint in the air. "Liz, I'm missing the connection. Couldn't the murder of Emiliano and the attempt on Ernesto be two different Unsubs? I mean, why are you connecting them because both the murder and the attempt were on a birthday?"

"Lee, I know I'm speculating here but singletons' birthdays are not as important as identical twins are. For a singleton, it's just one person's birthday. Conversely, for twins, especially identical twins, a birthday is plural. It's always celebrated together, in union. And they are rarely apart on that day. We know these two twins were not together on their last birthday. In fact, for the second twin, he was a singleton yesterday because his twin is dead. The fact that the surviving twin almost died yesterday, on the day he and his twin were born, makes this case a bit easier to solve."

"Easier? You think so?" Brick asked.

"Brick, and everyone, I know this sounds wacky. But when we diagnose mental illness, we look for parallel and repeated behavior, and second takes on everything. It's not good science— to speculate the way I am here with you. But the motive for the murder a year ago might turn out to be the same motive for the attempt yesterday. If we find the motive for the actual murder, we will have new ground to plow in looking for the attempted murder yesterday."

MANCHESTER, NEW HAMPSHIRE

Neither Brick nor Liz had been to Manchester. They flew to Boston, the regional HQ for four states—Maine, Massachusetts, New Hampshire, and Rhode Island. It was about a forty-five-minute drive up US 93. Both sensed why people loved New Hampshire. Natural beauty was everywhere. Mountains, forests, lakes, and a small stretch of Atlantic coastline. Wikipedia said 'Manchester' was the largest city in the state. Brick's iPad, running on Wi-Fi in the rental car, said it was the most populous city in Maine, New Hampshire, and Vermont.

"About 115 thousand souls," Brick said.

Liz said wryly, "Every city in California is bigger than that. And we have more than a thousand cities."

"Whatever," Brick murmured. "My focus is on how strong their local police department is. And I have a bad feeling the FBI won't be considered a welcome guest. I checked their demographics. They have a one in thirty-six chance of facing a violent or property crime here. Our data says it's definitely not one of the safest communities in America. New Hampshire is relatively safe, but its biggest city has a crime rate higher than 97 percent of the rest of the state."

Manchester Police Chief Thaddeus Kronzrk had razor cut hair standing at attention and close-set small eyes that magnified his most noticeable features. His bold nose and prominent cheekbones gave him the look of a prow. He stood behind his desk when a hurried junior officer ushered Brick and Liz into his office. Not offering to shake hands was purposeful.

"I'm Thad Kronzrk," he said without smiling or grimacing. "My officers are here to help you understand that dustup last night at the Estancia house. I have to say I'm surprised the FBI wants a piece of this, but I'm told it's because of the murder of the man's brother about a year ago. Is that it?

"Have a seat," he said over his shoulder as he took his place at the head of the nine-foot-long table.

Brick tried to assure the stern man in front of him that the FBI's Boston Regional Office would be the takeover agency on this case, but even at this preliminary stage he could see resistance, if not outright hostility. This guy's scared of us, he thought. He's confrontational because we might find something he missed when the first Estancia twin was murdered a year ago. Worse yet, he knows his office gave short shrift to yesterday's attack on the survivor twin. And if we tell on him, when we go to the mayor's office this afternoon, we will take sides in a political battle going on in downtown Manchester. So, he put on his big smile and answered in measured tones.

"Nice to meet you, Chief. I'm Special Agent Brick Cato and this is Dr. Elisbeth Socorro. And, yes, Chief, our interest in this case is because we're investigating a series of serial murders in three New England states. The Ernesto Estancia case wasn't just a murder, it was a hostile gun attack. If I may, can I ask you to clarify what happened night before last? You called it a dustup. It was a crime, right?"

"Aw hell, Special Agent, don't take offense by how I describe things. It was a violent attempt, but nothing about it says it's part of another murder. I'm told your office has our entire file on the shooting last year of this guy's brother. We don't pair them up but sounds like you do."

"Well, Chief, we'd sincerely appreciate your insight on both cases. We won't take up much of your time. The FBI regional office in Boston is officially taking over the investigation as of now. We'll be working with the SAIC there. We're sort of the advance team—we work out of Quantico, Virginia. The first thing we need to do is sit and talk to all of the officers that were at the scene. And we need digital copies of all forensic evidence secured, all notes, videos from lapel cameras, and all witness statements or summaries. There is a federal building here and we've arranged for temporary space there. Will this work for your officers and forensic people?"

"Well, we're always happy to turn over local crimes to the FBI. I don't know just how much you know now, but in anticipation of your visit, I had the staff prepare a copy of everything we have so far. It's there, in that brown envelope."

"Good start, Chief. But we'll need digital copies as well, pdfs, jpegs, and digital audio and video files. I understand someone scheduled a press conference here for 1:00 pm this afternoon. So . . ."

"You'd best hold on, Agent. We scheduled that press conference because the mayor's office, or probably his eager young campaign manager, wanted to showcase the mayor's interest in reducing gun violence in Manchester. Now that you're taking over, I canceled our end in that political side show. You'd best call their office. But don't be surprised if they back off now. They won't like to hear what the feds are thinking about our fair city."

"What the feds are thinking? What is it you think we're here for?"

"Hell, Agent, you're easily riled, aren't you? No offense was meant. You just said you think this is connected to a serial murderer. And one that's on the loose, I assume. We don't do murders across state lines. If that's what this is, then we are mighty glad you're taking over. And if you're right, I'm also guessing the mayor's political aide won't want you talking like that to everyone in town and putting it on Channel Nine for the six o'clock news tonight."

As predicted, the mayor's office saw no need to cause concern over speculation about serial murderers in Manchester. Brick's Quantico staff arranged for Brick and Liz to meet with the Estancia family at four o'clock that afternoon. He suggested that he make the introductions, start the interviews, and let Liz take the lead with the parents.

The Estancia home was in the middle-income part of town and radiated the care and attention given to the house, its occupants, and visitors. All the houses on their block were stuccoed and washed in shades of salmon, blue, and tan. All had front porches, small lawns, now dead in the face of last week's snow. Some had pointed fifties roofs. Others were two story with brick chimneys. Every porch had a swing, and all had welcoming doormats.

Brick used the brass door knocker on the right side of the screen door. In less than thirty seconds the door opened, and a doll-faced woman tried to smile and stuttered, "Come in, please. My husband is waiting."

As they'd planned when parking the car in the quiet street, Liz took the lead.

"Mrs. Estancia? We are so sorry to bother you. This is Special Agent Brick Cato and I'm Doctor Lisbeth Socorro."

"Yes, we know. A policeman told us you'd be here. Come in, please. Our son is upstairs, but he will come down when you're ready to talk to him. Come in, please."

Brick took special notice of her third "come in, please." This is a gentle soul whose life has taken the worst of all turns. He reminded himself to interview, not interrogate, and to listen more than talk.

Mr. Estancia introduced himself as Elmer, but said, "Call me Edward. It's my middle name. My parents named me Elmer Edward Estancia, EEE for short. My dad used to joke and say Mom screamed 'Eee' when they told her she was having twins."

They sat in the living room with an unlit fire in the fireplace, hot tea served on a silver try, and five minutes of small talk to put off the serious conversation they all knew would come soon. Brick explained that his office and a special team of FBI agents had taken over the local police investigation because they thought it was possible that the murder of Emiliano and the attempted shooting of Ernesto were connected. He let them take that in. Then he told them that a single person, who the FBI designated as an unidentified subject, or Unsub, might be involved in both cases.

Mr. Estancia said, "Unsub? Okay, we know that show on NBC. It's still playing on NBC. We've watched it many times."

Brick did not tell them about the other two cases they'd linked to the Estancia twins.

Mr. and Mrs. Estancia looked more like brother and sister than husband and wife. Both were thin and worn looking, the man slightly gaunter than his wife. Both were short, stubby, like twin fire plugs. Their skin was leathery, hers loose but his still taut. Both were dark eyed, but hers were red lined. They nodded in unison to yes questions, and squinted at difficult questions calling for feelings, hunches, and reactions to the horror of a murdered child and a wounded twin brother.

"Mrs. Estancia," Liz asked, "I know some of my questions will be uncomfortable, but I hope you understand that we need to know some intimate and important things about your sons. You don't have to talk about anything that hurts. Okay?"

Looking across the coffee table, five feet away from Mrs. Estancia, Liz let her words settle.

"When your boys were young, before kindergarten, how close were they? I mean emotionally. Did they seem settled with one another? Did they cry when separated for any reason? Did they . . . ?"

"Doctor Socorro, do you know twin families, like us?"

"Yes, I do. I'm a clinical psychiatrist and have studied and interacted with twins most of my career and . . ."

"Interacted? What do you mean by that word?"

"That's a good question, ma'am, a very good one. By interacting I mean I have spent long periods of time interviewing twin families in difficult circumstances. Mental illness in twins is no greater than in singleton families, but the stress and tension in raising twins, especially identical twins, sometimes causes family problems not seen in homes where the uniqueness and closeness of twins explains how they see themselves and how their parents see them."

But," Mrs. Estancia continued, "is that your experience— treating mental illness in twins' families? Can I ask a personal question of you?"

"Yes, you may."

"Do you have children, and are there twins in your immediate family?"

"No. My first husband died before we decided to start a family. So, you know . . ."

"Doctor, I hate to interrupt but it's important that you understand how parents feel about their children. That's why I'm imposing and asking personal questions."

"You're not imposing, Mrs. Estancia. You are asking the same questions I almost always get from parents who have lost a child. After my husband died, I never married. But I adopted a daughter. She came to me when she was just a baby. She's now in college in San Diego, California."

"Ah, that's a long way from here, San Diego."

"I live there. I'm just helping Agent Cato's investigation here on what we call the other coast because I've studied and known many twins' families in my work."

"Okay, doctor, okay, I think you can learn a lot from study and research, and I know that loving and raising an adopted child is just as wonderful as birth children are. Ask me what you need to know. I'll try not to interrupt."

"Thank you, Mrs. Estancia. Let me break down my first question. When your boys were just babies, before learning to talk, how did they react when you separated them—say, for bathing or feeding or anything else?"

"They were happy babies as long as they could see and hear one another. I could change them, feed them, hold them, walk them, as long as they were together. You know about that from your study, right? The need to be together was there at the beginning and lasted until they went to preschool."

"And how did they act when at preschool? I'm sure you talked to their teachers then, when they were four or five."

"Yes, we did, both Ed and me. He's a high school math teacher and part-time coach, you know."

Mr. Estancia smiled. "Well, honestly, I teach math part time and coach full time. I taught the boys math, and it took in Emiliano but not for Ernesto. It was the reverse in coaching. Emiliano was athletic and loved banging and hitting. Ernie was too gentle to tackle and too short to make three-pointers."

"So, here's a question for both of you. You know your boys are identical twins with shared DNA, but they are also mirror images of one another. Which boy was left-handed and which parted his hair on the opposite side of his twin?"

Almost in unison, they said, "Emiliano was right-handed."

Mr. Estancia kept talking. "Right away, when they started walking, I could tell Emiliano would be hitting right-handed and

Ernie left. But neither liked baseball, so it didn't matter. Actually, I think Ernie would have been a switch hitter because . . ."

Mrs. Estancia interrupted. "Edward, don't start with the baseball basketball thing. We'll bore these poor people to death."

"No, not at all, folks," Brick said. "For me it was football. Maybe Ed and I can talk about that later."

The four spent a little over an hour asking questions. Brick and Liz made notes. Then they heard noise from the top of the stairway.

A husky voice said, "I hear you all talking about me down there. When can I defend myself? A left-handed rock climber, that's me."

Ernie Estancia had a basso voice and a sparkling personality. He struck Brick as a handsome young man and Liz as fetching. He looked taller than his parents, but that was easy since his dad was barely five foot eight and his mom four inches shorter. He was thick in all the right places. His jet-black hair reached the nape of his neck, and his grin stretched from ear to ear.

He came down the carpeted steps carefully with a blue hard plastic brace fitted with spandex and nylon straps. Brick knew those braces in a very personal way and how they inhibit movement of the shoulder joint. It was a physical reminder of the media coverage reporting he'd been grazed by a bullet in his upper torso but didn't say where.

"The bullet," he said, "just grazed my right shoulder. That's not my climbing shoulder, you know. Rock climbers lean in and out when we climb, and my style is to use my right shoulder to balance my climb and my left to swing. But you're not here to talk about rocks are you? You want to know about my brother, right?"

Brick took over.

"Call me Brick, please. I've never been a rock climber but I'm an avid sailor, so I know a little about ropes and swinging into the wind on a three-meter sailboat."

"Okay, we have that in common. Dad said you'd be here, and that the FBI is taking over my case, not that it's much of a case. You know I hardly saw the guy that shot me. I sort of got the jump on him right from the start."

They were standing at the bottom of the stairs. Mrs. Estancia said, "Mr. Cato, would you like to use Ed's little office to talk to Ernie? It has a little table so you and Dr. Socorro can take notes."

"Yes, if you don't mind."

Once settled in, Liz offered a coming-attraction comment. "Ernie, maybe I should tell you a little about myself. I'm not an agent of the FBI. I'm a clinical psychiatrist. I work for the US Bureau of Prisons but am on loan to the FBI for this particular case, or should I say, cases plural?"

Ernie interrupted, "You mean my case *and* my brother Emiliano's case too?"

Brick answered. "Not only yours and your brother's case. Let me tell you something we must ask you to keep private for now. We are actively investigating three murder cases, all occurring under similar circumstances, starting with your brother's murder on December 14, 2014."

"Get out. You have three murder cases! But nobody knows about them? Holy smoke. Could I ask what you mean by 'similar' circumstances? Like all three are twins, like Emil and me?"

"Yes, that's exactly it. In each case an identical twin brother was shot by the same suspect. We know almost nothing about the killer because no one saw the shootings and there were no security cameras at the three crime scenes. But we have bullets from each case, and we think all six came from the same gun."

"Six bullets? Why six?"

"Each victim, including your brother, was shot twice. And in each case, the bullets were .22 caliber shorts. Based on the police file, your parents were told about this evidence last year."

"Well, nobody told me. I'll be talking to my dad about that. So, you know I wasn't home when my brother was killed. In fact, I wasn't living here then. I guess I never asked enough questions later."

Liz took over. "Right, Ernie, we know you weren't home. We want to talk about two things, first your case the night before last—Brick will do that. Then, I have questions about growing up with Emiliano. I know it's well past dinner time, so if it's okay with you, I'll start with my part, growing up with your brother, and then we'll come back tomorrow morning, and Brick will cover what happened night before last."

"Sure," Ernie said, dropping his chin to his chest.

"I used to love talking about growing up with Emil, he was born first, by almost three minutes according to Mom, so he insisted on being the big brother. Me, I was always the little brother, even though I was way smarter."

"You called him Emil. Was that a nickname that family and friends used, or just you?"

"Mom and Dad called him by his full name, Emiliano. So did our teachers and other family names. He liked it that way—Emiliano sounded more important to him than Emil. He wanted to be important, you know. A guy with bigger plans than I had. I called him Emil because it was shorter, just like Ernie is shorter than Ernesto. And sometimes I called him Emule because he was stubborn as a mule."

"Can you give me an example of how he was stubborn?"

"Well, like lots of stuff, you know. He wanted to stand first in line at the taco truck. He wanted to be in the middle of group pictures. Like if he took a selfie, you could always see he aimed mostly at himself, and the other person was sort of beside the point. Know what I mean?"

Liz moved on. "Yes, I know. I'm not trying to pry into your private life, Ernie, but my first question to an identical twin, especially a mirror-image brother is asking the impossible. How close were you to Emil, that's what you called him right, say when you were in junior high?"

"Okay, that's good we're not talking about grade school. I felt pretty free in grade school and so did Emil. But he changed in junior high, you know."

"Changed how?"

"Well, it's something Mom and Dad never knew. Still don't. In junior high I had my first date with a girl. My first kiss. And my first, you know, my first hard-on. Emil never had a date with a girl or kissed one, but he had a perpetual hard-on. Know what I'm saying?"

"Yes," Liz said, feeling the need to offer an explanation that Ernesto couldn't articulate. "What is not widely known about identical twins is that shared DNA doesn't mean shared sexual identity. Identity is not simple. Over the last forty or so years, doctors and researchers recognize that not everybody fits into the clear-cut categories of 'straight' and 'gay.' For all the same reasons that some singletons are attracted to both sexes, it also happens to twins. Some are not attracted to either; they are asexual. Some are bisexual. And many feel that traditional gender roles don't really fit them. Was Emil gay? Is that what you're telling us?"

"Hey, ma'am, I'm not telling you anything. You asked about junior high. I guess it's fair to say I was really worried about Emil starting then. I had my suspicions, but he wouldn't talk about it. When we went to high school, he had a couple of dates, one girl at a time. But by the time we were seniors, I was pretty sure he wasn't a stud. Know what I mean? And here's another thing. We started going separate ways by the time we were seniors. Like I was into sports and hunting and fishing and stuff real men did. He hated all of that. We were identical but different, you know?"

"Yes," Liz said, closing her lab book and screwing the top back onto her fountain pen. "Science now recognizes that lots of people do not fall into binary categories. There are studies that are debatable, and politics always gets in the way. We can talk more tomorrow, after Brick has asked you some questions about the attack. I would only ask one more thing now. You never lost the deep love and affection you had for Emil, did you? I have consulted with and recommended therapy for many twins that faced similar situations you discovered in junior high school. In every case, the twins may have made different life choices, but it never broke that rare relationship twins have—they loved one another, no matter what. Is that true for you and Emil?"

"Positively! We were as close when we graduated high school as we were when we were six. But we started seeing the world differently in terms of girls, and our futures. He wanted a quiet future not involving too many other people and doing something intellectual. He never wanted to work with his hands, only his brain. I wanted to be outside, making noise, and not worrying about money. I guess you can say Emil was introverted and I was convoluted."

QUANTICO, VIRGINIA
FREST HEADQUARTERS

Brick and Liz spent three days in Manchester gathering data, interviewing cops, family members, and searching for anyone who might have seen, heard, or even guessed what happened to the Estancia family. They asked about both the first murder in December 2014 and the attack in December 2015. They prepared separate reports and file documents and came to different conclusions. The FREST team spent a half-day reading and marking up print copies of their file entries. Then they gathered in the conference room to discuss and assess.

Brick started. "As everybody knows by now, the time spent in Manchester didn't give us much more than the original police reports did. I guess I shouldn't be surprised that everyone there is as mystified as we are. What we need to do now is *regroup*. I mean we need to think like our Unsub does and feel our way to him without much help from the law enforcement agencies that have done the groundwork in four attacks, three of which were deadly. My gut's telling me these are still murder cases and the fact that the victims are all identical twins should not matter.

But after meeting their parents and Ernie Estancia, I am leaning towards a very different investigation—one where we look beyond the crimes and dig deeper into the motives. That means we need an explanation that fits all four attacks because they are *so* bloody identical. If we focus today on the first murder, maybe the next three attacks will fall into line. Lee, you're senior by six months over Abe, so why don't you start?"

Lee got up, went to the far end of the room, and switched on the interactive whiteboard attached to the wall. She took a black marker from the tray. With her back to the group, she began by drawing four large circles in the four corners of the four-by-five white plastic board. In the upper left corner, she printed *Emiliano's Murder.* Stepping to her right she printed *Unsub.* In the lower left circle, she printed *Need.* Then, with a flourish, she printed *Rage* in the lower right circle. She drew diagonal lines from each circle to four square boxes she made next to the circles, about one-quarter of the way towards the middle of the board. Then she turned to her colleagues at the table.

"I'm not offering this so much as my assessment but only as the way my brain works when I cannot see how disparate events are connected. The top left circle is clear—*Emiliano's Murd*er. The top right circle is equally clear—*Unsub.* The bottom right circle is not only unclear, but also merely my opinion. Based on what Brick and Liz learned in Manchester this week, I think Mr. Estancia's killer acted out of pure *rage*, not robbery, not getting even, not mistake, and not grudge. The bottom left circle is another personal opinion. I think our Unsub *needed* to kill Mr. Estancia. I mean this in the subjective sense. Unless he killed this man, he would go through life with a job not done, a life spared, or something that made it vital for him to do—our Unsub needed to shoot a man he may never have known or seen until that night."

Abe raised his hand and said, "But . . ."

Brick waved his hand, palm down, at Abe.

"Let her finish, Abe."

"And if my thesis is even half right, these four overarching factors are followed by the squares you see moving inward and upward towards the middle of the board."

Lee turned her back on the group and stepped back to the Whiteboard. In the square just below the left corner square, she wrote *.22 shorts.* Moving to her right, she scribbled inside the right square, *two hollow points to the head.* Then, looking down at her iPad notes, she inserted two words into the lower left square, *Dark & Open.* She went silent for thirty seconds, then slowly printed *Barrel Muzzle Blast on Skin.* She went back to her chair and sipped on the Diet Coke can and then walked back to the Whiteboard and picked up a red marker. She drew a smaller circle inward from the four square boxes and filled them in from left to right. In the upper left box leading from *.22 shorts,* she printed, *Not a Pro.* Leading down from the right side, she inserted *Must Die.* In the lower right, leading from the *Barrel Muzzle on Skin,* she wrote *Can't Miss.* And jotting inside the left small circle she wrote, *Get Away.* Finally, with a heavy hand on the red marker she drew a large oblong-shaped box running from the sides of the board and covering the entire middle part. The four red lines pointed up and down at the box. The empty oblong box.

"So, guys, this is an architectural sketch of who our Unsub is, why he did what he did, and how he did it. The open box in the middle is what we have to fill in. Questions?"

Abe, as usual, barked.

"Lee, darling, I get your meaning on the top two circles, *Emiliano's Murder* and *Unsub,* but the four smaller drop-down boxes are facts from which crime scene? Aren't we starting with just the first murder and then working our way to the other three? I mean, holy shit, the forensics on all four cases would take four Whiteboards, right?"

Brick, answering Lee, stepped in. "Abe, I was thinking like you were as Lee filled in the circles and boxes. But, as you put it, HOLY SHIT! Lee is not jumping ahead here; she's starting from scratch. I've talked to her about this new approach, and I don't know what she has in mind for the big center box, but as I see the upper circles and drop-down small boxes, she's identified twelve known facts that are common to all three cases. We've already speculated that we're looking at the same Unsub for all three cases based on the ballistics at each scene—one gun—one gunman. But she's piecing together eleven other commonalities that point to the *same* Unsub. Okay, quick vote here. Hands up if you think Lee is right—eleven facts in common give us the same Unsub in all three cases."

Everyone raised their hands. To clinch it, Liz raised both hands and started clapping. "Can I insert a non-FBI element here, without interrupting Lee's smart assessment?"

Lee nodded. Liz tried to be succinct knowing that nothing's short for the FBI; they can spend all day on the smallest piece of evidence. "In your first year of med school, you're taught to rule out things before diagnosing something."

Abe mumbled, "Hey doc, we're not diagnosing the Unsub, we're trying to catch him."

"Right, Abe, but don't we have to rule out other suspects, other motives, other needs, and things that make the Unsub livid before we can select one person who meets all criteria? The common med school example is that a normal chest x-ray can 'rule out' pneumonia. By analogy, what Liz has done here is use her x-ray vision to rule out people that could not be the Unsub in these four cases."

Lee knew when to take center stage back. "Abe, you've talked about the certainty of ballistics science and the uncertainty of identifying one person responsible for three murders in three states over a period of less than two years. I'm digging for motive here. Because if we know the motive and it's the same motive in all four attacks, then we can move on to the Unsub's need to kill and the rage that explains why and how he kills. Let me give you some rule-outs my simple chart suggests. Because a handgun was used, we can rule out rifles, lynching, bombs, knives, drugs, drunk drivers, and chainsaws. Because our Unsub shot twice in each case, we can rule out misfire, accidental shootings, arguments, and ordinary American mayhem. Because he took care to use hollow point bullets, we can rule out less-thoughtful shooters. This guy wanted to kill, not wound. Modern ER rooms rush gunshot victims upstairs to surgery, and many are saved because the regular dome-like bullets with pointed tips fired from a high-velocity handgun loaded with often go into the skull on one side and exit on the other. The purpose of a hollow point is to allow it to expand upon impact and destroy brain tissue by bouncing around inside your skull. And we also know our Unsub held the muzzle of the barrel directly onto the skin of each victim. There at least two things we can infer from that. One, he hated the Vic. Two, he didn't want to take a chance of missing. That often happens in small, close-in spaces where the Vic tilts his head a split second before the trigger is pulled. Altogether these forensic data points suggest to an enraged, determined shooter who planned his killing carefully. That makes our job easier. You know better than anyone that most murders are fits of anger and decisions of the moment. Not so for our Unsub."

"Okay," Brick said. "Let's do this in rounds. Everybody has had one round but Cynthia. So, Cynthia, what's your take on Lee's Whiteboard chart?"

"Well, as everybody knows, I know zero about guns, even less about bullets, but as a mental health therapist, I have had my share of highly focused and intelligent people whose mental issues sometimes led to the level of rage that caused fights of all kinds. Rage is a first cousin to violence, and where we see repeated instances of that, we can reasonably predict violence. The biggest point I can make here is not that mentally ill people become violent. It's that most mentally ill people do not resort to violence. And here's another thing to remember, anger is common and very often not tied to mental health. Perfectly normal people with healthy attitudes about life get mad and feel angry. But when it escalates up to uncontrollable rage, then a mental health diagnosis can be made."

Brick said, "Give us an example where rage is a common element of someone who is deemed to mentally ill."

"Okay," she said. "Anger is a key criterion in five diagnoses within DSM-5: Intermittent Explosive Disorder, Oppositional Defiant Disorder, Disruptive Mood Dysregulation Disorder, Borderline Personality Disorder, and Bipolar Disorder. But that's anger. Rage is a horse of a different color. I know that's cliché, but my professor at nursing school used it all the time. She defined rage always in the context of violent anger. Anger alone is not enough. Rage is a total discharge of the sympathetic portion of the autonomic nervous system . . ."

Abe always interrupted when he didn't understand what someone said. "What's that? I didn't know the nervous system was automatic. Ya know, I thought you had to jump start it like changing gears or something."

"No," Cynthia said, "I said autonomic, not automatic. Autonomics are part of the nervous system. When the autonomic nerves aren't working properly, the patient can experience physical symptoms like lightheadedness, brain fog, or fainting. I'm not a neurologist, but when a person is in a state of rage, a lot of things are going in his body, brain, and breathing. If they are so enraged that they harm another person, we would know they are both mentally *and* physically at risk."

Cynthia was still shy in open meetings and leaned back in her chair and folded her arms across her chest. Brick thanked her for giving them a mental health perspective and asked if she had more to say about Lee's Whiteboard diagram. "Well, there is one small thing I can see up there," she said, pointing to the front of the room. "The lower left circle says, *Need*. I'm not sure, but maybe that should be *Needs*, plural, not just *Need*, singular. We always look for and are guided by what we see as basic psychological needs. There are different lists, but most texts identify four basic needs to make all of us mentally healthy, or at least mentally stable. First, attachment. Second, control, sometimes described as orientation. Next, pleasure, which is really the avoidance of pain. And last, we need self-enhancement. Absent any one of these needs, we feel want and weakness. Absent two or more, we need help. But if a person needs all four, no telling what they are capable of."

Liz chimed in.

"That's excellent, Cynthia. You know your stuff. I could only add the fact that these four needs are somewhat sequential, a little bit chronological. Attachment and control are developed at a very young age and are strong drivers of how we behave. But beyond adolescence we see the need for both pleasure and avoidance of pain. Self-enhancement comes last. Children don't have that need but young adults do. And those whose brains and personalities develop later, say at eighteen, often struggle with self-esteem, which is a reciprocal of self-enhancement."

Liz and Cynthia had sparked a thirty-minute, back-and-forth discussion about the Unsub. What could explain killing three young men? Did the Unsub lose his attachment with his own family? What about his "pleasure" quotient? Did he seek and was denied some weird pleasure? Did he take pleasure in killing people? Was he a psycho? And what is self-esteem in the criminal world? Abe thought the Unsub was a vicious bastard. Lee thought he was acting out male dysfunction. Brick held his tongue while Liz switched to lecture mode.

"I think," she said, looking a little exasperated, "that we are mistaking moral judgments for psychiatric basic processes. In our science-based assessment of one's acts, there is a basic process of evaluating what is 'good' and what is 'bad.' We use those words loosely as motivation to maximize our experience of the 'good' and limit the 'bad.' You and everyone in law enforcement know the phrase, 'suffering for the greater good.' In psychoanalysis, that's the denial of some pleasures to reach something of greater worth as a patient works through a defined program of treatment. That program is predicated on this basic need in all of us. What is good, pleasurable, beautiful, excreta, depends upon the individual and how the experience of things follows the satisfaction of their other basic needs. Here we don't know the Unsub, or whether he's been diagnosed or treated. If I had to bet, I'd say he was a loner, not well liked, maybe attacked and living under life's radar. I'd bet he may have been interviewed by a mental health specialist but never treated by one. And he doesn't look like a guy that's done time in group therapy."

"Life's radar," Abe said louder than he needed to in the small room. "I dunno know about you, Doc, I don't see life having some kind of radar. I've arrested a hundred or more criminals in my time and half of 'em lived their whole life hiding from all cops. The other half were out there in plain sight. I have no idea what you mean by living under life's radar."

Liz loved this exchange. It was like being back in a university lecture hall with excited voices floating down to the lectern from the seats high up in the back of the hall. "Abe, I think you've just given us a perfect example of what I meant by life's radar. Individuals who are either criminals on the run or innocent people unjustly accused of something live in hiding—they change their names, locales, looks, and habits to avoid being caught if guilty, or accused if innocent. The Unsub we are trying to find is clearly living below life's radar and surfaces only when he commits another crime, another killing. Our advantage is, thanks to Lee, that we are zeroing in on who he might be by excluding large parts of the population that are not on the Whiteboard."

Brick, thinking the discussion was veering too far from FBI protocols and too deep into psychoanalytical bantering, called a fifteen-minute refreshment break.

Lee said, "Make it thirty. I want to fill in the blanks on the Whiteboard while the rest of you are refreshing in the men's and ladies' rooms."

As they came back to the conference room, they saw that Lee had created a new large square on a separate page of her Whiteboard diagram.

1. Unsub is not related, not a lover, not living close by, and not known to civil authorities.
2. He is smart but not experienced in violent conflict.
3. He needs to kill these twins because they are doing something he hates.
4. He will kill again because whatever they did to enrage him will happen again.
5. The fourth murder will happen, almost certainly, in New England.

Lee was still standing as the others took their seats. "Okay, I've added five opinions, my opinions, to the big blank box you now see on the Whiteboard. Some of these come from my reading of all four local police files. And some come from the exchange between Liz and Cynthia. And lastly, a little bit comes from my own family—my sister has a much-loved son who is schizophrenic and . . ."

Always eager to jump in when others were trying to explain something, Abe interrupted. "Whoa there, Lee. You saying our Unsub is a schizo?"

Lee gritted her teeth, shook her head a little, and took a deep breath. "Abe, my friend, schizo is slang. I said my nephew suffers from schizophrenia. He's not a danger to anyone except possibly himself when his meds don't work. He's really a lovely twenty-five-year-old who lives at home. Liz, I'm sure you can explain this better than I can, so . . ."

Liz took the cue. "Of course, Lee. I know the identifiers and outliers well. So, everybody, here's a short story about schizophrenia. It's a chronic brain disorder. A tiny percentage of the country is affected by it. The movies make too much of it. When it's active, symptoms are delusions, hallucinations, disorganized speech. Unmedicated patients have difficulty thinking. They often lack motivation or interest in anything. But with meds and ongoing therapy, usually in group sessions, most symptoms disappear, and patients' moods are diminished."

Abe insisted.

"I heard it was like, ya know, split personality and they can go crazy, ya know?"

"No, Abe," Liz said patiently with a nodding head and a smile.

"It's a complex disease. Genre writers and film producers have made it into something to fear. It does not mean split personality or multiple personality. Schizophrenics are not any more dangerous or violent than people in the general population. While they are few in number, and some end up homeless, with frequent hospitalizations, most people afflicted with schizophrenia live with their families, in group homes, or on their own."

Lee renewed her explanations. "I don't think our Unsub is related to the Vic's family because they've all been cleared by forensics or alibis. He does not love the young men he killed; he hates them. The methodology and crime scene data confirm that. You can see under Item Two that I see him as smart but new to violence. All four crime scene files document both attributes. He was smart enough to get in and get out without leaving a trail. He carefully picked his time and place. But nothing about these killings suggest he's experienced. These killings were planned but not hired out, and not done in a way a pro or a paid assassin would have done them. Look again at Item Three. See there, I've underlined the word *Needs*. I'm using the term in the psychological sense. I think his need to watch them die, up close and in a very personal way, is driven by his obvious rage in the act of killing them. He could have planted a bomb, cut their cars' brake lines, or used a high-powered rifle from a hundred yards away. But he didn't. He stuck his gun into the sides of their head and fired twice with bullets engineered to destroy brain tissues and stay behind as his signature. That alone convinces me they did something he hates . . ."

Cynthia raised her hand at Brick. Lee saw it and paused.

"It's okay, Cynthia, I'm sure Lee wants questions when they pop up in our heads."

"Yes, sir, thank you. Lee, do you mean that the killer hated them personally, like he *knew* them?"

"No, Cynthia, I don't. But you raise a good point that needs clarifying. I mean each Vic did something that the Unsub knows about even though he might not know them. And it's a really big deal for the Unsub, big enough for him to kill the Vic for doing it."

Brick asked his first question of the session. "Lee, I want to hear your wildest speculation on what the twin could have done that so enraged the Unsub and how he knew about it if we assume he didn't know any of the victims until he killed them."

"I think they did some 'twin' thing that was publicly known. Maybe in the press. Maybe from social media sites. I looked and there are websites and social media sources that are of special interest to twins, triplets, and maybe even quintuplets. Today's social media reality, and nuttiness as I see it, is that we all have social media acquaintances, friends, colleagues, and even lovers that we never know in person."

"So," Brick asked, "might we learn more about the Unsub on social media than in police records or old-fashioned knocking on doors?"

"Can't say that, boss, but social media rules the lives of many Americans these days. One of us ought to be going down rabbit holes on Google because it's likely that all of the Vics did. Maybe that's where the Unsub found them."

Brick nodded. "Okay, we can do that. I'll get help from the front office—research help. But here's another question about Item Number Three. You theorize he killed because the Vics did something he hates. Is this something likely to be on social media? And if it is, could we zero in a little bit by raking through social media sites to find out things that twins' hate but still do?"

"No, Brick," Liz said quickly, "I didn't mean the victims did something they hate. I mean they did something the Unsub hates and he knows they did it. To them, it may be perfectly normal, nothing bad."

Cynthia raised her hand. "Well, here's a thought. What do twins really love, besides one another? Two of my best friends in high school were twins. I don't think identical because they didn't resemble one another. No one ever mixed them up. They were somewhat independent and didn't have to be together all the time, and . . ."

Liz interrupted. "Hey, Cynthia, you've just hit on something. Identical twins, especially mirror-image twins, are world famous for their interdependence with one another. They can often literally read their twin's mind. As babies, they have to be close, physically close—close enough to smell and hear one another. Separation at a young age is always disastrous for them. You've all seen bassinets at hospital delivery rooms where they put twins in the same basket. There's a reason for that."

Lee moved a bit forward, closer to Liz. "Expand that a little, Liz. What happens when twins are separated later in life? Like, God forbid, one twin dies when they are teenagers. Is their grief different than would be experienced by a singleton teenager?"

"Well, that's something widely researched. In fact, there are international support groups entirely directed at this issue. One of them is called the Twinless Twins Support Group International. Think about their name—*twinless twins*. When a twin dies, the survivor is no longer a *twin*. They hold annual conventions all over the world. My research tells me the death of a twin creates a level of grief different from the death of a singleton brother or sister."

Lee shuddered and dropped her Whiteboard marker. "How different, Liz?"

"I don't have the details in mind, but I attended the 2009, or maybe it was 2010, *Twinless Twins Convention*, held in Denver Colorado. The meeting hall was full of bereaved twins and some parents of twins. I've got it on my own iPad and can find it in a few secs."

While Liz was touching the iPad screen, Cynthia dug into her briefcase, pulled out a Mac notebook, and asked Brick if she could log on to FREST's Wi-Fi. He gave her a temporary login. While she typed her way through that, Abe got up.

"Right back, boss. You gotta do what ya gotta do, right?"

Before he returned, Liz found her conference notes on her iPad. "Okay, I noted two key findings on twin loss. I think I copied this right off the program summary. 'Identical twins experience the loss somewhat more intensely than fraternal twins although there is considerable overlap—the loss experience may be just as devastating for some fraternal twins. There is also evidence of less grief reduction over time for identical than fraternal twins, on average. The second finding is that the loss of a twin is associated with greater grief than the loss of any other relative, with the exception of a spouse."

Brick stood up at the end of the table and held both palms up.

"Yes, but how does that relate to the mystery we're trying to solve here? I guess I'm missing an important element. Three of our four cases involve identical twins who were murdered. Your research says the survivor twin's grief is likely greater than it would be for non-twins. How does research help us solve murder cases? I'm presuming very few of the cases in that study were murders, right?"

"Good point, Brick," Liz said. "Maybe this is crazy. But maybe we ought to take a look at twins as suspects where they lost a twin and now, somehow, blame it on the world. Maybe grief, accidental death, or really violent death has turned into rage at the world."

"Hey, Boss," Lee said. "Maybe our Unsub *is* a twin! Maybe he's killing other twins because he has some deep need to kill that we cannot imagine, much less know."

Cynthia put a ribbon on the discussion.

"Maybe the Unsub lost his twin. And now he hates other twins who still have their twin, so he kills one to give grief to the other. Yeah, I know, crazy."

Brick closed the file folder on the desk in front of him. "Okay, this is not FBI protocol, but crazy Cynthia and crazy Lee—and crazy Liz—are on to something. We're all researchers here. We're not field agents anymore. So, let's all research separately and meet here tomorrow, late afternoon, say 4 p.m.?"

Liz spread the three large file folders across the back bar of her cubicle. She'd read them carefully last week, but this time she thought about what she was missing, not what she'd learned the first time. Someone had left a small booklet on the desk titled, *FREST Approach.* Thumbing through it, she saw something on the inside cover that struck her as a different way to think about the twins' murder cases.

> FREST Officers & Criminal Investigations. We should address new case assignments as more than an investigation of a specific crime or a series of similar criminal activities. FREST must apply a multi-faceted, problem-solving, research-based, analytical assessment. We must rapidly make critical decisions, sometimes involving life and death, based on limited information in a dynamic environment of active and still-evolving events. After a criminal event has occurred, our role in solving crimes will depend on local law enforcement preserving crime scenes and collecting evidence. Our take-over role is to devise an investigative plan that will identify reasonable grounds to identify and arrest the person or persons responsible. FREST may involve consultants to aid and abet solutions beyond the traditional training experience offered by the FBI and local law enforcement agencies.

That's me, she thought. I'm here not to solve the crime but to offer a research-based approach to identifying an Unsub that might not seem obvious to highly trained FBI agents. They are relying on my background and psychiatric focus to complement and aid their police focus. It occurred to her that she'd been thinking mostly about the criminal himself and not enough about his victim. Since all victims were twins, her focus should be tightly focused on that element of all three cases. What aspect of being an identical twin could have possibly led someone to murder identical twins?

She did what she'd often done in San Diego after a therapy session or an individual interview with a prisoner. She'd turn off her cell phone, leave the documents on her desk, go outside, and take a walk, alone. The crisp air and still damp streets around the BAU building were inviting since her mind felt clustered. She caught glimpses here and there of men in military garb, women in sensible shoes, jackets, and wool caps, and vehicles of every make and color. In the distance she could see treetops, electric lines supporting small birds and pigeons by the score. Somehow the complexity of buildings, people, humid chilled air, and birds led her to a place she'd had not given a second's worth of time in the last ten days. She thought of one other criminal case, a prisoner named Arthur Cheshire, and his steadfast sense of loyalty and fealty to his deceased identical twin brother. Once there, she walked as rapidly as she could back to her cubicle and her iPad.

She spent a half-hour logged in to her San Diego desktop computer via Wi-Fi. She made notes on a three-by-five note card, picked up the landline phone, and tapped out Brick's four-number extension. He answered immediately. Everyone on the team was spending the day isolated in their offices digging into what they might have missed.

"Brick, can I pop into your office now, please?"

"Well, okay. You sound a little out of breath. You alright?"

"I'm just fine. I'll be there in a sec."

She grabbed a bottle of water in the cubicle area of FREST's part of the floor, drank it half down, and walked at quick-march speed, 120 steps per minute, to Brick's corner office. She knocked, got a come-on-in, and pushed open the door. Lee was sitting across the desk with a folder on her lap and a Sharpie in her hand.

"Hey, Liz, what's up? You got our man in sight, I hope?"

She smiled at Lee, sat down in the other desk facing chair, and took a deep breath.

"You're not gonna believe this, but I think I might *know* your Unsub. I actually was also his mental health consultant while he was in a holding cell in San Diego two and a half years ago. His name is Arthur Cheshire, and he lives in Portland, Maine."

"Jeeze Louise," Brick said, closing the folder in front of him. "How in holy hell did you figure this out?"

"Well, more or less by accident. I took a walk outside to clear my head. And three blocks from here it hit me like a ton of bricks. I felt a flush of adrenaline and ran back here to call you. So, Arthur Cheshire! I just checked my iPad notes on his case. It's quite complicated but here's an elevator version. He was arrested under the name Martin Cheshire in Portland, Maine, by the FBI. Your Boston office will have a substantial file on him. He was extradited to San Diego and held there on a first-degree murder charge for killing his twin brother. But it didn't work. Two months later, after spending a dozen or so sessions with me, he walked out a free man. The FBI screwed it up and . . ."

Lee waved her hand. "Hold up, I got it here," she said, pointing to her iPad. "It was prosecuted initially by Boston FBI HQ. Here's the cover sheet. Docket Number 2003-CR-218519-FJM, *United States of America v. Martin Cheshire*. Extradited from federal court, Portland, Maine, to federal court, San Diego, California. US Assistant Attorney Stran Cabelson was the prosecutor out there and US Deputy Federal Defender Gordon Kemper represented Mr. Cheshire. And, by golly, you are right! Your formal title and name, Dr. Lisbeth Socorro, Court Psychiatric Services, is on page one."

Brick lit up like an old-fashioned Zippo in a dark room.

"Liz, do you think this guy, Martin Cheshire, is our Unsub? Is that what you're saying?"

"No, Brick. And thanks, Lee, for finding the FBI file so quickly. I never saw that. I only saw the initial pleadings in San Diego, but I wrote a fairly long report for the judge. Let me say right now, our Unsub is definitely *not* Martin Cheshire. He died several months before his twin brother, Arthur Cheshire, was arrested . . ."

Lee was perplexed.

"But Liz, the docket, and our file references a man named Martin Cheshire. He was arrested. He gave a long statement to our charging team in Portland and . . ."

"No," Liz said, squaring her shoulders and taking a deep breath. "Everyone in Portland got it wrong. Some of the people in San Diego, namely United States Magistrate Eli Hightower, got it right. Let me give you the front page of a spellbinder of a case. The US government thought the man they arrested was Martin Cheshire, but in fact he was Arthur Cheshire. They thought he was Martin because that's the name he used at that time in Portland. He had a job and a girlfriend there and they identified him as Martin. But when he was extradited to San Diego, he insisted he was Arthur. Now get this—Martin was charged with murdering his twin brother, Arthur. It took a good bit of court time and a lot of my time trying to unwind a bizarre case. The hearing before Judge Hightower was dubbed as an identity hearing. I was the only witness called to the stand in the case."

"What happened?" Brick asked.

"After a few months, the court accepted my testimony and assessment that the man arrested in Portland was actually Arthur, and the body found in Mexico was actually that of Martin, not Arthur. So, there was no murder. The identity hearing resulted in the government dropping all charges. It spawned a civil suit for wrongful arrest, wrongful imprisonment, and violation of civil rights. We heard the plaintiff got a large settlement, thanks to a big-name lawyer in San Diego."

"Okay, but how does that history relate to our cases here?"

"Well," Liz said, "it wasn't the charges or the way the case ended. I am persuaded by what I learned from the defendant, Arthur, in a dozen or so therapy and assessment sessions. I've been involved with maybe fifty or sixty identical twins one way or another over the last ten years. But Arthur Cheshire's relationship with his twin, Martin, was off the charts. They didn't just look like mirror-image twins, they switched identities frequently. They did it so often and so skillfully that even people close to them never knew exactly which one was the room, or even in the same bed. They invented a game as children they called *Hide and Be.* One would do something bad, the other would take the blame. One would get something nice, the other would claim it. They were absolutely bound together as if they had been conjoined at birth like Siamese twins and . . ."

Lee's face took on an ashen pale.

"Even so, even so united, how does that fit the things we know about the murders of a twin back here?"

"Of course, Lee, I see the doubt in your eyes. Me too. I'm doubtful too. But what triggered my memory of Arthur was our discussion yesterday and our talk about 'need' and 'rage.' Science and studies support those psychological elements in twins. We talked about that in terms of killing twins. But what is digging at me right now is whether our Unsub is *himself* an identical twin."

Brick stuck up one palm.

"So, if the Unsub is also a twin, how does that fit killing another twin's twin?"

"Brick, it would not fit except where the killer himself also lost a twin and cannot accept that fact. In the Cheshire case, I became convinced that either one of those boys, Arthur, or Martin, would have killed in a fit of gigantic rage to protect his brother. So deep was that bond that they often acted out the life of the other. And in the end, in Arthur's case, I had the feeling over and over that even after losing his brother in a boating accident, he could not accept that reality. So, he became his brother. That's a need rarely seen in human behavior. He needed to be Martin to keep Martin alive. And he would have become enraged if he knew some other twins were, shall we say, not 100 percent committed to one another. And then, the final clue for me was the simple fact that all three killings shared one more strange coincidence. They all happened on the twin's birthdays. That means nothing to law enforcement, but it meant something to the Unsub. He picked that day for a reason. I have the awful feeling that it might be Arthur Cheshire. Here's why. He and Martin spent every birthday together. Neither of them would have understood another set of twins voluntarily spending their birthday apart."

PORTLAND, MAINE

Brick called the SAIC in Portland and arranged a quick trip. He asked Liz to go along because she already knew the Cheshire case and had basic charging documents in his federal case in San Diego. She knew things about Arthur Cheshire that were in her interview notes but not in the abbreviated court records in either Portland or San Diego. While a longshot, he hoped that the Portland office could find Arthur, whose last known address was a fishing camp on the Damariscotta River, about fifty miles north of Portland. And he was eager to see an old friend, the SAIC in the Portland office.

They flew to Portland in a Marine Corps UC-35 jet from Quantico to the US Marine Corps Liaison Station in Portland. They were met by the youngest agent in the Portland office, who said this was his twenty-ninth birthday. Brick asked if he was a twin. The man said no, and Brick changed the subject to what he knew about fishing camps on the Damariscotta River. The agent said nothing.

Liz asked him if he liked living in Portland. He said it wasn't bad in July, but the winters were not like his hometown, which turned out to be San Antonio, Texas. The conversation on the twenty-minute drive to the FBI office on Middle Street was limited to restaurants and whether the Hampton Inn in Portland was a good place to stay. He said it was a block off the waterfront, but he'd never been inside. When they got to the FBI office on Middle Street, they learned it was within walking distance of their hotel, the Portland Police Office, and the only restaurant the agent could recommend—Boone's Fish House.

They checked in at their hotel, got their keys, left their roller bags with the bellman, who smelled a little like fresh fish, and walked to the FBI office. Once they got through security, Brick's old friend, Normandie Washington, met them in the hallway.

"Brick, you haven't changed a lick since I last saw you on that Canadian drug case we had up in Bangor."

"Good of you to say that in front of Dr. Socorro. She's on TDY assignment with us on just this one case and calls San Diego her home base. Liz, meet Normandie Washington. He was the black panther agent with me on a drug case it took us two years to finally eradicate."

"Nice to meet you, doctor. I saw your assessment this morning on the digital files Brick's temp sent in last night. Looks like a case that needs a good shrink—starting with whether my old buddy Brick is as crazy as he used to be when he was an in-the-dirt field agent. Did you know he was once under cover? Even from me, his classmate at the Academy."

Liz enjoyed the banter among old friends. She asked how long Normandie had been the SAIC in Portland. He said five and a half years. She asked about the Martin Cheshire case. He said, ugh.

But," he said through clenched teeth, "it was a teaching moment. Who would have thought that a young man, well known here, could be someone no one really knew here? Of course, I never met him in person, but I reviewed all of the 302s on him—we have a stack of them—they are waiting for you, laid out in alphabetical order in the small conference room next to my office."

"Three-oh-twos?" Liz asked.

Brick answered for Normandie.

"That's the short name for FD-302. All witnesses are interviewed without recording and all details from interviews are typed on an FD-302. They are the nuts, bolts, cranks, and shanks of every FBI investigation."

"Wouldn't it be easier to use digital audio recorders?"

"Yes, and we occasionally do record some people. But you need to understand that about 80 percent of a field agent's job is to interview people. The official policy is that when doing background investigations, criminal and intelligence investigations, or source debriefings, we make notes in the field and use those notes to create full-length summaries as soon as possible. And unlike most other law enforcement agencies, we document everything we learn in a 302 Case File, whether positive or negative."

The defensive looks Liz was getting caused her to backtrack.

"Hey, guys, I'm on your side, remember. I work with suspects and convicted defendants daily and am very pro-police, but I also argue for technology when it makes the job easier. Is there some deep-set reluctance for the FBI to avoid audio recording that colors the insistence on handwritten notes and typewritten 302s?"

Normandie smiled. "Liz, you're here just in time. Remember that the first twins' murder you guys are working on occurred in December 2014. Just a few months before that, in July of 2014, the FBI joined the modern tech world, at least partly. Here's the deal. Teddy Roosevelt created the FBI in 1908. When tape recorders came into widespread use in the early fifties, J. Edgar Hoover didn't trust them because they missed the nuance in interviews and took up lots of space. Of course, he had other reasons not to like them too. For his forty-eight years at the helm of the FBI, we were type, print, and store investigators and liked 302s much better than audio tapes. But we made a big change in 2014. The Department of Justice reversed that policy for all DOJ entities, including yours—the Federal Bureau of Prisons. Now, when we interview or interrogate suspects in custody, we use digital audio, preferably with video. There are special exceptions made, but almost all suspects are taped. But we don't tape or video witnesses, victims, family, or friendly psychiatrists."

"Thank goodness," Liz said with a grin. "I don't use audio or video when talking to prisoners. So, which federal law agencies are now using high tech on suspects?"

"It applies to us, the DEA, ATF, and the US Marshals Service. It's important to remember, though, the recording policy only applies to individuals in custody."

"So, as long as we're on the subject, are agents wearing body cams?"

"Funny you should ask. We hear that's coming. HQ is ramping up a BWC program."

"BWC?"

"Stands for body worn cameras. Some of my guys here think it should be WOBC—Worn Out Body Cameras. We've been wearing out our bodies ever since 911."

Brick turned the conversation back to the case at hand.

"Norm, we're here because Liz spent a good deal of time with Arthur Cheshire while he was in custody in San Diego. I'll let her tell you how the San Diego case might be the key to the twins' murder cases here in New England."

"Agent Washington," Liz said," you may think I'm crazy, but here is what sparked me to think that Arthur Cheshire might be more than what your office here saw in him two years ago and what Brick's team in Quantico is faced with now. Arthur Cheshire was so deeply committed to his twin brother, Martin, that he virtually became his brother after Martin drowned in a boating accident not far from here. He pretended to be Martin while he was here in Portland, but had a new life as himself, Arthur, in San Diego. He lived with and slept with Martin's girlfriend, Rosie Andersen, here while amazingly managing to start a new sexual relationship with another girl, Marcella Munoz, in San Diego. All of that was unraveled in a court case, called an *identity hearing*, in federal court. You know about all of that because your office was involved in Arthur's arrest here and extradition to San Diego. Now fast forward to today. Brick's team in Quantico is searching for an Unsub who killed three twins in the last eighteen months. I came to realize that the perfect person to commit those crimes here on the East Coast might be the same man that I spent a good deal of time with on the West Coast. Here the team has a set of known facts that give us a broad look at the Unsub. Those same facts fit Arthur Cheshire to a T."

Norm listened with his jaw lowered, his eyes blinking, and his comfort zone exposed. He pushed his chair back from the table, stood, and rocked back and forth on his heels looking more at the floor than Brick and Liz.

"Dr. Socorro, I have great respect for your profession and am sure your intentions here are the best. But I gotta tell you, the dominoes in your evidentiary chain are miles apart. Hell, they are three thousand miles apart. As I hear it from you, it's what you learned in psychoanalysis two years ago that leads you to suspect Arthur Cheshire of murdering other twins two years after he was released and absolved of a murder charge in California. That's not only far fletched, but it's also three thousand miles short of probable cause. What if you do find him here, somewhere on the East Coast, do you expect the FBI to file charges here? On what basis?"

Brick reacted.

"Now hold up, Norm. She's suspicious for good reason. My team thinks she may be right, but we're not placing bets yet.

This is an open FBI investigation. We're looking for suspects. We won't arrest Arthur Cheshire or anyone else unless we have a rock-solid evidentiary basis to support an arrest *and* charges. We're not asking you or anyone here to do the work. We want to look at your 302s and talk to a few local citizens. That's all. If we can't connect Mr. Cheshire to our cases, then we'll continue to investigate. Actually, all we're doing now is the work that might rule Mr. Cheshire out."

Brick and Liz spent the rest of the day reading 302s, looking at photo scans, asking one another questions, and taking calls from Quantico. By mid-afternoon, they had a short list of people in Portland they wanted to interview. Employees at *AmHull Insurance*. Teachers and local people who may have known the twins before Arthur was arrested. Anyone who might know where Arthur is now. People living near the fishing camp the Cheshire twins owned on the Damariscotta River. Someone who can provide access to the fishing camp itself because Brick wanted to look under the floorboards that covered Martin Cheshire's remains, before Arthur moved them to Mexico. Last, and most important, anyone in town who can add to the lore about the game the Cheshire twins called "Hide and Be."

AUGUSTA, MAINE

Portland has a population of about 65,000. It's a peninsula extending into Casco Bay, once a busy commercial fishing port. But now the Old Port waterfront consists mostly of some working fishing wharves, with warehouses converted into shops and restaurants. By comparison, Maine's capital city, Augusta, has about 16,000 people. Maine has lots of land, lots of fish, not very many people, and almost no diversity. Its population is stable. Many families had close relationships with other Down Easters from the Canadian border on the north to New Hampshire on its southern border.

Brick took less than five minutes to find Rosie Andersen's new address and workplace. She'd moved from Portland to Augusta a year earlier and bought a nice little brick house on Winthrop Street. Zillow listed her buy at $360,000. She was an assistant manager at a busy Starbucks. Her cell phone was not listed anywhere, and she had no reference on CODIS or NDIS, the DOJ federal search engines. So, Brick and Liz went to her Starbucks store at noon, identified her from her Facebook postings, and waited until she got off shift at 3 p.m. They followed her home, noting her license plate. Ten minutes after her garage door closed, they knocked on the front door.

It took several minutes for Ms. Andersen to open the door. Brick held up his FBI credentials card and badge to the peep hole in the door. He was about to knock a third time when the door inched open against the chain lock on the inside.

"Who are you?" a female voice called out.

"Miss Anderson, I'm Agent Brick Cato with the FBI. We would like to talk to you about a case we're investigating."

"Well, I guess so. Just a minute, please."

They waited on the doorstep for another three or four minutes before the door opened and the young woman facing them said, "Is this official or are you just talking to people in the neighborhood?"

She opened the door wide, motioning for them to come in, but not looking directly at either of them.

"Sorry to intrude, Miss, but we are here on FBI business. Of course, you do not have to talk to us. We could arrange to talk to you downtown if you'd prefer that. You are not a suspect; we only want to talk to you about a person of interest in an ongoing investigation."

"Okay," she said, still looking around them and pointing them into a small living room with what seemed to be period furniture. A tapestry hung on the far wall, an ornate fireplace with a heavy bronze screen was centered the near wall, and a finely carved oak chest of drawers was offset, covered on top with several crocheted doilies.

Pointing to a heavy couch, she said in low tones, "You can sit there. I hope this won't take long; I have things to do, you know."

"Thanks a lot, we won't be long. You know my name. This is Doctor Lisbeth Socorro. I work out of our Quantico Virginia office, and she works in a different DOJ office in San Diego. We're interested in Arthur Cheshire."

"Well, I'm afraid I can't be of much help. I haven't seen him for almost two, maybe two and a half years."

"Do know where he is?"

"You mean now, where is he now? No, I absolutely don't. The last I heard of him was when they arrested him, thinking he was Martin, his twin. You know about the Cheshire twins, right?"

"We do, Miss Anderson. In fact, that's exactly what we would like to talk to you about—Arthur and his twin brother, Martin. We know they played tricks on people here in Portland for years—something they called Hide and Be. Do you know about that?"

"Well, yes, the dirty bastards did it once to me—those two thought it was so cute. But it was just a game for them. And then later when Martin and I were . . ."

She put her hand over her mouth as though she had revealed a secret and felt bad about it.

"None of what they did was my fault. Why are you after me? I'm the victim, right? And besides . . ."

Brick started to answer when Liz touched him on the arm.

"Rosie . . . can I call you that? Maybe I can ease your nerves a little bit. We're not here to accuse you of anything. I met Arthur Cheshire when he was in custody in San Diego following his arrest here. I spent a good bit of time with him as a consulting psychiatrist, but not as a treating physician. He talked some about you and about another woman Marcella. That's part of what we are here for. But I can assure you we are not investigating you, or Marcella. We are trying to understand Arthur's relationship with Martin before the boating accident. Maybe we could start there. Is that okay with you?"

Rosie Anderson nodded at Liz and turned to face her more directly.

"Well, if you talked to him, you know that I did not know about the boating accident. No one here did. Martin and I were just getting to know one another. I had only moved into Martin's apartment a week or two when . . . well, when—oh God, are you going to put me through that? You know, when we slept together, I thought it was Martin. But it was Arthur—he fooled me while making love to me! That's a crime, isn't it? Why didn't the FBI charge him with that? And you probably know he totally fooled Marcella too. He told her Martin was alive all the time. What in God's name are you doing here in my living room? I told some other FBI officer; I don't remember his name, but he worked downtown and . . ."

Brick tried to get back into the conversation.

"Miss, you're exactly right. You have every right to be incensed at what he did. We know about some of it because we read interview notes about your relationship back when he was arrested. We don't need to put you through any of that again. All we would appreciate is asking you some questions about how he managed to pull off the hoaxes he played on you, and several others, like people at AmHull Insurance."

"You're talking about Alice Singworth, right? He fooled her too, but at least he didn't sleep with her."

"You're right," Brick said. "We read her interview notes too and we had hoped to talk to her tomorrow morning. But as you probably know, she doesn't work for AmHull anymore. We understand she works in Boston now."

"Well, good for her. She was so nice to me, and to Marcella. We hardly knew one another at all and yet those twin idiots, the Cheshire brothers, fooled all three of us. Okay, can you just ask your questions and then leave me alone?"

Liz knew that if they didn't take this opportunity, she might never again open that ornate front door.

"Rosie, would you say that Martin and Arthur were so close to one another that they could fool anyone? Like one of them pretending to be the other. Would you say they did that to protect themselves or just to fool people?"

"Protect themselves? What do you mean? From what?"

"Well, we know they used their game, Hide and Be, to protect one of them by the other one pretending to be the one that did something bad. They protected one another that way, didn't they?"

"Hell I know. They played their game to fool people. That's all I know. They put me through hell. And this visit by both of you is bringing all that hell back. I'm gonna be sick. Please leave, but you can call me. I'll give you my cell number and just hope you don't call."

Brick got up and put his notebook back into his briefcase.

"Thanks, Miss, sorry to be a bother."

Liz got up, walked over to Rosie, and handed her a business card.

"Rosie, this is my San Diego card, but you can always reach me on the cell number. You know I talked to your friend Marcella in San Diego because Arthur told me a lot about her. You have nothing to fear from the FBI, or me."

Rosie didn't walk them to the door, but she said something unexpected to Liz as she looked at her card.

"Thank you, doctor. I talk to Marcella occasionally. She and I shared a romance with Arthur, except I didn't know he *was* Arthur. And she never met Martin, but she told me knowing one Cheshire twin was knowing the other. They lived for one another—us girls never mattered to either one of them. They hated anyone who didn't think like they did. We got even in the end."

PORTLAND, MAINE

American Hull Insurance, Inc., was one of Maine's many small insurance companies, specializing in selling "hull" insurance. Harold Hull's grandfather, Henry Hull, started the company in the 1880s. He was a master seaman. Family legend said he survived the sinking of the family's fishing boat with a vow to never set foot on another boat, and to make money from those damn fools who did. Technically, "hull insurance" protects boat owners against loss caused by damage or destruction of water borne craft. Airplanes have hulls too, but Henry Hull started his company nineteen years before the Wright Brothers came on the scene in 1903.

Harold Hull's inheritance of the family company began in 1973; he was still at the helm in 2014. More or less. His sons liked the branch office in San Diego, and his faithful book-keeper slash office manager, Alice Singworth, quit a year ago. Her replacement was an ambitious young entrepreneur named Stralinski. When Brick called to set an appointment with Mr. Harold Hull, Stralinski gave him a landline number for the owner's waterfront home on Munjoy Hill in Portland's East End. It had stunning views of Casco Bay and downtown. It was an 1893 two-story wood slab house with multiple decks on three sides.

Brick and Liz decided in the taxi ride that Brick would take the lead and she would take notes. A teenager answered the door knocker and said his grandfather was waiting for them in the downstairs study. It turned out to be a tiny museum of Portland's boating history.

Harold Hull was a heavily whiskered man who didn't look his age, eighty-five. But his age-related hearing loss proved to be an interviewing challenge.

After the usual preliminaries about the FBI's interest in his former employee, Arthur Cheshire, Harold perked up.

"Oh, them. You're asking about the twins. They worked for me for maybe ten years. Maybe less. Alice mostly dealt with them even though she could not tell them apart any more than one oyster looks like all the other oysters. She said he stole from us. Is that why you're here?"

"No, not exactly, Mr. Hull. We'd like to locate him in connection with other possible involvement in crimes that have nothing to do with your business."

"Well, good then," Mr. Hull said, "I don't know him now any better than I did then. Come to think on it, I never knew him or his twin—whose name I'm forgetting."

"His brother's name was Martin, Mr. Hull," Liz offered.

Still looking at Brick, but answering Liz's comment, the man flexed his eyes up and down.

"Their names confused people. You see, they weren't truthful about that—their names I mean. They switched back and forth—I know that because Alice said so. She thought it funny. I thought it suspicious. You can't trust people in the insurance business who lie about their names, can you? When I was young, I sold hull policies to people in the fishing business. My father taught me the business. He said always make buyers show you a social security card and if they won't, don't insure them. I could go on and on and . . ."

"Yes, Mr. Hull, I'm sure you're right about that. But we know their names and a little about the games they played and . . ."

"Was it a game? You say that. You know I can remember the names of boat owners back in the seventies because I remember looking at their social security cards. My father was sure right about that. Now it's a little different for me. These days everyone who visits me here at the house, you know I don't go downtown much anymore, wants to know what I know. I have to tell you I remember swirling waters and crashing waves in Casco Bay out that window over there. But customers and employees are not so clear to me these days. Did you talk to Alice about them?"

Over breakfast that morning, Liz had talked to Brick in her "lecture" voice. She told him that remembering and forgetting is taken for granted, like breathing. The power of memory lets us remember children, birthdays, terrible losses, and happy days. But in counseling or group therapy, moments, events, and people are remembered or forgotten depending on age, history, and personal experience. The challenge, she said, is embedded in the fabric of mystery and tragedy. No one likes to be disbelieved because it shatters our confidence. When we forget and realize we have forgotten something we once knew well, it can shut down an interview or a therapy session. Opens old wounds, she said.

They spent another fifteen minutes learning about the hulls of fishing boats and yachts. They thanked Mr. Hull and left after he identified the names of a dozen beautiful boats from old photos in his study. He was proud his company had insured them and hundreds more in the twentieth century. Brick said that will be a five sentence 302. Liz said they needed to find Alice Singworth.

When they got back to the FBI office in Portland, they found a fax from Lee in Quantico. She had located Alice Singworth in Boston. She worked half-time as a bookkeeper for a locally owned bookstore and lived in an apartment on Myrtle Street, about a mile from the bookstore. She apparently worked mostly from home but came into the store every Saturday morning. Lee had tried to arrange an in-person interview, but Ms. Singworth sounded hesitant since it involved her former employer, American Hull Insurance, Inc. She said she would talk on the phone.

Brick thought maybe she'd be less resistant if Liz talked with him on the line as a listener and note taker. So, she called the number Lee had given them.

"Miss Singworth, my name is Dr. Elisbeth Socorro, we got your number from our Quantico office. You talked to Agent Lee Cheong yesterday. Is this a good time to talk for a few minutes with us?"

"Ah, well, I don't know anything about what the FBI lady asked about yesterday. I mean, ah, are you with the FBI too?"

"Well, I'm not an agent or a law enforcement officer. Actually, I'm a psychiatrist working with the FBI on an important case. It might involve someone you knew in Portland; his name is Arthur Cheshire."

The line went dead for a moment. They could hear rustling and what sounded like heavy breathing. Liz waited thirty seconds and said, "Miss Singworth, are you still on the line?"

"Well, yeah, but you said 'we.' Is someone else listening in?"

"Yes, I was about to explain that," Liz said, speaking crisply but cautiously.

"Special Agent Brick Cato is on the line, and he may have some questions, but mostly you'll be talking to me."

"Do I need a lawyer or something? I never did anything wrong and cannot imagine why the FBI wants to talk to me about the Cheshire twins. They were never nice to me, and besides I was already talked to by the FBI in Portland. But you and the FBI lady yesterday said you are from Virginia. So, . . ."

"Miss Singworth, you do not have to talk to us. You are not a suspect or anything. We're only interested in finding and talking to Arthur Cheshire. Our FBI office in Portland kept notes about your interviews last year. We're just following up on some new things that might involve Arthur Cheshire."

"Well, okay, but I haven't seen or talked to him hardly at all since Mr. Hull sent him to San Diego. I know he got arrested and all, but I don't know where he is. Good riddance, I'd say. He could only see his brother, no one else in the office, even Mr. Hull who was kind to him and Martin. They thought they were so smart, always trying to fool everybody all the time and, well, I don't know what you want from me, and . . ."

"Miss Singworth, I'm so sorry to disturb you. We know you didn't do anything wrong. Let me just ask two questions. First, can you tell us anything about Arthur embezzling money from your company? Second, can you give us any information about where he is now? Can you help us with that?"

"It wasn't Arthur. It was Martin. He cheated the company, but it wasn't my company, like you said. I just worked there."

"Yes, you're right about the name under which he was arrested in Portland—it was Martin. Do you know any of the details about embezzlement from AmHull? You were the bookkeeper there, right?"

"So, now I don't know what you want. Arthur or Martin, whatever, embezzled money. What does that have to do with me? Tell me that."

Liz waved at Brick signaling him to take over.

"Miss, this is Agent Brick Cato. We have no information that suggests you had anything to do with the embezzlement at AmHull. You are not a suspect, and this is not an interrogation.

We won't be reading your Miranda rights to you, but I always tell everyone I interview that you must be truthful in what you tell us."

The line went dead again for a half-minute, but Brick thought he could hear whispering in the background.

"Miss Singworth, do you have someone there with you? If so, it might be wise for you to identify him or her. This is an official interview, and we ask this sort of question routinely. Are you okay?"

Thirty seconds passed.

"No, I'm sorry, Mr. Cato. I'm sorry I can't help you, but I don't know where Arthur is. And I don't really want to be involved in anything those Cheshire boys did. I told you they were always trying to fool me and everybody. I can't stand them. Is it okay if I just hang up now?"

Liz answered.

"Yes, of course you can hang up. But if you think of anything you can call me at my personal number. It's 858-788-34—"

The line went dead. Brick clicked off his iPhone and scratched his forehead.

"Okay, Dr. Socorro, what just happened?"

"Dunno, Brick, but three possibilities pop up. Maybe Miss Singworth knows something she doesn't want us to know. Maybe she knows more about Arthur than we do. Or maybe she is afraid to talk to us because she's afraid of Arthur. I think the FBI needs to find out more about her than I saw in the Portland file."

"Well, you might be right; maybe she knows something we don't. We need to keep close tabs on her. All we know about Arthur Cheshire is that he fits our Unsub profile based on your research and your extended interviews of him in the lockup at San Diego. And if your second thesis is right—she knows him better than we do—then she could be a real asset for us. And third, if she's afraid of Arthur, she might be a potential victim, even though she's not a twin. Let's get the full team on this tomorrow."

ARTHUR TALKING TO HIMSELF

Eh? The bucket? What bucket? Ah, that bucket, the one where we used to put our shoes so no one would know we got 'em dirty climbing over the drainage ditch in the back of that foster-moster house. Right? Marty, God man, I miss you. Except when I am you, right? You know that, right? Remember when we hid and then I'd be, and no one knew? Or even better for the fumbucks, you'd be me while I was hiding in plain sight! Those days . . . those days . . . well, they are back. You wanna know why? Because I'm watching us every goddamn day, every goddamn day. And while you're hiding out, I'm punishing, punishing our inner kin, those mirrors that look the same but don't live the same. You know what I'm talking about, right? See, I been in the Facebook, in the Facebook, and you know what? Some twins, same as us, don't follow the rules. They have birthdays just like we do but they fumbuck it up BIG TIME. BIG TIME. They don't live in the same house, open their presents together, live for each other, each other like we do now even though you're dead, man. You're dead but nobody knows it because they think you're me and I'm you and we're NOT DEAD, NOT DEAD. So, there were two of our kin that lived down New Hampshire way, down New Hampshire way in shitty Manchester. We went there and double-tapped a sinful twin who would not come to the Crucifix, didn't even know the Crucifix! You remember that Crucifix—the one where the bastard-bastard had the good-boy strap and he'd strap me thinking I was you and that was good because I was you that time, that time. Anyhow, this twin down New Hampshire way was a Puerto Rican or something like that cause his name was Emiliano Estancia. I called him EE and I gave him two hollows in the head for not loving his twin like he had to, had to, you know. You hid off the porch and I blasted his brains all over that porch. Now he cannot dis-love his brother. That word, dis-love, was never used by us, was it! Never. Never. We didn't die because we loved ourselves, didn't we?

QUANTICO, VIRGINIA
PRESENT TIME

At 0900 hours the next morning, Brick called for another AHOD and gave the FREST team an update.

"Okay, guys, you all know from the status briefing I emailed to you last night that we didn't learn much in Portland. Mr. Hull has no idea where our potential Unsub, Arthur Cheshire, is. Alice Singworth is, at best, a reluctant informant. She is either afraid of us, the FBI, Arthur Cheshire, or she has something to hide. But none of that is of much consequence to us since her reticence is unconnected to our challenge—finding our Unsub. So . . ."

Liz, seated at the end of the table, next to Cynthia, raised her hand.

"Brick, sorry to interrupt, but I've been thinking about our visit with Ms. Singworth. I agree 100 percent with your assessment—she's scared of something. But what if she knows something that is directly connected to everything that happened between Arthur Cheshire, who might be our Unsub, and his former employer, American Hull Insurance Company?"

Brick, who usually invited team members to pipe up when the spirit moved them, frowned. Like all decisive men, he had a natural reluctance to change course when the current path was underperforming.

"Liz, I thought we agreed that neither Harold Hull nor Alice Singworth could help us find Arthur Cheshire. Right? And to make that a trio, Rosie Anderson essentially blew us off with a definite shrug. So, the three people in Portland that knew Arthur Cheshire best are evasive and uncooperative. What does that tell us and what are we missing in Portland?"

Liz picked up her lab book and thumbed through it for a few seconds.

"Well, there's still a history track to follow. Remember that the Portland FBI team's first look at Arthur Cheshire was because they thought he *was* Martin Cheshire and that he'd embezzled a quarter of a million dollars from the company. It was only later that a court in San Diego identified the man they arrested as Arthur, not Martin. And they thought he had killed Arthur. The embezzlement charges involving insurance payments died when they learned that Martin died in a boating accident that Arthur hid because, for psychological reasons we've discussed, he *became* his brother, sort of. Martin may or may not have embezzled anything. That crime—embezzlement—was never fully investigated, much less solved. That may be why Alice Singworth is scared to talk to us."

"Liz, suppose you're right about Miss Singworth. So what? What does her fear or her complicity, if that's what you're suggesting, give us in terms of finding Arthur Cheshire?"

"Nothing, Brick. Nothing at all. But I spent two months interviewing Arthur in San Diego. I can promise everyone here that he believes he is his brother, even though Martin died in a boat accident. Psychologically, Arthur is Martin. He cannot separate his past from his present. Alice Singworth's reluctance to help us might be explained if she was somehow involved in or knew about Martin's embezzlement. We know she talked to Rosie Anderson. We know she quit AmHull not long after Martin was arrested and before Arthur was dismissed as a defendant in San Diego. Are those events connected?"

Brick dropped his ballpoint on the desk and raised both hands, palms up, in the air.

"Hey, Liz, this is the FBI. You and Cynthia are a giant help here, especially on such a murky psycho case like a dude killing three young men because they happen to be identical twins on their birthdays. But we're law enforcement. We investigate on reasonable suspicion and prosecute only on probable cause. This investigation is based on evidence of serial murders happening in three different states. That's our jurisdiction. We have no jurisdiction in a state crime that may have been committed in Maine under state embezzlement statutes. Am I right about where you want us to go? You think we might find our Unsub if we dig into the AmHull embezzlement case, which a federal court in Portland dismissed almost two years ago?"

Lee, sensing that things could get out of control if the boss and the doctor were to take separate paths, eased into the argument.

"Brick, like you, I'm FBI to the bone; we can't pursue state embezzlement charges. But Liz seems to me to be right in thinking maybe the old embezzlement case explains Miss Singworth's avoidance during your interview. I read your 302. You got it right. What puzzles me is why Arthur Cheshire, who was never suspected of stealing anything, might have scared Miss Singworth. As I read your 302 and talked to Liz about it, last night, I wondered if maybe Arthur somehow did know about the embezzlement and lied about it to protect his brother Martin. Isn't that what they always did, protect one another against the world? And while I'm offering my two bits, let me up the ante by a quarter. The 302s on the interview with Rosie Andersen were similar, now that I've reread what she said in the context of what Alice Singworth said. In short, both women who had every reason to hate Arthur, now won't help us find him."

Liz resisted smiling. "You know, everybody, Brick is correct. This is an FBI case—murder in the first—like they say in the movies. But I forgot something important that I learned from Arthur in one of our counseling sessions in San Diego. We were talking about his guilt over the boating accident. I tried to assure him it was an accident. He didn't kill Martin. He drowned because he was thrown out of a boat in a huge rainstorm. But in the middle of that, Arthur went almost blank on me. Like I was telling him something new. He said, no you're wrong, doc. I killed Arthur while I was being Martin. You remember right after the accident I went back down to Portland and made love to Rosie. Rosie was Martin's girl. I was Martin right there in our apartment two days after that storm on the Damariscotta. And you know about the money, only twenty-six grand Martin said he siphoned off AmHull. They said it was embezzlement. But Martin was charged with embezzling about a quarter million. He said he did it right under Alice Singworth's nose. Arthur told me in my office that maybe he did it because he was Martin. Remember, he played Martin in Portland and himself in San Diego. He told me he must have stolen that money because he was Martin in Portland and *only* Arthur in San Diego, and . . ."

Abe, sometimes confused but never in doubt, snarled.

"Hey guys, let's button this up. Both of you are right, just about different things. I don't want to investigate a robbery that never happened or a witness that is scared shitless about some state embezzlement scheme. But if Liz is right, like I think she is, in tagging this Arthur Cheshire as our Unsub, then we ought to take a long look at two women who aren't cooperating with us. This Singworth babe is sending vibes to both of you. And then there's Arthur—the twin Liz thinks might be our Unsub. We are the FBI, famous for finding criminals on every continent, even the North Pole. But here's my thing. We ran a nationwide search for Arthur Cheshire, and we got zip. Nada. No jobs, bank accounts, SSNs, cars or jeeps, and the girls up there in Portland are scared. Maybe we're looking for the wrong twin."

Brick jumped up from his seat and knocked over his Starbucks cup.

"Abe, holy mother of God! Maybe you're right. Lee, can you hook up that electronic Whiteboard now, the one with the great diagram laying out our combined theories in this case?"

Lee turned the Whiteboard on, fished through recent saves on it, and beamed her original chart back up.

"See there, guys?" Brick said, beaming. "It's there just like Abe said. We're thinking Arthur might be our Unsub and we've searched high and low for him with zero sightings. What if he is there, in plain sight? What if this is another Hide and Be game? You know, Arthur does something bad, like killing three people. And we can't find him. Why? Well, Abe just said it. Maybe we're looking for the wrong twin. What if Martin is the Unsub? Remember, Arthur won his case in San Diego and walked out of court a free man. Where did he go when he exited that courthouse? Maybe he became Martin again. Let's ride the other horse—let's look for Martin Cheshire! The girls in Portland won't help us find Arthur. But maybe they will help us find Martin, without even knowing they are helping."

Brick sent a status via the FBI's internal fax system to all FREST team members outlining a process known as tap and trace. Liz and Cynthia were surprised that the FBI did not need a search warrant or judicial permission to access phone lines. The FBI cannot get a wiretap on phone conversations with either Rosie Anderson or Alice Singworth. But they could "tap and trace" and use "pen registers" on their cell phones. Neither device records nor "listens" to actual conversations. The tap-and-trace protocol simply taps the line and records phone numbers calling into a specific phone line. Pen registers let them record the phone numbers from outgoing calls. The hope was that might lead them to Arthur through a back door, without either Rosie or Alice's knowledge or permission.

Two days after getting back to Quantico, the taps and registers on both targeted lines revealed a flurry of calls back and forth between Alice and Rosie. That was a small surprise, but more interesting was that on the third day, there were a half-dozen teleconferences between Alice in Boston, Rosie in Portland, and Marcella Munoz in San Diego. Each call lasted about a half-hour.

Brick asked the team for comments on the three-way party line calls.

Lee as the ranking member asked Brick how Marcella was connected to the other two women.

"Well, here's where it gets really interesting. Marcella was the young lady Arthur dated, lived with, and constantly lied to about his brother Martin. He told her Martin was happy in Portland for months after the river boat accident. I'm not sure how she became part of the three-way flurry after we stirred things up in Portland last week."

Liz seemed very surprised about the recent phone calls and was eager to brief the team on Marcella.

"I saw her in court once and had a phone call or two with her during the time Arthur was in jail and I was engaging him in counseling sessions in my office. I'm surprised Marcella is now talking to Alice Singworth but not at all surprised that she's taking to Rosie. The Cheshire twins played their Hide and Be game on Rosie and Marcella, lied to them, and Arthur had sex with them; actually, he raped Rosie and had what I sensed was wild sex with Marcella. Of course, he knew Alice because they worked for the same company in Portland. It is very surprising that these three women are talking to one another right after the FBI talks to two of them. I can't help but think they were exchanging information about Arthur, since he was the focus of our interviews in Portland."

Abe jumped on that.

"Hey, there's an easy test we could do today. Liz, why don't you call Marcella in San Diego and ask about Arthur Cheshire? If Arthur is the subject of the three-way conversation, we ought to see a trap and trace shortly thereafter on their three-way chats."

Brick agreed and took it one step further.

"You're right, Abe, but do you think we ought to boost that a little bit? What could Liz say to Marcella that might put her in same 'don't call me' frame of mind that Alice and Rosie latched onto as soon as their front doors slammed shut?"

Cynthia, ever the social media advocate, chimed in. "Liz could say that she talked to Alice and Rosie, and they are helping us find Arthur. They aren't, but Marcella will already know that to be wrong. Right? If she's talking to them, she knows they are not going to help us. And here's another thing that pops into my social media brain. Why don't we get a full-blown search of all three of them connecting on social media? If their three-way tele chats are just for fun, some of it will leak onto their SM pages. If not, then they will be quiet on SM and Marcella will tell Liz on her first call that she doesn't know where Arthur is and doesn't want to be bothered by our hunt for him."

Brick was pumped.

"Great input guys, now let me poke a little deeper. Neither Alice nor Rosie had any inkling we were looking for Arthur as a possible serial murderer in New England. There's no way Marcella could know that in San Diego. So, what if Liz asks Marcella a question that leaks the murder cases? Will Marcella be surprised? I'm betting she won't; the New England girls will have spilled the beans on that. If she is surprised, but admits she's talking to Alice and Rosie, then we know they are talking about Arthur in their three-ways. There are probably other trigger questions we can ask. Why don't we all think on it tonight, then fax or call Liz? She can make the call tomorrow morning. Liz, that okay with you?"

ARTHUR TALKING TO HIMSELF

Who, me? Bud, you are *me! Why are you asking about that turncoat twin named Caleb? You were there with me when I gave him his just deserts. You were in my ear when I stuck the muzzle of our old .22 caliber Sears and Roebuck revolver in his ear. You flinched when I double tapped his head—Jesus, it nearly blew his head off his worthless body. Say what? He seemed nice. You shittin' me 'bout that? It was their birthday, and he was happy to celebrate by himself? His brother, Chaim, hundreds of miles away? I wonder which was the oldest. You think about that when we did him? Remember, you wanted to stay with the bike when we did Emiliano on our first kill. But you were me when we did Caleb. Your fingers were not on the keyboard when I liked his FaceFuckingBook page, but your thumb was on the hammer while my finger was on the trigger—we shot him to that special hell ungrateful twins go to. We did it! And we're proud, aren't we?*

"Hello," a groggy voice said.

"Marcella? Hi. This is Dr. Socorro. I hope you remember me—I was the mental health consultant on the federal case involving Arthur Cheshire. I'm sorry to call so early."

"Who? Why are you calling me when it's still dark outside?"

"I'm sorry, Miss Munoz. I'm in Virginia right now and I completely forget about the three-hour time difference. It's eleven here so . . ."

"Oh, but I see a San Diego number on my phone; that's why I picked up. Yes, Dr. Socorro, I remember you. Why are you calling me?"

"I am really so sorry, but I'm working on an FBI case here on the East Coast and Arthur's name came up so I thought . . ."

"I do not want to talk about him. You should know that. Do not call me again."

The line went dead, and Liz made an entry in her lab book.

11/14/18 . . . FBI Case File # _____ Tele call to Marcella Munoz in SD. Called her 0700 hrs—three-hour time diff fm Virginia. Call lasted maybe 1 min max. I said the call was about Arthur Cheshire. Ms. Munoz was angry. Refused to talk. Said "Do not call me again." Based on past contact re the murder charge in SD, Subject is evasive—very different from last encounter in court—she clearly wants to avoid self-revelation. I could not see her (not face time call). Paranoia symptomology. Noted in earlier case—she harbors deep feelings of guilt in being deceived by Arthur—very angry—may want to get even—sbjct will be difficult to engage via phone—in person contact recommended.

She left a voicemail for Brick, called her office in SD, left another one for her supervisor there, and reread some of her notes about Marcella. She logged into her US Bureau of Prisons account and brought up the Martin Cheshire case file. There were nine entries tagged with M Munoz in file names in the subfolder Gov/Witnesses.

The first file was one of her first interviews with Arthur when he was jailed in San Diego. She'd asked him to explain his relationship with Marcella. He started with a physical description of her. She was "short but taut. Shiny hair like silver but black as coal tar. Looked damp. All the time. A permanent tan, more tea than coffee, and opalescent. No one in Maine ever had that skin. Pronounced eyes, set well apart. Like she could look at you with one eye, or the other."

When she asked Arthur what he meant by Marcella's one-eyed look, he said, "She'd look through you. See your secrets. If she stared at you, you felt thrilled, or twitchy. Depends on why she's sighted in on you. Is she hunting, or just grazing? Man, those eyes. Some girls, most I ever knew, had eyes with some kind of light color. But Marcella had eyes like giant bruises inside milky white ovals. Livid eyes—black *and* blue. First glance—her best feature. Then, second glance—her lips. Like Rosie, Marcella's lips were full. But Rosie wore lipstick. Marcella's lips glistened. Probably something in a tube, I admit that. But it never faded. She never applied anything. I watched her do her makeup late in the afternoon. Six in the morning. Didn't matter. Liquid lips, like magic, ya know?"

Arthur's language and attitude about Marcella were mildly interesting to her in San Diego, but now that she saw him as a possible serial killer, his words about Marcella took on new meanings. Now it occurred to her that Marcella was another unmet need on Arthur's part. His descriptions were interesting then but now seemed more menacing. He was working through his manic grief over Martin's death by engaging two women simultaneously and lying to both to hide what was tearing him apart.

She had asked him questions about both women, Rosie, and Marcella. Her notes said, "Rosie was soft, soft everywhere. Marcella hard. Hard like sheet steel, only polished. Nothing matters. Slick, smooth, but impenetrable. Temperament? Not sure what you mean. Marcella was a screamer, in or out of bed. Feelings ruled actions. Rosie was a planner. Slow to burn, tempered herself down. Took her time about it. Marcella flashed like a fit whirling out of a wasp's nest."

In retrospect, Arthur now projected the difference between being the hero to Martin he thought he was and the villain he now felt himself to be. His comparison of the two women was an inner effort at denying his past, denying his traumatic wound. Now his wound was in his frontal lobe all the time, forcing him to fight the true reality—he did not kill his twin brother—with an altered reality—yes, he killed his brother, and it was all their fault—these two women.

She'd studied case histories in med school about people becoming violent because an emotional switch in their brains had been turned on to meet a repressed need for redemption. This kind of reversal often turned deadly, either for the patient or innocent people in his way. As she moused her way through her notes and scrolled down the digital images on her screen, she leaned back in her chair when she came to an entry she'd long forgotten. Arthur told her, "Lemme give you a metaphor for Marcella. Fire and Ice. Like the house specialty drink at Chuy's—Tequila, a splash of Habanero juice, pepperoncini, over crushed ice. Crank your flame or cool you down. Up to you. That's why I just visited Marcella at first. You know—get laid and get out. Fire can burn you. Ice can chill you down. Give you a brain freeze."

Her final entry on the file was chilling. Arthur summed up the woman he called *Marcella Wella*. "Best thing about her. She was predictable. Don't mess with her."

She picked up the phone in her hotel room and called Brick at his office.

QUANTICO, VIRGINIA

"Good morning, Liz ," Brick said when his office line buzzed. "It's Sunday, I hope you're taking the day off."

"Are you taking it off, Mr. F B I? I'd planned a day of leisure with a good book and maybe a visit to the Marine Museum. It's only about three miles from the Wood Springs Suites, and my lovely little BR suite. You were a Marine, right? Do they have a picture of you there?"

"I doubt it. The FBI has lots of jarheads in the ranks. The DOJ frowns on hanging our pictures up in public places. So, what's up, doc?"

"I called Marcella Munoz this morning, but she was hostile and insistent. She said, 'Do not call me again.' Then she slammed the phone down."

"And your diagnosis is . . ."

"I wouldn't call it a diagnosis, but my assessment is she is exactly where Rosie is when it comes to Arthur Cheshire. She's afraid of him."

"Why? Do you think either one of them knows we're looking for him in a criminal context?"

"No, it doesn't feel that way to me. They might be afraid of him because of something they did to him or to his brother Martin. Or they might be afraid because he humiliated them. He made them look like disreputable women, easily fooled by a conman."

"What might they have done to him? I get how badly he treated them, but are you saying they got even somehow?"

"I don't know, but there is a nagging back story that I haven't thought about since the judge released him and the government dropped all charges. Remember, Martin embezzled money from AmHull Insurance. It was a small amount, something in the mid-twenty-thousand range. But AmHull lost a lot more. If memory serves, it was ten times that amount. Arthur knew that Martin had figured out how to siphon about 10 percent of premiums paid and put them in a New Hampshire bank. But Arthur told me, and the federal judge in San Diego, that he was not part of Martin's scheme and had no explanation for why the federal prosecutors thought it was ten times as much as Martin had explained to him on that last visit to Portland. Martin called it a *'Hide and Be the Money Game.'*"

"Okay, but so what?"

"It's thin, but I remember Arthur telling me what Martin told him about siphoning off premium checks. He said Alice, the bookkeeper and front desk receptionist, got the mail, including premium checks from clients. She would often irritate him at his desk in the back office by bringing in mail that looked like premium payments rather than just general inquiries to Mr. Hull. I remember Arthur using funny language describing Alice and the way she worked in the office. He called her *Alice Blue Gown* and said she'd 'tippy toe in, hold the mail packet, properly rubber-banded, as high as she could, and drop it on his desk.' She warned him to be careful you don't lose any."

"You're losing me, Liz. What's all that mean?"

"It's just a wild guess, Brick, but what if Alice somehow figured out what Martin was doing—that is, embezzling premium money from AmHull?"

"Well, in that case, we could go back to the FBI initial investigation in Portland and look for—well, I'm not sure what. I doubt the investigation went that far—they thought all the money was embezzled by Martin and didn't look at other employees as accessories."

"Yes, but Alice quit working for AmHull right after Arthur was arrested in Portland. She moved to Boston. Seems to me, she's living a richer life now than she did in Portland. And she refuses to help us find Arthur. She seemed angry with him, but what if there's more to that? What if she's afraid of Arthur finding out that some of the money AmHull lost was not embezzled by Martin? Who else might have been able to do the same thing—siphon off premium checks, knowing that Mr. Hull paid no attention to bookkeeping or missing premium checks?"

"What makes you suspect Alice Singworth?"

"It's not suspicion—that's a good word in your world, Brick. I'm just theorizing. I'm curious about Miss Singworth because she was a bookkeeper from high school to her early thirties. Her only job was at AmHull. She eventually became the back-office bookkeeper and the front office face of the company. Think about the business traits that fit that work profile. She has to be self-controlled, make a good impression, introverted, serious, responsible, and a conformist. She did all of that for fifteen or so years. Then, when Martin's embezzlement became known to the FBI, and no doubt the office staff, she stays on the job for only a month and then abruptly quits. What led to that? Why is she now afraid of Arthur? Might she have known that Martin was stealing money? Did she help him? Is that why she's now afraid of his twin brother?"

"Okay, Liz, you may be on to something. But how would that connect to Rosie and Marcella? They didn't work at AmHull, and they couldn't have known about Martin's Hide-and-Be-the-money scheme."

"I am totally guessing here, Brick, but what if Alice is talking to both Rosie and Marcella? Suddenly, we have three women refusing to help us find Arthur. What does Arthur know to make them afraid of him?"

"Maybe it's what Arthur knows about the embezzlement that scares all three?"

Liz signaled to Brick she was about to change the subject.

"By the way, if we do find Arthur, who arrests him, the FBI, or is that done by police in whatever state he's in when we catch him?"

"Well, Liz, maybe we should sign you up for a remedial course in constitutional law. They probably didn't cover that in med school, right? Just kidding. Here's how federal arrests work. We make arrests for federal offenses committed in our presence. And we arrest when we have reasonable grounds the suspect has committed a felony violation of US law. In this case, we investigate, charge, and arrest violent crimes such as mass killings, sniper murders, and serial killings. That's because those particular crimes paralyze entire states and stretch state and local law enforcement resources to their limits."

"Yes, Brick, I know that, but how do you get arrest warrants for local crimes? Do your agents ask state judges to issue warrants?"

"No, we go to federal courts to do that. Federal judges or magistrates issue arrest warrants based on sworn affidavits showing probable cause that a specific crime has been committed. I've written a draft affidavit detailing what we believe about Arthur Cheshire and his involvement in the three cases we've been assigned by FBI HQ. If someone spots him, or our tipster hotlines and websites click on him, my draft affidavit will be finalized with exact details. Then we'll get a warrant for that state and initiate find-and-arrest protocols."

Four days later, the FBI's famous telephone number 1-800-CALL-FBI got a tip from Leary MacIntosh, a retired US Coast Guard sailor in South Bristol, Maine. He said he looked at the list of fugitives on *www.fbi.gov/tips* and recognized a recent photo of a man he thought lived over on the tip of Jones Island. He'd spotted the man two days before buying bait and tackle. He saw him again that morning in the South Bristol post office standing in line waiting to mail a package. The recorded phone call was clipped and emailed as a wave mp3 file to FREST in Quantico.

> Hello, FBI, this is Chief Petty Officer Leary MacIntosh calling. I'm retired US Coast Guard and live in South Bristol, Maine. I think I just saw a man on your fugitive wanted list over to the bait shop here in South Bristol. The name on your list is Arthur Cheshire, but I think the picture is his brother Martin. I knew those boys when they were teenagers living in a fishing camp over to Jones Island. Here's my number to call me by. I'm not home that much if the fishing is good, but it's not too good today.

The call was redlined to FBI HQ and relayed immediately to Brick at Quantico. Brick called the SAIC in Portland and requested that a team, including a US Marshal, and local law enforcement be on standby for an immediate arrest after talking to the tipster Coast Guard caller in South Bristol. Then Brick arranged for a Marine flight to Portland. He got there four hours after the tipster's call. The arrest team drove with lights and siren to the bait shop identified by the tipster in South Bristol. It was a rainy day, as noted by the tipster's comment that fishing was not good. Brick showed Mr. MacIntosh other pictures of Martin at the time of his arrest, and a high school annual picture of Arthur.

"Yeah, sure," MacIntosh told Brick. "That's your man alright. I don't remember those boys' names now, but I remember they were two peas in a pod. They came in the bait shop where I work when I'm not fishing, which I do whenever I want. I own the bait shop, but the wife runs it. She knows the boys too. We haven't seen 'em for a year or two."

Brick asked him if he'd go to Jones Point and show them the fishing camp. MacIntosh said okay, but not in his boat, which would have been the quickest way to get there. But he didn't want to go upriver in rainy weather. The arrest team had two FBI SUVs, a Lincoln County Sheriff's Department truck, and an unmarked sedan. The first unit to arrive on scene was the sheriff's truck. Brick put their informant, MacIntosh, in the sedan, which would not be involved in the arrest. They drove from South Bristol up Highway 129 to Jones Point. The drive was 2.2 miles by GPS; they made the trip in just over four minutes.

Brick radioed MacIntosh's directions to the four-car arrest team as they approached the narrow asphalt road down to Jones Point. Even through the drizzle, they could see the fishing camps from a half mile away. The camp closest to the end of the small peninsula was owned by the Cheshire boys. The other two were vacant.

The Cheshire camp was a single clapboard building with dark windows and a brick chimney on the far side of the house. It had a covered boat dock and a boat ramp down into the Dramiscotta River. An old white Tacoma pickup, with a broken rear plate glass window was diagonally parked on the gravel driveway in front of the cabin. Smoke lifted upward from the cabin's chimney.

MacIntosh said, "Everyone's got a wood stove in these parts; that smoke says somebody's home."

Brick created a roadblock a hundred yards up from the pickup. The blacktop road was heavily forested on both sides. He sent the sedan back to South Bristol with Mr. MacIntosh. The four FBI agents, the US Deputy marshal, and two sheriff's deputies got out of their vehicles and took up shooting positions over the hoods of the black vehicles. Brick and a sheriff's deputy crept slowly down the road toward the camps. They only got about twenty yards from the blockade when the rear lights of the pickup in the driveway came on. The driver backed out and turned slowly onto the asphalt pavement.

Brick and the deputy ran back to the roadblock. When the oncoming pickup got about a hundred yards away, Brick radioed the team to light up the area with their spotlights. The pickup driver, grizzled with a beard under a dark baseball cap, stopped in the middle of the road and made a U-turn back toward the cabin.

Brick clicked on his bull horn and yelled at the driver, "Stop! Stop right now! This is the FBI. You are under arrest!"

The driver didn't stop right away, causing the Lincoln County deputy to fire two shots at the back of the truck. One shot hit with a clang of bullet on metal. The other apparently missed. But one shot was enough; the truck stopped. The driver lowered his window and stuck both hands out the driver's side window. He didn't move. The six-man team spread out and slow-walked toward him. He just sat there till they got ten yards away.

Brick yelled, "All right! Easy now. With one hand, open your door and push it out. Then step out slowly with your hands in front of you with palms up toward us."

Once he was out, the officers ran toward him, yelling, "Freeze, don't move!"

The first agent to reach him asked, "Are you armed?"

"No, sir, I'm not. What's this about?"

Brick was ten feet away with his iPhone in one hand and his Glock in the other. He looked at the mug photo from the San Diego FBI office. It confirmed the man in front of him in the black baseball cap was Arthur Cheshire.

"We are FBI. We have a warrant to arrest you, Arthur Cheshire, for murder. Is your identification on you, or in your truck?"

"It's in my right rear pants pocket, in my wallet," the man said. "My insurance card on my truck is in the glove box. I don't know where my brother Arthur is. You're got the wrong twin. I'm Martin Cheshire."

Brick was perplexed but not rattled. He holstered his gun, spun the man around, and motioned to the agent alongside him. "Cuff this man."

Once that was done Brick removed the wallet and extracted a driver's license issued to Martin Cheshire. The license was two years old but still valid, and the picture was of a shaven man who looked like the man in front of them but for the scraggy black full beard and the five o'clock shadow below his nose and above his upper lip. His tan shirt was dirty, and he smelled like a man who hadn't showered for a month. The glove box revealed an insurance card on the Tacoma and identified the owner as Martin Cheshire.

Turning back to the driver, Brick said, "You are under arrest for murder. We will take you to Portland for booking into the city jail, pending removal to a federal institution as soon as possible. The card I am about to read to you contains your constitutional rights. 'You have the right to remain silent. Anything you say can be used against you in a court of law. You have the right to the presence of an attorney. If you cannot afford an attorney, one will be appointed for you.' Do you have any questions?"

The bearded man said, "Yes. Why are you reading me my rights? I'm not Arthur. That's who you want, right?"

They buckled him up in the rear seat of the sedan.

PORTLAND, MAINE

Arthur Cheshire was arrested based on a warrant issued by US Magistrate Juliana Rachlyn following his arrest two weeks earlier. Brick wrote the affidavit supporting the grand jury's earlier indictment and was present in court to testify at the arraignment before Judge Rachlyn.

Normally, defendants are brought to court almost immediately following indictment for an arraignment. But this hearing was delayed by the defendant's insistence he was not the person named in the search warrant. Typically, the judge gives the defendant a detailed explanation about federal court process, including his constitutional rights, the charges filed, information about legal representation, and bail issues. Then the defendant tells the court whether he wishes to plead guilty or not guilty to the charges. Bail is rarely available in serious felony cases because defendants are a flight risk or a danger to the community.

"All rise, please, the Honorable Juliana Rachlyn presiding," the bailiff said.

Judge Rachlyn was a petite woman with a confident stride from her chamber's door on the right side of the courtroom. She skipped up the two steps up to her bench, set down her manila folders , and nodded to the court clerk. The court called the case by name, number, date, and purpose in official federal court monotone.

With the preliminaries done, Judge Rachlyn said, "Thank you, ladies and gentlemen. Good morning, Miss Persuanoli, nice to have you back in my court. And good morning to you as well, Mr. Cheshire. It appears you are not represented by counsel, sir. Are you able to afford counsel? If not, I will appoint the federal defender's office to visit you immediately, today, or tomorrow, and we will adjourn this initial hearing."

Arthur sat alone at the defense table. The prosecutor sat to his right at the table on the other side of the podium. Brick sat directly behind Assistant US Attorney Letty Persuanoli. The court clerk sat at his desk to the right of the bench as did the bailiff at a long evidence table in front of him. The federal detention officer sat directly behind Arthur Cheshire, whose hand cuffs had been removed but his leg shackles were still affixed. There were neither ladies nor gentlemen in the pews behind the courtroom bar.

Arthur looked up at the judge but didn't respond to her question.

"Mr. Cheshire, if you didn't hear or understand my question, I'd be happy to repeat it."

Arthur looked around as though maybe someone else might say something. He tried to stand but seemed to get caught up in the leg shackles. So, he just sat back down and remained silent.

The judge leaned forward on her bench, with a ballpoint pen in her left hand, and increased her volume slightly.

"You need not stand, Mr. Cheshire. If those leg shackles make you uncomfortable, I'll have the detention officer remove them. I have a file on you here on my desk. Nothing in it suggests you have a language difficulty or other impediment. If you choose not to answer my questions, I'll adjourn this hearing and return you to detention. Do you understand me, sir?"

Arthur looked back at his detention officer and then turned back toward the bench. Not looking directly at her, he focused on the court clerk.

"Does it say my name on the court record? It's Martin Cheshire. When they arrested me, that tall man sitting over there, he called me by my brother's name. So, who is on trial here? Me, or my brother Arthur?"

The clerk looked up to the bench for instructions. The judge looked at the prosecutor and said, "Miss Persuanoli, are you aware of this, what do I call it, denial of identify, or mistaken identity?"

The prosecutor rose, saying, "May it please the court. May I take the podium, Your Honor?"

Judge Rachlyn nodded to her, and she took the four steps to the ornate podium in the twenty-five by forty-foot courtroom.

"Judge," she said loud enough to be heard at the rear of the courtroom, "the government is aware this defendant denies he is the person named in the grand jury's indictment or the arrest warrant you issued in this case. Nonetheless, we are confident he is Arthur Cheshire and definitely not his twin brother, Martin Cheshire. On the day of his arrest, he was identified as Arthur by Special Agent Cato, who is here in the courtroom and ready to testify. That identification was confirmed when the man seated to my right at the defense table was finger-printed, photographed, and questioned as to his identity at the federal jail adjoining this courthouse. He told the booking judge he was Martin Cheshire. We have Martin's fingerprints on file as well as *this* man's fingerprints. The prints confirm the defendant here in court is Arthur Cheshire. He is Martin's twin. Both twins have criminal records on CODIS, in this court's files, *and* in the US District Court files in San Diego, California."

Judge Rachlyn opened one of the files on her bench, flipped to a page, and turned toward the defendant.

"Mr. Cheshire, were you charged in a State of Maine criminal action with violation of Title 17-A, Maine Criminal Code, Section 353-A, Theft by Unauthorized Taking or Transfer, an embezzlement charge filed by your former employer, AmHull Insurance Company?"

Smiling, Arthur answered, "Thank you, Your Honor, I presume that's my file in your hand. And yes, I am Martin Cheshire. I don't remember all those numbers you just read to me, but yes, the State of Maine did falsely charge me with siphoning off premium checks about two years ago. But later they threw the charges out, acquitting me. It's in your file, Judge. I'm sure. Maybe somebody stole $269,000 from AmHull, but it was not me, or Arthur. The man the FBI think killed somebody is my brother. So, they arrested me for him. But they are plain wrong and I'm ready to testify for my brother Arthur. He's not a killer, Your Honor. They got the wrong man in jail, me, and they don't have any evidence against my brother. He told me so."

The prosecutor rose in objection mode. "Your Honor, the defendant's statements are out of order and . . ."

Judge Rachlyn said sharply, "Miss Persuanoli, I'm the judge of what is or is not in order here. Mr. Cheshire, listen to me very carefully. You have the right to remain silent, the right to counsel, due process of law, and the presumption of innocence. You risk those rights by making statements that might be considered inculpatory if made without the advice of counsel. I'm going appoint a US public defender, temporarily, to meet with you today so your rights are protected. Then, at our next meeting, tomorrow morning in this courtroom at 9 a.m., you can waive your rights and represent yourself if that is your choice. We are adjourned."

Back at the Portland FBI office, Brick and Normandie made a conference call to Liz.

"Hey, Liz, it's Brick. I've got Normandie, the SAIC here in Portland. We need your advice on Arthur Cheshire."

"Oh, hi Brick. How did this morning's court hearing go?"

"It didn't go, it stalled like a jeep out of gas. It sputtered a little and then just died."

"What happened?"

"The judge called the docket. Her job this morning was to appoint a PD for Arthur unless he had retained someone privately. He was in court by himself and took the opportunity to tell the court she had the wrong man. Remember when I arrested him two weeks ago, he insisted he was Martin, not Arthur? Well, he repeated that in court this morning, with a couple of twists. He said he wasn't Arthur, he was Martin, and he asked who was on trial—him or his brother? Then the judge tried to shush him, but he pushed on like he was an actor on stage. He pointed a finger at me as the man who arrested him, and get this, he thinks he was acquitted two years ago of all embezzlement charges. Imagine that!"

Liz was on the phone call. She inserted herself. "Brick, and hello to you too, Normandie. I heard about the premium siphoning from Arthur back in my San Diego office, but the details escape me now. I mean I know he was charged and that somehow the case went away. There was a dispute about the amount, right?"

"Right, but Liz, now he is not only claiming to be Martin, but he also told the judge that maybe somebody else stole $269,000 from AmHull, not the Cheshire brothers. There was an insinuation that maybe it was some other employee. Does that ring any bells with you?"

"Oh, my lord, is he talking about Alice Singworth?"

"We don't know, but we need you to come back here to Portland and be ready to testify if the identity issue still dominates the federal court. We don't want another nightmare or a so-called identity hearing here, like the debacle your Judge Hightower had out there in sunny California."

"Okay, sure. I can get to Portland tomorrow if you can arrange air transfer for me from the Marine air base here."

"I can do that. But there's another twist in the case. Came in yesterday afternoon but I haven't been able to brief you and Lee on it yet. The trap and trace we're doing on Alice Singworth's line fired up three times in the last four days. Alice placed calls to Rosie in Boston and Marcella in San Diego. And the calls are long—more than thirty minutes for each call. I'm going to expand the tap and trace to see who Rosie and Marcella might be calling in response to whatever Alice is telling them. I wish we could get wire taps, but that's out of the question. And bring your detailed notes on those sessions you had with Arthur. I'm meeting with the prosecutor at two this afternoon in her office. See you when you get here. Maybe dinner with me and Normandie?"

"Yes, sir, that fish place maybe?"

"Okay, but wait a sec. I almost forgot to tell you what else Arthur told the judge. He said, and I quote, 'I am ready to testify for my brother Arthur. He's not a killer, Your Honor. They got the wrong man in jail, me, and they don't have any evidence against my brother, *he told me so.*'"

"Well, as you know, research data supports the concept of telepathy from one identical twin to the other. But there's no reliable data linking a telepathic message from a deceased twin to a survivor twin. His courtroom statement raises two possibilities, neither of which are good for the prosecution. First, if Arthur is getting messages in his head from his deceased twin, he may be in deep psychosis and incompetent to stand trial. Second, his brother, Martin, is still alive. Remember, the San Diego judge accepted the DNA found on the bones in the fishing shack in Mexico were from Martin, not Arthur. I always thought that was logical since it was Arthur who was alive and testifying in court. But if both are alive, now, and the boating accident was all bogus, then the FBI and the US Department of Justice have a pile of you know what in their laps."

CUMBERLAND COUNTY JAIL

Hey hey hey, that's what you say, say! Brother of mine thinking fine fine! The bad cops and lickety-split capital F bee eye think that they got the goods on me for settling hash on those disrespecting twins who discelebrate their happy happy birthdays down to New Hamp and Old Boston and out there Vermont Vermont. Well not skin off our ass Brother of mine. Not. I'm in another cell but out shortly shortly like we did under the porch. You remember the porch, creaky, dust, spiders, and that big strap! I told you I ate but I never did, never did. I did not sit still and be quiet quiet. No No Brother of mine—I told her what you told me, told me—I am you for now. Being Martin while Arthur, Arthur, is hiding hiding. Tomorrow tomorrow the judge says again again. Maybe new lawyer man or lawyer woman then then. Won't matter will it, brother of mine brother of mine.

QUANTICO, VIRGINIA

At 6:45 p.m. Eastern standard, Brick started an encrypted video call with his team in Quantico.

"Hello everyone, thanks for standing by so that we could catch up between Portland and Quantico. I have the smiling faces of Lee, Cynthia, and Abe on my screen. You should all be able to see me, Liz, Normandie, and his lead communications aide on your screens. We're using government-enabled encrypted video for this session. Give me a hand wave if you can see and hear one another. Okay, that worked. Abe, you're not smiling. What's up, Bud? The Marines got you down again for using their private mess hall?"

"Hell no, Brick. I'm trying not to smile too much on recorded video, even if it is encrypted up the gazoo. The more people see me smile, the grumpier I feel. Being happy is for today's generation. My generation likes grumpiness. Wearing gun belts with tasers, Glocks, and handcuffs is a serious biz—nothing happy about it."

"Okay, Abe. As for everyone else, I have happy news. We are building a case for wiretapping Alice, Rosie, and Marcella because they are engaging in what might be some sort of international crime based on calls they are making."

"Brick, this is Lee, I'm not sure you can hear me. Can you?" she asked, waving her hand to her right ear.

"Lee, I see you, but your mike is still on mute. Switch it on, okay?"

A few seconds went by before everyone could hear Lee.

"Okay, Brick, I toggled the mute button with my mouse. Can you hear me now?"

"Right got it. Okay, everyone here's the tap-and-trace situation. You all know they made a flurry of calls right amongst the three of them right after we talked to Alice at her new house in Boston. The next day, Alice made three calls to Panama. Rosie made one call to the Cook Island Bank of Trust. Rosie called a travel agency in Columbia known to be connected to drug smugglers. Two of the three are on AT&T and it's cooperating with us. Verizon is less helpful but is taking our calls and may soon be on board—the SAIC in Brooklyn is making noise at Verizon's NYC home office. Their general counsel is in consultation. The pattern and timing of these calls suggests that these women, either singularly or as a group, are using offshore banks to do what criminals and high wealth people do—open secretive offshore banks. None of them are wealthy, so we're assuming they are up to no good talking to hiding places for ill got gains."

Lee asked, "Ill got? What's your thinking there?"

Brick answered, "Well, the record says Martin embezzled about $26,000 from AmHull by using a bank in New Hampshire. He denied it, but just barely before he sort of disappeared. Or died. One or the other. By the time the State of Maine charged the case, the losses at AmHull were up to exactly $269,000. The state investigators think there may have been more than one person embezzling money. We never followed up because the man we thought was Martin was extradited to San Diego and claimed to be Arthur there—remember, that was on the screwed-up murder case against the guy we thought was the other brother. Anyhow, we're now investigating the possibility that Alice was the embezzler and she is somehow connected with Arthur's girlfriend in San Diego—Marcella and Martin's girlfriend in Portland—Rosie. All three of them have shunned us like we had the pox. That smells to me like they have something to hide. We don't think they are serial murderers, but they might be embezzlers and are afraid Arthur knows about them."

Abe said, "Say you're right, Brick, you usually are. How does that get us a wiretap on them?"

"Because calling offshore banks and doing criminal business internationally may invoke money laundering."

"How does money laundering fit into our serial murder case?" Cynthia asked with palms up in the air.

"It's admittedly a stretch, but the thinking in Portland, after talks with Harrold Hull, is that AmHull only did business with local banks here in Portland. But we know at least one account in New Hampshire was also set up for AmHull. But Mr. Hull says no one in his office opened it. We think the embezzler sent the money to New Hampshire, and from there to a known laundering bank in Panama. And we know Alice and her friends are making calls not to the same offshore banks. That makes the criminal effort international and may get us a federal wiretap order. We're working on that."

"But," Cynthia said, looking perplexed, "how is that connected to the twins' murder cases?"

Brick answered. "It might not be connected. But these three women are unwilling to help us find Arthur. Now that we have him, he says he's Martin. But to prove that he's really Arthur, we are going to need these women's cooperation. So, the money laundering they might be doing could be an influencing factor in changing their minds and getting them to help us nail Arthur in the murder cases."

"Is that legal?" Cynthia asked.

Abe jumped in. "Cyn," as he had recently started calling her, "The FBI needs all the help we can get on the murders. The state can handle the embezzlement case. No harm in us helping them with their state charges if they help us on our murder case. We're all friends, right?"

PORTLAND, MAINE

As hastily arranged the prior afternoon, the prosecution team met at 7:30 a.m. in the US Attorney's office on the second floor to prepare for Judge Rachlyn's rescheduled arraignment. Brick, Norm, and Liz arrived separately with notebooks, preliminary pleadings, and a good deal of uncertainty. Liz was keen to hear more about what the judge had in mind for the confusion created by Arthur's announcements. Had he really told her he was Martin? Liz was the only one who slept poorly thinking about all the parameters of the Hide and Be game that to some extent defined the personalities Arthur and Martin Cheshire had absorbed.

When they passed through the metal detectors, the guard told them to take the circular stairs to the second floor and a receptionist would take it from there. They climbed the beautiful one-hundred-year-old stairwell with glistening red maple hand-rails and eastern white pine planks. The majestic area featured a reception area with wall-to-wall portraits of several dozen chief judges. In short order they were escorted to a conference room, with more judicial portraits on the wall and a carved oak table that seated six per side with two chairs at each end. A coffee and water table offered hot coffee, water bottles in a large bowl of ice, and a rack of professional cards of the seventeen members of the US Attorney's Office.

As soon as they were seated with coffee mugs in place, Letica Persuanoli came through the double door with an armload of manila folders and a blank yellow legal pad. As they started to get up, the lead prosecutor shooed them back down.

"Don't get up, please. Good morning, Norm, and Agent Cato."

"Morning, Letty," Norm said.

"I'd like you to meet Dr. Lisbeth Socorro. I think Brick said something about her yesterday while we were in court."

"She did indeed. Dr. Socorro, please call me Letty. I'm delighted to meet you. This building is burdened with male lawyers in dark suits who lack any real knowledge of psychiatry or feminine leadership."

Liz got up and reached across the table to shake hands.

"I'm Liz and I can attest to how little all the crazy lawyers I know care about psychiatry, present company excepted, of course."

Letty was dressed in jeans and a silk long-sleeved shirt. Liz wore her go-to-court pants suit with a fluffy white collar. Letty explained her casual wear.

"First thing I have to tell you is the email I got last night from Judge Rachlyn. She canceled this morning's hearing. Said the PD's office was now representing Mr. Cheshire, but they had not yet assigned a specific lawyer, and had not yet arranged a meeting with him. So, she asked us to advise her JA as to when we would like to reschedule the prelim. Norm, are you in the lead for the FBI side of this case?"

"No, Letty, that would be Brick and his FREST team in Quantico. They are deep into the serial murders we have charged Arthur Cheshire with and . . ."

Letty waved him off.

"Norm, sorry to interrupt but that's the central issue before us and the main reason I wanted you here at seven-thirty even though I knew we're off today's calendar. I am perplexed, to put it mildly, about that gong show yesterday. I mean, my god, does the defendant actually believe he is Martin, when all tests and dates mark him as Arthur? What in the world is going on here?"

Brick said, "I was as taken aback yesterday as you were, and I know a good deal about the Cheshire twins. But honestly, the real expert on identity issues for the Cheshire twins is Dr. Socorro. She knows Arthur both clinically and personally because she spent months talking to him and advising the judge in San Diego on a very similar stunt that he played out there."

"Stunt? What stunt?" Letty asked.

Liz volunteered. "I wouldn't call it a stunt but only because I spent about thirty-two hours in consultation with the defendant. On the first day in court, the defendant, Martin Cheshire, told the court he was not Martin Cheshire and insisted that he was Arthur Cheshire; he and Martin were twin brothers. I was asked to evaluate him because I was the jail psychiatrist. Still am, by the way. I did a full written eval and filed it with the court. Also, I studied all of the court filings and his polygraph results. I can assure you that the man in court yesterday was Arthur, but I also think it's likely that he *believes* he is Martin. He is deeply wounded in a traumatic sense. Do you want me to expound on this or would you rather ask me questions? I do tend to go on and on in cases like this."

"I want his full story no matter how long it takes for you to tell it, but there is a central question I need to ask first. Do you think he, by either first name, is competent to stand trial?"

"I can give you a diagnosis based on tests I gave him, but there is no medical test for competency, especially in a legal environment."

Norm interjected.

"Letty, maybe you can give us the legal definition first, then together we can cobble together a plan, assuming for the moment that the PD's office comes up with an insanity defense out of the gate."

"Well, gentlemen, and you too Liz, the legal definition is easy to say and nearly impossible to either establish or quash. The modern protocol is straightforward. If the defense raises competency to stand trial, then the judge will order a mental health assessment to determine how much the defendant remembers and understands about his charges. Additionally, the judge will want an expert opinion on whether the defendant has sufficient mental capacity to understand court proceedings and assist his lawyer in defending the case."

Brick said, "Okay, we have a starting point for you, Letty. Of course, I'll let Liz fill in the blanks, but I think the existing record in San Diego, plus the work she did, will take care of the last part—does Arthur understand court proceedings and can he assist his PD? He can, right Liz?"

"Right," Liz said, "but that seems to me to be irrelevant here. The pivotal question is, does Arthur believe he is Martin? If he does, then he's probably competent to stand trial as Martin. But if the judge or counsel insist on calling him Arthur, he will revert, resist, and remonstrate. Given what I know about the Cheshire relationships from early childhood to now, that's a real possibility. All that said, I'm not at all sure that also means he is incompetent. All humans can be competent—that is, functional—to do millions of things, and yet be so traumatically wounded that their belief system takes over their essence, which is, who am I?"

Letty's face seemed tight. Her jaw was taut, and her eyelashes lifted.

"Dr. Socorro, can you give me an abbreviated version of what you mean when you said when we started this meeting that the defendant has a traumatic wound? I mean is that a DSM diagnosis, as in mentally ill?"

"Not exactly," Liz said, hoping not to either offend nor to dismiss. "As I'm sure you know, the DSM is a handbook we use as an authoritative guide to the diagnosis of mental disorders. It gives the clinician an array of descriptions, symptoms, and other criteria for diagnosing mental disorders. It gives a common language to use in explaining a diagnosis. But it is not itself a diagnostic tool. We use it to assess patients. But it is not a guideline for treatment, or court testimony."

"Okay," Letty said, "let's add another dot to the dilemma. Let's assume, whoever he believes he is—don't his fingerprints on record in Maine, as well as the federal court here in Portland, clearly define him as Martin Cheshire? I mean, he was investigated, indicted, arrested, and charged here as Martin two years ago. Then last week he was arrested, indicted, charged, and brought to this same courthouse, for the second time. Both booking files identify the same man by the same fingerprints, photos, and identification on him at the time of his arrest. What am I missing here?"

Brick said, "Letty, I said the same thing a month ago when FREST was assigned the triple twins murder cases. But the San Diego court and FBI files confirm that a hearing was held there, and the presiding judge found that the man extradited from Maine to California was *not* Martin, he was Arthur. And to add to the dilemma, making it a trilemma, the court found that Martin was deceased and that his sole surviving relative was Arthur. To make it over-the-top-weird, the judge out there also held that since Arthur was alive, he could not be charged with either his own death, or the death of his twin brother, Martin."

Letty got up and went to the water/coffee side table and pumped a fresh cup of coffee into her mug.

"Anybody got a flask on 'em?" she asked. "I don't drink in the morning but this one is giving me a migraine. Okay, Liz, back to you. I'm still wobbly on the traumatic wound that you diagnosed for Martin and Arthur when one or the other was before the court in California. Can you follow that thread for me?"

"Sure," Liz said, sipping her cold coffee. "Psychiatrists, psychologists, therapists, and mental health practitioners discover, define, diagnose, and sometimes treat people for emotional trauma. It could be getting trapped in an avalanche or seeing a parent die. But more often, its origins lie in repeated episodes of trauma. This, I think, is the trauma wound both Cheshire twins suffered—child abuse, adult abandonment, with their only solace being identical twins, reading one another's mind, and relying on themselves to weather their stormy young lives."

"Wow," Letty said.

"Is there a medical record to support all this traumatic wounding?"

"No, not in the sense I think you mean. I relied on my report to Judge Hightower in San Diego, which contained the story Arthur gave me over a three-month period. He had no medical records in support of what happened, but then I was not trying to diagnose or treat him. I was simply writing an evaluation of what he believed at the time he was extradited to California. I found no evidence of lying or manipulating. I have all the standard mental health tests, and I read his polygraph results. I believe he was deeply wounded but perfectly able to function in most worldly events and situations. He was competent in that he could explain his childhood and his teen-age years to me based on memory alone."

"Yes, Liz, I understand your process and am anxious to read your full reports, but here's the thing I'm struggling with. Is this man being truthful with Judge Rachlyn? Is he really Martin, or is that a lie he's telling to avoid the investigation the FBI conducted leading to the arrest and charging of Arthur? Is he lying or just mentally ill?"

"You make a good point, Letty. It's one that Brick and his team at Quantico raised early on. I explained to them that emotional trauma is terrible to experience. But I also said the brutal reality of emotional trauma is *not* the worst part. What underlies the wound is a lie in and of itself. In medical and scientific terms, we see it as a *false belief.* You could call it *misbelief.*"

Letty turned to Norm. "Has your office here followed up on any of this as you investigated the murders and zeroed in on Martin? What was your probable cause sense that justified an indictment and an arrest warrant? I mean, is your case based on the fact, the true fact, that the defendant we saw in court yesterday is Martin and that he is your serial killer?"

"Well, I know how stupid this might sound, but we didn't develop the evidence to support probable cause. That came from Brick's affidavit and the work his FREST team did."

"Okay, Brick, I'll bounce the ball to you—is the guy in court yesterday, Martin, your Unsub, or is he the twin, Arthur? No disrespect intended, but did the forensics support an arrest of only Martin?"

Brick, in a rare moment of hesitation, thumbed the table for a few seconds. Then, nodding his head, he said, "The Unsub left DNA at each crime scene. It was hair follicles. The hair follicles DNA were Arthur's. But as you know, identical twins share the same DNA. When we interviewed fact witnesses in this case, we asked about Arthur, not Martin. We did not ask about Martin because the court record says Martin died in a boating accident two years ago. We were not looking for him because we relied on the record—Martin is dead. There is no death certificate because there was no post-mortem or doctor present at his death. The only witness to his death was Arthur. And the court in San Diego found, as a matter of fact and law, that Martin was dead, and Arthur did not kill him. Frankly, I don't know where that leaves us."

"Liz," Letty said, "talk to me about the DNA issue in this case. Is there some way we can have the DNA the killer left at the scene retested to tie it to the man in jail?"

"Well, I'm a psychiatrist. I have an MD degree. But I'm not a geneticist and not an expert on DNA. But here are the basics. Identical twins share their DNA *code* with each other. They are born with the exact same sperm and egg from their father and mother. They were in an embryo. But, early in development, this embryo divides into two, creating two babies rather than one. Those two babies, let's call them Marty and Arty, as they were known as babies up until their late teens. While Marty Arty shares the same DNA code, there is more to genetics than just that. Letty, you will want to talk to a geneticist about this."

"Yeah, okay, I will. But we're under the gun here. Give me your sense of where to go."

"Sure, just remember I'm talking in general and making some assumptions along the way. During development in the womb and after birth, life changes us. Who we are, how we live, react, think, eat, and grow influences how our genes are *expressed*. Twins' bodies develop differently. Their minds work differently. Gene changes happen during the embryonic period or during development. It's possible that one identical twin has a genetic condition that his twin does not. The blurry answer is that genetic codes graph our makeup, but there are other factors, genetic and environmental, that produce unique, even novel human beings."

"Okay, let me ask it this way. I understand we have hair follicle evidence left at the scenes of all three crimes by the intruder, who we believe to be Arthur Cheshire. Can we definitively assert that this forensic evidence is absolutely identical to the guy in our jail today—the one who we think is Arthur but who insists he is Martin? That guy! The hair follicles at the crime scenes could be compared with a new hair plucked from the man in jail right now in Portland. Would that be scientific evidence?"

Liz, always confident in her work, smiled. "Well, there is real hope out there. I read an article in *Science Today* a few months ago. I'll find it and circulate it to everyone. It focused on a rape case from Florida or Alabama, I can't remember which. But the gist of the article was an answer to your question. If memory serves, the rapist was an identical twin. His lawyers challenged the DNA testing because they argued what has been called the twin defense for decades. The article was about genetic mutations. Apparently, changes in DNA sequencing make it possible to pinpoint those mutations. In other words, they can tell identical twins apart with deeper testing and sequencing. I'll get the article and send it to the team and of course to you too, Letty."

"All right, Liz," Letty said with a thumbs up motion. "Now, let's get back to yesterday's courtroom surprise. Pending more DNA sequencing, what does the FBI recommend vis-à-vis the announcement that Arthur is Martin, and we have no case against Martin because he is presumably dead? Brick let's start with you. Wadda ya think?"

"I arrested him so my testimony will have to be introduced in court. And I'll be subject to cross-examination as to why I'm sure he's Arthur. But I know that only from a research perspective, you know court filings and investigative results. When we talked to Alice Singworth, Rosie, and Marcella, we asked about Arthur, and they essentially refused to talk to us. Now that we have him in custody, they might not be afraid of him any longer. So, we'll reconnect with all of them. But I don't know . . ."

Liz pushed her chair back, and with a rising pitch said, "Wait a minute, hold the phone, guys. I feel like an idiot for not remembering a huge physical difference in the Cheshire twins. Only one of them has a tattoo! A real tattoo. And we can prove that it's Arthur and that he's the only one of the two to get one. He got it in San Diego from a tattoo artist whose name I can't remember, but Marcella was with him when he got it. I think the tattoo artist was a relative. When I called her just last week, she slammed the phone down on me when I barely mentioned Arthur's name. She has reason to hate him, I guess, but still . . ."

Brick said, "Well, she won't be slamming anything down next time she hears from us. We'll get two agents to knock on her door tomorrow, with badges flashing and getting her attention. Tell us how the tattoo came to be and why it distinguishes Arthur from Martin."

"It does for a reason that needs full explanation. I never saw it, but it's part of his intake record at the federal jail in San Diego. I think it's a sea animal or something like that with a capital 'M' in the middle."

Letty gasped, "Oh no, don't tell me Arthur put an 'M' on his tattoo standing for his brother Martin!"

"No, that's not it. As I remember the story Arthur relayed, the guy who tattooed him was a cousin or something. He was pretty drunk at the time. He said Marcella told her cousin, or whatever he was, to put a 'M' for Marcella, sort of as a joke. The back story is not very important, but the fact is that Martin never had a tattoo. She didn't want to talk to us either, but Marcella told her about the tattoo when she came to San Diego for the fake funeral. Remember that, Brick?"

Brick didn't remember that part of the record, but it sparked another question.

"Let's assume, just for the moment that we can prove to the court here in Portland that the man in jail is Arthur and he's pretending to be Martin to avoid the triple murder charge. I mean, we've charged Arthur, not Martin. Are the facts that were established in San Diego, when he was before that federal court, binding on what the federal court here does? I mean, part of the struggle there was establishing who the defendant really was—the guy arrested and charged was Martin, but it turned out he was really Arthur. That's what the court held, right? Does that work in our favor here or against us?"

Letty made a half-sign of the cross. "If I was a religious woman, I'd say praise the lord, we have a legal question. But my heathen tendencies won't allow that. So, I'll just thank you very much for posing something in my jurisdiction—the law. If a case is resolved by a judge without a jury, and they make factual findings in the case, those findings are limited to that case. They are not binding on a different court, even if both cases are federal district courts. Occasionally, that presumption is challenged when the district courts are in the same federal circuit, but that's not the case here. California is in the Ninth Circuit. Maine is in the First Circuit. So, the factual findings out there on the Pacific Coast are not binding on us here on the Atlantic Coast. Praise the lord."

Letty looked at her watch. "Well, we've managed to blow most of the morning. What say we quit while we're ahead? I'll let you know when the next hearing is scheduled. I'm sure we'll be talking back and forth as this case heats up. And Brick, I need to know a lot more about probable cause. I've taken a quick look at your affidavit. I'll look at it more carefully and call you, okay?"

CUMBERLAND COUNTY JAIL

"Good afternoon, Mr. Cheshire, my name is Ephraim Tutt. I've been appointed by the court to represent you."

"Which court?"

"The United States District Court for the District of Maine. I'm with the federal public defender's office. Magistrate Judge Juliana Rachlyn appointed our office to represent you yesterday. I was able to look at the charges against you online this morning and . . ."

"Do you know who I am, Mr. Tutt?"

"You are identified on the court docket as Arthur Cheshire, but the judge's office told my boss there is a question about whether you are correctly identified on the charging documents. You may call me Eppy, everyone does. Now, sir . . ."

"Eppy? What kinda name is that, 'Eppy'?"

"It's short for Ephraim, which is hard to say or spell, so my whole life I've just been called Eppy."

"Okay," Arthur said. "Back to my question. Do you know who I am?"

"Well, as I was explaining, there is a documents question . . ."

"No, dammit! It's a simple-ass question. Do you know or not? What's my name and don't tell me about some document in a courthouse."

Eppy tugged at the edge of his collar pulling it out a little from his throat.

"No, sir, I am not sure who you are. That is precisely why I'm here this early in your case. The judge's clerk told me on the telephone this morning that you say you are Martin Cheshire but that the court docket identifies you as Arthur Cheshire. I don't work for the court. My appointment is to represent you and to resolve as soon as possible the question before the court—are you Arthur Cheshire or are you Martin Cheshire? Tell me who you are, and I'll go from there."

"Okay, that's fair. I'm Martin Cheshire. They think I'm Arthur, my twin brother. But I'm not. I know the FBI officer that arrested me called me out as Arthur, and the detention cop that dragged me out of my cell to court says I'm listed as Arthur on his clip board, but that's fumbucked. If you think I'm Arthur, then you've got the wrong prisoner. Maybe he's up on the fourth-floor cell block. Hell I know."

"Is it okay with you if I refer to you as Mister Cheshire for this interview, so I can get some basic information?"

"Yeah."

"Mr. Cheshire, do you know the charges against you?"

"They gave me what they called a charging document and a copy of an arresting warrant or some damn thing. But they're wrong—they are looking for Arthur, my brother. He told me so. We don't kill people, but people never did us any favors either. How long you been a lawyer? And while I'm asking, how long you lived in Portland?"

Eppy had been told by his first supervisor at the PD's office to maintain close eye contact with jailed prisoners and never act cocky or know-it-all. So, he locked eyes on the man on the other side of the steel-topped table.

"I graduated from the Boston College Law School in 2010 and have been practicing law for almost five years now. There will be a senior lawyer from our office if your case goes to trial. You are charged with multiple counts, including three first-degree murder counts. I'm not a death-qualified attorney yet, one will be appointed soon, and I'll be second chair. But for now, I'm your legal representative in court. I've been living here in Portland since 2011."

"You ever heard about a company called AmHull Insurance?"

"No, can't say I have."

"Well, me and Arthur worked there. But not anymore. We're between jobs, ya know?"

"I want to take a full personal and work history from you, but first let me make sure you know your rights. Do you remember the FBI reading your Miranda rights to you when you were arrested?"

"Yeah, they did. I know about Miranda from TV. You know, *Law and Order*? Based on what's happening to me right now, they ought to call it *Law and Disorder*. They said, the FBI said, I had a right to remain silent, but then he argued that I was my brother when he never even asked my brother's name? Is that legal, tell me that?"

"Well, there are actually four constitutional rights you have in criminal cases. You can remain silent. You don't have to talk to the FBI or the DOJ. You have the right to a lawyer, a free one if necessary. That would be me. And you are presumed innocent until you are found guilty in a court of law. Let's make sure you understand all of those rights. Now . . ."

As Eppy would come to know all too well, Arthur would weave in and out of conversations about one issue by inserting his own questions about what he wanted to talk about.

"Hey, I already told you what the freakin f bee eye said. What I want to know is whether you believe me."

Taking in a slow breath, Eppy opened the manila file he had brought with him.

"I believe you when you say you are Arthur, not Martin. But my beliefs are not enough for the court. You are charged in these documents *as* Martin, your twin brother. I took a really quick look at a past filing here in this courthouse against you almost two years ago. The case was *US versus Martin Cheshire.* Sometimes charges are mistakenly filed against people with the same name. So, are you the same Martin Cheshire that was named in the case two years ago—that was a theft charge? American Hull Insurance was the victim, and . . ."

"It's AmHull, not American Hull. And yeah, that's me. They said I stole money, but I didn't. And I told them Arthur didn't either. Same thing as in this case. I never killed anybody, and he didn't either. He told me that. I told the judge that he didn't kill anyone day before yesterday. Now here you come asking the same questions. Tell me this, do I have the right to a lawyer who believes what I say?"

"Mr. Cheshire, I have a legal obligation to take what you tell me as factual unless and until it's clear that you are mistaken. And I will argue to the court you are who you say you are. But I also owe the legal system an ethical obligation not to make false claims or false assurances in court. So that's why I have to ask you questions in order to give you full representation in court. My job is to represent you whether you are guilty or not. Let's talk about where you've been since the last case was dismissed three years ago. Have you been here in Maine the whole time, or . . . ?"

"Are you asking me if I went down to New Hampshire, or maybe to Boston, or over to Vermont? You wanna know that so you can see if maybe I did kill somebody over there? Is that what you're asking?"

"No, I'm not asking that. Let me ask this, did your brother, Arthur, ever go to California? I ask that because a warrant was issued for you three years ago and somehow your brother ended up in the federal case against you in California. What do you know about that?"

"What Arthur did is not your business, is it? What if he did? I talk to him every day and we trust each other. Why don't you ask me about whether I stole dough from AmHull or I killed anybody?"

"All right, I will. Did you go to California and appear before a judge there on the embezzlement case at AmHull?"

"No, that was Arthur."

"And did you kill anybody here, or in New Hampshire, Massachusetts, or Vermont?"

"No, and neither did Arthur. He told me that over and over."

"The grand jury indicted you based on forensic evidence, including DNA sequencing, found at three different crime scenes. The file here on the desk says you and Arthur are identical twins, which means you share DNA with Arthur. Do you know what shared DNA means?"

"Yeah, me and Arthur looked it up at the library. And people talked about it to us sometimes. But it is science; we were not so good at that in high school. Did you learn about that in law school?"

"No, not law school. But DNA specimens and gene sequencing is occasionally important in criminal cases. In simple terms it can be considered as the information storing molecule of your body. You are what you are because your DNA contains the information for what you are meant to be. I read up on this last night after I was assigned your case. The files in your case confirm you and Arthur are identical twins. But science says even identical twins pick up genetic mutations in the womb, as their cells weave new strands of DNA and then split into more and more cells. So, you're not 100-percent identical from a genetic perspective."

"Well, Eppy, you maybe read that somewhere, but I can tell you Arthur and I are 100-percent identical. We talk all the time without talking. We think the same. I know what Arthur is thinking at the exact second he thinks it. What do you know about clairvoyance?"

"I know what it means, but it doesn't come up much in the legal world."

"Well, I'll explain it to you like me and Arthur know it. It's the no-doubt-about-it ability to know what one twin thinks or wants or is about to do. We were told as little kids by foster parents that it was called extrasensory perception. One of our fosters said it came from Jesus. We knew that was bullshit, but we pretended they were right, so they didn't strap us."

"Alright, Mr. Cheshire. Are you saying that even when you are miles away from your brother, say like he was in California, and you were here in Portland, that you knew what he was thinking?"

"I just told you there was no-doubt-about-it. No doubt at all, none at all, is what I said and what Arthur says too. I'm thinking about him right now because he's close by right now, back up there in our third-floor cell block. He knows what I'm thinking even if he can't hear you talk. No doubt about it."

"Alright, Mr. Cheshire. I think I've got enough for now. There will be a hearing, called a preliminary hearing, on your case pretty soon. I'll come back here and give you all the details as soon as the court clerk picks a date. And I'm leaving my card right here on the table. You put it in your pocket and call me any time if you want to talk to me. I'll see you soon."

"Okay, Eppy. We'll be waiting for you."

The chief federal public defender in Maine, Yi Elon Ho, was mildly surprised when his secretary said Eppy Tutt was on line two. It wasn't rare to get a call from one of the junior lawyers in his office, but she said it was about the new triple murder case involving those identical twins. That got his attention.

"Good morning, Eppy, glad to see you're in the office so early. What's up?"

"Good morning, Mr. Ho, I've been here since about five. I knew you were here because I saw your car downstairs in the basement."

"Well, I'll let you in on a small secret. I left the car down there yesterday. My wife came downtown last night for that bar association dinner at the Press Hotel, so we drove home in her car, and I took an Uber this morning. Jean said you wanted to talk about the new capital case. What do you need?"

"Could I come upstairs now?"

"Now? Well, I've got a pretty full calendar today, Eppy, but I can give you ten minutes if you come up right away. I've got a Zoom call in twenty minutes."

The federal defender's office in every state is a balancing act. It teeters one way to defend indigent people and totters the other facing woefully insufficient resources. The end result is too often undermanned defense teams and overpowered prosecutors. That's what his Zoom call was about—a large-group business meeting with the Chief Administrative Officer for the First Circuit Court of Appeals. A little-known fact about federal public defenders was that the chief in each office is appointed to a four-year term by the United States Court of Appeals of the circuit in which the defender organization is located. They do it that way rather than the nomination system used for federal prosecutors. The goal is to insulate federal public defenders from the involvement of the court before which the defender principally practices.

Eppy raced up two flights of metal stairs and rushed into Mr. Ho's office a little flushed.

"Wow, that was fast, Mr. Tutt, go on in, the boss is waiting for you," Jean said.

Eppy nodded thanks to her and pushed his boss's half-open door all the way.

"Mr. Ho, thanks for letting me barge in, I know you're busy but I just . . ."

"How can I help you, Eppy? Take a seat."

Eppy burned up three or four of his ten minutes describing his jail session with a man he said had two names: "Martin and Arthur." He explained the client's insistence that he was Martin at the arrest site, at booking, and in court before the PD's office was appointed. He said he'd gone back over the affidavit written by Agent Cato and carefully read the indictment and the charging document. He answered Mr. Ho's question about who was prosecuting and learned that his boss and Letica Persuanoli were friends.

"So, Eppy, what's your take? Is our client believable or is this a duck-and-dodge maneuver designed to put off the inevitable?"

"Well, it could be both. He denies with a straight face and seems to genuinely believe that he is Martin, not Arthur. But I get the feeling that it would be the other way around if his twin were to be arrested. I didn't spend much time with him but somehow I believe he *thinks* he is Martin right now. He talked a lot about how close they are, and he believes in mental telepathy and clairvoyance. He uses the royal 'we' a lot."

"So, Eppy, why are you here in my office telling me about your first meeting with a new client? Isn't this something you should be bringing up with your trial team, and the department head of the felony/serious crime group? I rarely get involved in trial strategies or non-capital plea deals. I presume that's what you have in mind here, right?"

"No, I'm here because I have a novel idea about how to deal with the identity problem—is our client Arthur as charged by the government, or is he Martin, as he insists he is? See, it's as much a problem for the prosecutor as it is for us. They are not sure who they are prosecuting, even though the fingerprints, photos, driver's license, and other things seem solid—the man they investigated, indicted, charged, and brought before the court on a prelim is Arthur Cheshire. I bet the judge is also scratching her head on this one."

"Novel idea? Criminal defense gets novel cases once in a while, but our ability to defend is tightly controlled by statue and constitutional rights."

"Yes, sir, my point exactly. I think we should file a motion seeking a writ of *habeas corpus*, in lieu of a response to plea or even a plan of discovery and exchange of evidence."

Elon Ho took in a deep breath, tapped his finger on the manila folder slowly, and almost imperceptibly shook his head from side to side.

"Have you ever filed for a *habeas corpus* writ?"

Eppy said no.

"Well, I have. Once. In twenty-eight years of practice. Once. We have a half dozen full-time appellate lawyers in this office. I'd bet they collectively have not filed more than a dozen in the last several years. How would you even construct a prayer for relief if the writ were granted?"

"Mr. Ho, I think this is perfect factual scenario for habeas relief."

Eppy covered the essence of *habeas corpus* relief in five minutes. Mr. Ho buzzed Jean and told her to beg his pardon on the Zoom call. Then he told Eppy to expand on the basics and get into the nuts of *habeas* relief even before their client was tried and convicted. This kind of legal writ was usually the last effort at getting a murder defendant off death row.

Habeas corpus is Latin for "bring me the body." In federal courts, the writ is used to determine whether a state's detention of a prisoner is valid. Granting the writ forces whoever is detaining a prisoner to bring him or her before the court. The purpose is to determine whether the person's imprisonment or detention is lawful. It is particularly useful if there are questions about extradition, bail, and the jurisdiction of the court. Eppy cited three cases from the First Circuit.

He talked about James Madison arguing for the Bill of Rights, including *habeas corpus*, not long after the Constitution was written. He cited Chief Justice Marshall, who had emphasized the importance of *habeas corpus*, calling it a "great object" to liberate people imprisoned without sufficient cause. He cited dicta and law review articles recognizing *habeas corpus* as a fundamental instrument to safeguard individual freedom against arbitrary and lawless state action.

Mr. Ho wondered why Eppy thought it was important that a federal judge could dismiss the petition out of hand.

"Well, because federal judges are overworked and way behind. The docket is very crowded. Time is on the defendant's side in this case. A *habeas* proceeding could give the defense valuable time to fully investigate the clear mental health issue here, which could lead to a competence hearing."

"Why is time on our side, Eppy? Our client is entitled to a speedy trial and the government will push hard given that this is a serial murder case. There will be significant pressure from three families in three different states, right? Why delay the case on the merits?"

"Because I spent less than an hour with our client. I'm confident our client believes he is Martin on the face of credible evidence that he is Arthur. We might have a very hard time gathering evidence to prove his claim that he is Martin, not Arthur. But if we file for *habeas* relief right now, instead of just showing up at the prelim, the burden of proof will be on the government to prove *they* arrested Arthur, and that the man they arrested is the twin *they* think killed three people in three different states, before we get to the discovery and trial stages of the case. It puts the heat where it belongs, on the government, to prove every element of their case, beyond a reasonable doubt, including the true identity of the defendant."

"All right, Eppy, you've persuaded me. But let's jump ahead a mile or two. Let's say the government meets its burden and satisfies Judge Rachlyn that the defendant is Arthur Cheshire, then what?"

"Then we go to stall number two. Is Arthur competent to stand trial?"

"So, the burden shifts back to us on that issue, right?"

"Right, boss, but it's a mental health issue, not a legal issue. There is probably more than one psychiatrist out there that will say Arthur Cheshire is more than one bubble off plumb. And that may be our best defense for him. I mean, you once told me the only sure way to lose a criminal case was to take it to trial. Even if he is guilty, they can't try him if he's incompetent to help us defend him. He didn't help me much in our first meeting by telling me he talked to his dead twin brother every day."

Later that afternoon, in the same building, Brick and Liz met with the prosecution team in Letty Persuanoli's office.

"Happy Friday," she said to Brick and Liz as they were shown by the guard into the room.

"Wow, you're right, Letty," Brick said.

"This week went by like the last lap at the Indy 500. The Quantico team has been charging ahead to get all inculpatory evidence and forensics organized for you."

"Great, Brick, but I'm getting buzzing noise from upstairs as well as rumors floating over the federal jail walls about the defendant. I'm hearing he's staging a one-man play for detention officers and the jail population."

Liz nodded.

"No surprise to me. I've got my own buzzes. We need to have a longer conversation about the identity hearing we went through in San Diego with Arthur Cheshire. I can't forget that he came in shackles and handcuffs to my first visit with him, insisting he was Arthur and only mistaken for his twin, Martin. Now, as Yogi Berra might put it, we have *déjà vu* all over again."

"Yes, Liz," Letty said, "I'm getting the feeling I'm Alice and this case is more Wonderland than it is a capital murder case. I've seen references to a hearing in the California case to establish identity, but I have no idea what that meant. Can you fill us in?"

"Glad you asked, Letty. I spent maybe three hours last night going over my iPad files and typing a numbered list of how the San Diego case flowed from incarceration to release. It's of course a mental health list rather than legal history. I made five copies of it at the hotel copy center this morning. Can I give you two copies now so we can use it as a guide map, and skip over the items you don't need at this point?"

"Hey, Liz, that's a great idea. Are you sure you're not a closet lawyer, pretending to be a psychiatrist?"

"Heavens no. Actually, we don't have closets in mental health these days. The padded rooms have been replaced with prescription drug usage. I'll start with number one, and you can interrupt and ask questions or tell me to skip numbers on the list as we move through it. Okay, number one. This is the key event that dominates everything that happened in Judge Hightower's courtroom. Martin Cheshire died in a boating accident near here, at a place called Jones Point, near South Bristol . . ."

As often happens when five people in a room are looking at the same numbered list and one is talking, hands go up and interruptions are the rule, not the exception.

"Hey, that's where the arrest in our case occurred, right, Jones Point?" Letty's second-chair lawyer said.

"Yes, I think so," Liz said, adding, "The death of one of these two identical twins colors and shapes every fact that ultimately led to the identity hearing in San Diego. As you can see in number two, Arthur survived the accident, but his brother Martin died. That led to Arthur pretending to be his brother out of a combination of guilt, remorse, loss of self, and other comorbid associations . . ."

Brick spoke up. "Liz, what exactly do you mean by comorbid associations?"

"Comorbidity refers to the occurrence of more than one mental health disorder at the same time. It also relates to physical condition. We never got reliable health records on Arthur, but I gave him myriad mental health tests. He and his brother, Martin, were so mentally invested in one another that the unscientific things, like mental telepathy and clairvoyance, became clues to what I think Arthur suffers from, then and now. He's bi-polar. And he's got comorbid associations so deeply ingrained that he could pass a polygraph and convince the operator he is exactly who he says he is, at any given moment."

"Sorry to interrupt, Liz, but can you give us a quick update on bi-polar?" Letty said. "Am I right in thinking bipolar is a treatable mental disorder? So, was he on medication when you were assessing him in San Diego?"

"Yes, Letty, it is treatable with medications. He was not on any meds when I saw him in California. Bipolar meds are like eyeglasses. That's because bipolar disorder distorts your view of yourself and the world. The right meds help patients to see things more clearly. They don't cure the patient, but they help him keep his moods in balance. When they are off their meds they swing back and forth between mania and depression."

"Okay, Liz, that helps me. Did you determine his true identity through therapy in California?"

"No, I didn't 't give him any therapy, or diagnose him with a mental disorder. I only tried to establish his true identity by extensive questioning. While I'm guessing quite a bit here, I think he actually *was* Arthur in the San Diego jail. More importantly to this case, I think that he actually *thinks* he's Martin now that he's in jail here in Portland. That's comorbidity to the max."

Everyone at the table raised their hands signaling questions galore. Letty cautioned, "Okay guys, let's let Liz move through the list. Interrupt if you think it's important but make notes if you can. This list has eighteen reference points. So, Liz what's number two?"

"This is an easy one. Arthur survives the accident. He 'becomes' Martin out of guilt. When I say 'becomes,' I'm not being literal. He's the same human after the boating accident that he was before it happened. But his mind screams *Martin, Martin* at him. You'll see in point three that his brother had been living with Rosie Anderson for a short time when the accident happened. Arthur hid the accident and his brother by burying him under the floorboards of their fishing camp at Jones Point. Then he drives back to Portland and *pretends* to be Martin by sleeping with Rosie and convincing her and everyone else in town that Arthur went back to San Diego. Now, in point four I report how angry both twins were with AmHull Insurance because the boss there forced Arthur to go all the way across the country to San Diego and open a branch office."

Letty was obviously confused. "Liz, am I hearing this right? Arthur loses his twin in an accident and instead of intense grief, he acts out by fooling his brother's girlfriend into sex with him, and he's mad at his employer for some reason, but he still goes back to San Diego and, what, still runs the insurance business three thousand miles away?"

"Yes, Letty, you have it right but from a rational person's perspective. These twins, the Cheshire boys, were damaged goods, but nobody here knew that. They lived as though only one of them ever got blamed for anything. If Arthur did something bad,

Martin would take the blame for it. If Martin did something good, Arthur would take the credit. As hard as it is to imagine or believe, they lived a life of Hide and Be. That's a game they invented to shield themselves from the reality of child abuse, multiple foster homes, and the identical genetic and environmental demands that monozygotic, mirror-twins have . . ."

The second-chair lawyer raised his hand but was tamped down by a stern look from Letty. "Definitions can wait," she said.

"Right," Liz said. "Number four is a fact I have only limited knowledge of. I think Brick can brief you on that later. Martin's anger at AmHull sending Arthur out to San Diego caused him to do something foreign to these twin boys. He figured out a scheme to siphon off some insurance premiums from AmHull to get back at Harold Hull, the owner. I think someone told me he embezzled about $26,000. He may or may not have told Arthur about it when he came back to Portland for that tragic fishing trip. Everyone, including Rosie, accepted Arthur as Martin. No one here knew that Martin died in the boating accident, or that Martin had embezzled money for AmHull. Arthur had two secrets to hide from the world. And he thought the best place to hide those secrets was out there in California."

Letty broke her own rule about interrupting.

"I'm sorry, Liz, but I think all of us need info and maybe more perspective on this point. How in holy hell did so many people here believe that nothing had changed with the Cheshire twins? How did Arthur, who I'll just call the survivor twin, manage to carry this off until it got unwound in that identity hearing in San Diego?"

"Well, it's sketchy, but for maybe two months, Arthur flew back and forth between Portland and San Diego. Here in Portland, he pretended to be Martin and explained his absence on out-of-town business for AmHull involving claims adjustment or new policy sales in New England. In San Diego, he continued his real life with a woman named Marcella Munoz. He helped Harold Hull's two sons open a new AmHull branch office in San Diego. In San Diego, he continued to be who he really is, Arthur. In Portland, he pretended to be Martin. Everyone here fell for it because no one could tell the boys apart anyhow. He easily convinced them he is Martin even though he is actually Arthur."

Liz took a few sips from her government-supplied water bottle. Letty declared this was a good time for the afternoon pee break. The men went left down the long hall to the men's room. Liz and Letty went next door to the ladies'.

At the wash basin, Letty asked, "Liz, my god, how ever did you manage to sort all this out for your judge down there in San Diego?"

"Well, it certainly helped that I was in the middle of the most fascinating case of mental health crisis in my professional life. I thought that case would make a fascinating article in *Science Today*, but that never happened. Instead, I got that call from Brick to fly back east and do for his FREST team what I did in San Diego when I thought Arthur was telling me the whole truth and nothing but the truth."

"So," Letty said, applying a light pink lipstick to what looked like parched lips, "do you still believe Arthur when he says he is actually Martin and that we've got the wrong man in jail?"

"Well, I know this much for sure. The man in jail here in Portland is the same man I talked to in San Diego. But I think if I were to talk to him here, I would be talking to Martin. They are not the same man, but they have always lived one single life, even when there were two of them."

Back in the conference room, Liz continued with her numbered list.

"Okay, now let's talk about number five. It's fair to think of Arthur's short life in San Diego as a brilliant charade. Arthur, I think, realized that he could not continue to be himself in San Diego and be his twin in Portland. To him, it was just Hide and Be. They used it as a survival technique as children. They used it as a joke in junior and high school. And they used it to trick gullible women and unsuspecting men as young adults. One would *hide* and the other would *be*. That's how Arthur made the game work. When he was in Portland for six weeks or so after Martin died, he pretended to *be* his brother Martin. Then he'd *hide* by going to San Diego where he'd *be* himself. The game worked well as a shield when younger. As young adults they upgraded it as a sword against the world. They were never sick, physically, or mentally in Portland. They would not survive separation, by accident or otherwise. So, in Arthur's mind, they weren't separated. He became *them*."

The one-woman show stopped for almost thirty minutes while everyone chimed in with a question, answer, doubt, similar story, or denial. Letty got the group refocused by asking how the embezzlement charges morphed into a murder charge in San Diego.

"That gets us to number six. Arthur's solution to the risk of detection of Martin's death in Maine was to fake his own death in Mexico, fifty miles south of San Diego. He told me in one of our talks in my clinic room that he talked to Martin, and they agreed that he should be Martin in Portland and forget about his life as Arthur in San Diego. He thought no one in California would miss him, including a new girlfriend out there, Marcella Munoz. So, here's how the fake death worked. He rented an Avis truck in Portland that he could turn in at the Avis rental facility at the airport in San Diego. In the bed of the truck, he hid the remains of Martin's partially decomposed bones from the fishing camp at Jones Point and . . ."

Brick interrupted, "Liz, the FREST team knows how you came to know these facts, but I think you should explain to the Portland team how you're certain about the fake death plan."

Liz grimaced a little because she knew her explanation sounded more like a mental health lecture. "Maybe certain is not the right word. Let's say I'm confident that what Arthur told me about the fake death is true. He based it on the simple assumption that the authorities in Mexico would believe he died there in a fishing shack south of Ensenada because they would find his DNA in the bones. He knew he and Martin shared DNA and he thought DNA was dispositive. They would believe it was an accident he caused and died from. Back in Portland, Arthur, after faking his own death and pretending to be Martin, realized that it would only be a matter of time before Rosie realized he is Arthur and not her lover, Martin. So, before that happened, he left her but continued to work as Martin at AmHull. By then the employee he had mostly worked with, Alice Singworth, had quit and moved to Boston. So, she wasn't a problem anymore. What Arthur didn't know was that Alice had discovered his embezzlement and told Rosie Anderson about it. That ultimately led to the first arrest in Portland several months ago. His second arrest was on the road to Jones Point. Okay, that's enough of me expounding. Questions?"

Letty had several.

"Liz, thanks for those mostly unknown details. I have many questions. First, you told us Arthur told you about the AmHull embezzlement. You said it was $26,000. But the indictment here was for $269,000. Is that just a mistake on Arthur's part or a lie?"

"I think you'll find my answer evasive, but let me say first, there are two very different kinds of liars. Pathological liars tell compulsive lies without a clear motive. Arthur is not a pathological liar. Nonpathological lying is almost endemic today. It's a common feature of social interactions among humans. Essentially, we lie to achieve some benefit—to avoid embarrassment or to avoid being caught doing something wrong or unlawful. But it is not typically a sign of a mental health condition. Pathological lying is different. It may be a sign of an underlying mental health condition, such as a personality disorder. In Arthur's case, there is no evidence of pathological lying, and for the most part he was truthful to me in relaying his role in the lesser embezzlement, and his role in faking his own death. His reasons for taking over for Martin are a function of his profound mental illness, his obsession with protecting his twin, and his deep grief over, and self-blame for, Martin's death. On balance, he is much more truthful than he is deceitful."

"So," Letty pressed, "you say he is truthful when he now says he's Martin, not Arthur?"

"No, I'm not at all saying that. I'm saying he believes he is Martin. I think, in the beginning, starting with the boat accident, he knew he was Arthur and only pretended to be Martin as part of their Hide and Be game. But as his pretense became both impractical and in danger of not working to keep Martin alive to others, like Rosie, he did what he could to revert to his life as Arthur while psychologically and mentally sinking deeper and deeper into the illusion that he could be both alternately himself when possible and Martin when necessary."

"What do you mean, 'be' Martin when necessary?"

"Good question. The word necessary of course means required to be done, achieved, or present. It's synonymous with needed or essential. So, think about the new emotional wound that afflicts Arthur because of Martin's death. He already suffers from the many emotional wounds caused by cruel or ignorant foster parents as a child here in Portland. Now, because Martin is dead, he cannot accept that reality. He can't adapt to it. He needs Martin. Martin is essential to him. So, when he says to me, you, the court, or the world, that he *is* Martin, he says it because he believes it, because it's something he needs to say, and something essential to who he is."

Letty raised her left hand as a symbol to pause as she ran her ballpoint down the handout Liz had given them at the start of the meeting. Then, looking up, she opened up a new thread of legal issues.

"Okay, Liz and everyone, I want to shift gears now from views on Arthur's past and his persona to a more acute legal reality. Let's assume we get past the identity question and start the long process of evidentiary assessment, theory building, plea bargaining, and trial preparation. How does Arthur figure in? Is he a serial killer? Is he killing only twins who do not, for whatever reason, celebrate their birthdays together? Is Arthur evil or just demented? If we see his motivation as paranoia, is it enough to drive him to kill three people? Is his guilt so profound that he could seduce two women pretending to be someone he's not? Remember, we, the federal government once accused him of embezzlement in Portland and not long afterward simply gave up and walked away when he convinced a California federal judge that he was Arthur and therefore could not have killed himself in Mexico. Is his incessant use of the royal 'we' a dodge or an admission?"

The group exchanged tentative answers, guesses, speculations, and hopes. As the energy in the room melted, Letty posed the final question of the day.

"Brick and Norm, are both of you confident we can prove that we indicted and arrested the right Cheshire twin? It could come to that if the defense challenges the court's jurisdiction."

Norm asked how that might come about. Letty explained.

"The defense could argue that we claim Arthur was arrested. But the man we arrested claims he is Martin. So, the government has the burden of proof to clarify his identity. I know the court in San Diego went through a similar process—they called it an 'identity hearing.'"

Norm didn't agree. "Letty, we arrested the defendant under the name Arthur Cheshire. We have his bona fides on file here in Maine—driver's license, state taxes paid, fingerprints, photos, and DNA CODIS filings. They match the photo, driver's license, fingerprints, and DNA in the California case. There's no doubt about it—the man in our jail is Arthur Cheshire. Do you think the public defender will insist on an identity hearing here?"

"I don't know their plan or what their defense might be. But it won't be our burden to prove. If they claim we have the wrong man, they will have to prove the man in jail is Martin Cheshire. And if Liz's team in San Diego is right, we have documents from there that our court here will take judicial notice of. Seems airtight to me."

Liz asked, "Judicial notice? What is that?"

"Sorry, Liz, I keep thinking you're a lawyer, like the rest of this motley crew. Judicial notice is a rule in the law of evidence that allows a fact to be introduced in evidence if the truth of that fact is notorious, well known, or authoritatively attested. If it is, then it cannot reasonably be doubted. That works heavily in our favor."

At 5:15 they called it a day and met for drinks at an authentic O'Shea's, an English pub a block away from the courthouse.

Arthur was in the official custody of the Cumberland County Sheriff because there were no federal jails or prisons in Maine. He was housed in Portland's Cumberland County Jail at 50 County Way in Portland, about two miles from the federal courthouse. Three hundred sixty-two other adult males were there, awaiting trial, or serving less than one-year for misdemeanor convictions. Sixty-seven were federal prisoners awaiting trial. Like most jails, it was safe if every prisoner behaved, and none had a shank or the chance to use it.

On the third Monday after his arrest, Arthur exercised his sheriff-given right to walk from the chow hall into the exercise yard, an octagon no bigger than a mini-mart parking lot. A dozen other sullen prisoners were scuffing about, smoking, cussing, and kicking up dirt. Two uniformed but unarmed guards manned the checkpoint. Random searches were the order of the day. Arthur was not selected, and neither was the hulk with the shaven head leaning up against the block wall on the far side of the yard.

Ten minutes after Arthur got there, more prisoners poured out, and the yard got much louder. He ignored everyone. The others did not touch one another but exchanged greetings, slurs, hand signs, cigs, and spits. After studying Arthur for a few minutes, the hulk, weighing just under three hundred pounds sauntered his way slowly toward Arthur. His real name was largely unknown to other inmates; they called him Tank, but not to his face. He was almost the same age as Arthur, twenty-seven, with olive brown skin, dreadlocks, and enough prison tats to look like a walking mural.

Tank had grown up street banging in Charlestown, inside Boston proper, but widely recognized as the place to go for shoot-ings, drug dealing, and prostitution, especially at the eastern end. He strolled past his guards, shoulders swaying from side to side, and his size-thirteen clod hoppers kicking up dust.

"You the dude what killed them white boys on their happy birthdays?"

Arthur blinked and backed up a step. He started to form an answer but had little experience with street crime, much less jail yard confrontation.

"I'm sorry, but . . ."

Before he could finish the sentence, the center of the yard erupted. The sound of knuckles snapping against bare flesh. Arthur went down to his knees, raising his arms over his head. Tank launched a battery of fist-flurries at Arthur. Another white federal prisoner joined the fray for a minute or two until the two checkpoint guards, who had their pepper spray, aimed their tasers.

"All right, come on, guys. Knock it off."

Their first warning was passive. None of the now-encircled prisoners paid attention. Four more uniformed guards, wearing flak jackets and carrying long black billy clubs rushed through the door, providing backup.

The passive guard ordered, "OK, Tank, that's enough. Get on the ground, Arthur. Both of you now, goddamn it! On the ground!"

Turned out that the shank Tank taped to his palm didn't do much harm to Arthur, only surface slashes on his forearm. When Arthur's blood sprayed out, they tasered Tank. Three more guards rushed outside, but the fight was over. It had lasted about a minute. A guard with blue stripes on his brown shirt said, "The fed dude's going to med unit, Tank's going to lockdown and will get another twelve-month flop."

A *flop* meant you had one foot out the door, as long as you stayed out of trouble for your year. Now's he's headed to the big yard, the state prison, another guard mumbled. The other guy, the fed defendant, went to the infirmary and from there to detention where a jail lieutenant asked Arthur what he said to Tank that so infuriated him.

"What did we say to that fat slob with the dreads and tats? Nothing. Not a single syllable. He screamed something about a white dude killing somebody. No sense to me or Arthur. You know? We're only here temporarily. That's because the freakin' f bee eye think I'm my brother. We know better and nothing they have is going to stick on me or Martin. Nothing, you see. We will be shown the door out of here any day now. Any day now."

After getting the go-ahead from Mr. Ho, Eppy spent the next day and a half reading, indexing, and identifying statutes and cases to cite in his *habeas corpus* writ. He asked other up-and-coming public defenders, none of whom had any experience with *habeas* law to send him forms and ideas. No one thought the famous rule could be used to simply identify a defendant by name—Arthur or Martin.

Eppy had scribbled a research list on a legal pad. Item one his list read, "Scope of *Habeas Corpus*." He knew the basics—*habeas* relief depended on specific legal issues arising out of a federal prisoner's rights. The writ wasn't available to review errors of law or irregularities of procedural rules in a lower court's resolution of guilt or innocence. But here there was no lower court. Arthur was facing a federal district court trial. He found a US Supreme Court case, *Waley v. Johnson*, handed down in 1942 that allowed a *habeas* writ where the defendant's constitutional rights were not considered at all phases of the lower court's handling of the case. That gave him standing to seek the writ at the outset, he thought.

He read a long 1948 law review article titled, "The Freedom Writ—The Expanding Use of Federal *Habeas Corpus*." Both supported his view that a prisoner's claims of confession or discrimination, or other prosecutorial failures, were within the jurisdiction of a federal court at any stage of the proceeding. What could be more unconstitutional, he thought, than forcing a man to stand trial based on the *assumption* he was actually the man charged and indicted under a name he denied? Martin had informed the arrest team he was Martin, not Arthur. He had raised that same argument at the first, quickly terminated preliminary hearing. The upcoming hearing would also be formally and officially against Arthur, notwithstanding the defendant in the dock's insistence he was *not* Arthur. He *was* Martin.

For Eppy, the most important legal issue was jurisdiction. Did the federal court have jurisdiction over a man who insisted he was not Arthur Cheshire, but rather Arthur's twin brother, Martin Cheshire? If there was jurisdiction, who had the burden of proving identity—the defendant—or the government? The difference was enormous. The government had to prove its case beyond a reasonable doubt. The defendant had to prove his identity by a mere preponderance of the evidence. Was it the government's obligation?

He found many cases over the last fifty years all debating and inconsistently resolving identity issues. None answered the question he thought was most important. Could he insist on the government proving identity before moving forward with the merits of their case? If the court agreed, then who had the burden of proving competency to stand trial? The government? And does it shift to the defendant once he's properly identified?

Common law principles and some case law holdings supported the argument that the government had the burden of proof of the defendant's identity *and* the duty to prove he was competent to stand trial. Other cases said the court had the obligation to clearly identify the defendant by name, but the defendant had to prove incompetency to stand trial.

His research produced seven cases from three states with favorable holdings in each case. None were from Maine, but all involved the same issue Arthur faced in the triple murder case.

Eppy found an Oregon case with similar facts. In *Starskie,* twin brothers were arrested and charged with felony theft and burglary. The state charged them with stealing more than $12,000 worth of guns and ammunition from a well-known sporting goods store. Two masked and gloved thieves were caught on surveillance video breaking into the store through a large skylight, gliding down ropes, turning off motion detectors, and hauling up seven expensive rifles, one pistol, and several cases of ammunition. The local press called it, "A complicated and well-orchestrated heist." The prosecution told the grand jury the heist was performed perfectly, except for one mistake: one twin had left behind drops of sweat on a glass top display case. The police ran it through CODIS and got two hits. They identified one of the two twins. It was the only piece of forensic evidence to identify the thieves. In a pretrial motion, the twins' lawyers argued that, given that the DNA matched both twins, identification could not be matched under the government's no-reasonable-doubt standard. No other identification differentiated the twins. Neither waived their constitutional rights. The twins went free.

In an Ohio case, *Ohio v. Moise Veebar, et. al.*, someone threw a Molotov cocktail into a busy nightclub on a Saturday night, before closing time. One identical twin brother was identified by a security camera sitting in his car in the alley behind the nightclub when the fire started inside the club. They arrested him while the fire was ravaging the building. The other identical twin had a solid alibi; he was twenty-one miles away, in an emergency room, waiting to see the doctor for a painful gall bladder attack. The prosecution arrested both twins, one for criminal arson and the other for aiding and abetting. At a preliminary hearing the defense challenged the indictment against both twins for failure to prove which twin was on the video. No credible evidence differentiated one from the other. The video showed a man who looked like both twins. The court dismissed the case for failure to identify which twin committed the crime.

At the end of a long day spent reading cases and statues, Eppy wrote out four arguments he thought supported his theories of how best to start this case. He would ask the court to order the government to prove the man at the defense table was actually Arthur Cheshire. They had good evidence on this issue in the form of fingerprints taken when Arthur was initially charged in Maine and subsequently extradited to San Diego. And the government would argue the San Diego court was right when it identified Arthur as the defendant before the court. But that was, he hoped, a trap they would regret.

If the federal judge in Maine agreed with the federal judge in San Diego, then Eppy would shift gears and insist that his client, who believed he was Martin, not Arthur, was not competent to stand trial as his brother. He had four arguments for this position. It is fundamentally unfair to try an incompetent defendant. It is inhumane to subject an incompetent defendant to trial. The trial of an incompetent defendant contradicts the law's disfavor of trials in absentia. And most important, the pathetic spectacle of the trial of an incompetent defendant diminishes society's respect for the dignity of the criminal justice process. And if all else failed, he would argue that the due process clause of the Fifth, Sixth, and Fourteenth Amendments demanded fairness as the underlying principle of criminal prosecution. How could he defend his client if the client believed he was his brother, even if the government proved he was Arthur, not Martin? Didn't they have to prove both? First prove the man in the dock *was* Arthur. And second he was *not* Martin.

With his notes and legal documents securely in his briefcase, Eppy went to the Cumberland County Jail, and asked to see his client, Martin Cheshire. The jailer said they had a Cheshire in custody named Arthur Cheshire. Eppy said, "Yes, same guy."

Once settled in a small room behind a bolted steel door with his client, Eppy spent the maximum time allotted for legal sessions, fifty-five minutes. He told the man who insisted he was Martin Cheshire what a writ of *habeas corpus* was. His client insisted he could prove he was Martin by telling the judge in no uncertain terms who he was. "I am Martin Cheshire. I am because that's what we both want, me and Arthur. Even before I was arrested at our fishing camp by the f bee eye, Arthur told me I was Martin."

Eppy asked, "When did you talk to Arthur?"

"Just before Slo, the day-detention officer on my cell block, came to get me, maybe ten minutes ago. Maybe one minute ago. Time's different in jail, you know?"

"So, you and Arthur want the same thing, to be let out of jail and not found guilty of anything in court?"

"Yeah, damn straight. And we want to be declared by the court by our right names. I'm Martin and he's Arthur. We are innocent."

Eppy went back to his office, spread out his notes and drafts on his desk, and stared at them, hoping he could do what he thought was impossible. How could he tell the court what his client wants without suggesting the client was an insane man who might never know who he really was? And to add an ethical dilemma to the calculus, was he ethically obligated to proceed against the feeling that his client was actually Arthur, as charged, and that he was merely a pawn in the charade being advanced by the Cheshire twins? He no sooner thought that than he slammed his ballpoint down on the desk, breaking the tip. Under his breath, he said to himself, I represent the man in jail, and I have taken his word for who he is, without thinking about what he may have done.

With good constitutional, statutory, and case law in support, Eppy drafted a four-page motion seeking *habeas corpus* relief. He identified the name and location of the court. He identified his client as Martin but labeled the case as Arthur's case. With the formalities of federal pleading done, he did what all lawyers everywhere do. He pleaded for relief, albeit in a style rarely seen in federal court pleadings or writs.

Martin Cheshire, erroneously named herein, being a proud citizen of these United States and in particular the State of Maine, seeks relief from this court to establish, confirm, and address the US Department of Justice, the Federal Bureau of Investigation, and the federal prosecutors identified in the case at large that the accused defendant is in fact, by reason of his birth and his existence on planet Earth, the son of unavailable and uncaring parents as so identified on his certificate of birth as Martin Cheshire, having no middle initial, and that he is legally not the person otherwise identified in this case as Arthur Cheshire, having no middle initial, and that any crimes or misdemeanors committed by Arthur Cheshire are not and cannot be legally ascribed, assumed, or blamed on Martin Cheshire. Martin Cheshire respectfully reminds this court that a writ of *habeas corpus* is an ages-old mechanism designed by the framers of our United States Constitution carried from England to enable all confined persons the absolute right to challenge the circumstances that led to their confinement and to force the government of the United States to prove each and every element of its charges beyond a reasonable doubt. Martin Cheshire also respectfully reminds this honorable court that he is by law and circumstance entitled to the vaunted right that he is presumed to be innocent until proven guilty and that he cannot be prosecuted for any crimes perpetrated by the aforenamed Arthur Cheshire, notwithstanding the affinity and love shared between the natural born twin brothers whose names have been misidentified and confused by the government agencies named above to the detriment of the petitioner Martin Cheshire. Wherefore the petitioner demands the Sheriff of Cumberland County be commanded to produce Martin Cheshire, wrongly identified as Artur Cheshire in the indictment giving rise to these proceedings, in and before this Court at its first and immediate opportunity. And Martin Cheshire respectfully reminds this honorable court that this and all writs of *habeas corpus* are lawsuits between two parties, and governed by civil, not criminal law. Accordingly, Martin Cheshire asks this court to refer to him henceforth as the "Petitioner" and not the "Defendant." The Petitioner asks that unless and until his true identity is established by the court, all criminal charges and process against him be abated, pending the jurisdictional and competency issues raised in this petition for a writ of *habeas corpus*.

The day after Eppy filed his Petition for Writ of *habeas corpus*, Letty called Norm at his office in Portland. She said she had news, but she wanted Brick on the line as well because their case had just hit a hole in the road. Once all three were on the line, Letty told them Mr. Tutt had filed a *habeas* writ.

Brick said, "What? A *habeas* writ. The last time I even thought about a *habeas* writ was when I took the bar exam twenty-seven years ago."

Norm laughed.

"Yeah, and as I remember it, you whined about that bar exam for the next full year. Remember that study group we had? Con law was not your best subject."

"So," Letty interrupted, "you guys were in law school together?"

Brick mumbled something about Norm kissing up to the con-law professor, who was the shortest con-law professor at Duke. And Norm rebutted that she was short and bare footed but with her Marine brogans on, she scared the crap out of everyone in her class. Letty got them back on track.

"Okay, guys but let's save the law school war stories for some other time. Eppy Tutt's petition is going to get Judge Rachlyn's full attention and not in a good way. Let me parse it out for you.

"The defense is casting the case as one of mistaken identity. As you both know, the defendant is now claiming that he is not Arthur Cheshire. He now insists he is Martin Cheshire and . . ."

"Yeah, Letty, that's what he said to me when I said hands-up at Jones Point and arrested him. But you sound concerned. He has no chance of pulling a switch-off. He is Arthur and we can easily prove that."

"I know that, Brick, but Norm, just for the hell of it, walk me through the factual evidence we have to prove he is Arthur Cheshire."

"Right. When he was first arrested in Portland two years ago and booked into the same jail where he's now blowing smoke about *habeas corpus*, he was fingerprinted, photographed, identified by his employer, and freely admitted who he was by signing jail custody forms, including a receipt for his personal stuff. You know, watch, neck chain, wallet, et cetera. His wallet contained his driver's license, business cards, credit cards, and a picture of him and his brother in a pub bar. We matched things up with his girlfriend, Rosie Andersen. We did not do much more because there was never any question—he was who he said was. There's a presumption of law about that, am I right?"

"You're right, Norm, there is a rebuttable presumption that you are who you say you are. I spent a couple hours last night on Lexis-Nexis trying to find the source for that odd notion—you are who you say you are. In part it stems from what many think is the most important principle in criminal law—the presumption of innocence. It's a legal principle that every person accused of any crime is considered innocent until proven guilty. While he doesn't say that exactly in his petition for a writ, Mr. Tutt is headed straight for the jugular of any criminal case—forcing the prosecution to rebut the presumption of innocence by presenting compelling evidence to the judge. If we don't convince the judge that Arthur Cheshire is the man sitting at the defense table, then he could walk out of court, scot-free, so to speak. To prevent that, we have to offer proof of both identity and guilt beyond a reasonable doubt."

Brick said, "Well, I may be a few years behind on my con law but aren't these completely separate issues—identity and guilt?"

"They are, but in this case, the defense is raising a reasonable doubt by simply telling the court that it has the wrong twin brother. That raises the legal presumption that you are who you say are. The man you arrested said you have the wrong man, I'm Martin, you're looking for my brother Arthur. You put that in your report and the man you arrested told the booking judge his name was Martin. The jailed man is telling everyone there he's Martin, not Arthur. Now his lawyer is repeating that defense to the trial judge. I am sure you are right about the strength of the evidence—fingerprints, history, personal identification. But the personal identification will be doubtful, and fingerprints can be very tricky in a full-blown jurisdictional defense. So . . ."

"Letty," Norm interrupted, "if I remember right, there was a hearing on a similar issue in San Diego. There, the man we extradited on a murder charge was Martin Cheshire, but when he got there, he claimed he was Arthur Cheshire. The judge out there bought it hook, line, and sinker. He decided the man was Arthur, and since he was alive and well in court, he could not be charged with his own murder. That record will clear this up, right? I mean, Arthur could not have killed himself. But he did prove he was Arthur, and now we have evidence he killed three young men here in New England. Once we prove that the guy we arrested and jailed is that same guy the judge declared in San Diego was Arthur, we win, right?"

"No, Norm it's not that simple. I think you're correct about our evidence and that we can use that to persuade Judge Rachlyn that the man on trial in her court is Arthur Cheshire. But now comes the hammer. We prove he's Arthur and that proves the man is incompetent to stand trial, by whatever name. I think Mr. Tutt is a young and very inventive lawyer. He will use our evidence against us and ultimately argue that his client does not know who he is, that he cannot assist in his own defense because he thinks he's someone else, and that until he regains sufficient competence, he cannot be tried. That takes him out of court in a serial murder case and into a mental institution for the next few decades."

QUANTICO, VIRGINIA

rick walked into the conference room ten minutes late. Lee had just texted him, worried that something might be wrong.

"No," he said in her general direction as he dropped the expandable folder at the head of the table, "I just spent twenty minutes with the gang in Portland where they added a pile of backfill for us to do while they try to outguess a nutcase disguised as a sane man who kills but doesn't know who he really is."

Abe chided, "Hey boss, outguessing a nutcase is a bitch. My wife tells me that all the time."

"Okay, guys," Brick said, electing to ignore Abe's thinly veiled taunt. "The US attorney in Portland is wringing her hands and pounding the table at the same time. The big news is that Arthur Cheshire has a public defender, a young man full of piss and vinegar, and he's filed a petition for a writ of *habeas corpus*. The disguise is that Letty thinks he's really aiming to get the court to declare Arthur Cheshire mentally incompetent and avoid trial. And she has decided *we* are the solution, as in *you*, Liz."

"Me?" Liz said. "I'm a psychiatrist, and I spent a good deal of time trying to figure out who he was in my office in San Diego. But at that time, he insisted his name was Arthur and that he lived in California, and that his twin brother, Martin, died in a boating accident. Now he's driving in reverse insisting he is Martin, which I suppose means that the body parts in the fishing shack in Mexico belonged to Arthur."

Abe smiled.

"Yeah, yeah, this Humphrey Dumpty guy fell off his wall and Portland wants us to pick him up. How we gonna do that, boss?"

"Their idea is to use the same team to identify Arthur now that identified him as Arthur in California. Starting with Liz. They want her to testify before Judge Rachlyn because she spent several months with him in therapy. And they want us to persuade Alice, Rosie, and Marcella to appear in court and identify Arthur as Arthur because they all knew him well, no matter what game he's playing now."

Liz waved her hand in the air.

"Brick, for the record the name of the game he's playing is 'Hide and Be.' But this is no game. In California the FBI thought he killed his brother. In Portland, the FBI thinks he killed three young men in three New England states. I did not see Arthur Cheshire in therapy. I was a court consultant and wrote a detailed report explaining why I believed he was Arthur and incorrectly identified as his brother Martin. Now he says he is Martin. Little of what he said in consultation back in San Diego would relate to his current claim that he's Martin."

Lee said, "But Liz, who could assist Judge Rachlyn better than you? The judge there asked you to meet with a defendant, assess his identity, and report to the court. Isn't that exactly what the judge here might want you to do? Meet with the defendant, assess his identity, and report to the court? What am I missing here?"

"Okay," Liz said with a sigh, "I take your point, but identifying a person as a defendant before a court of law is very different from identifying someone as a 'person.' Let me take a few minutes to explain. Identity is the distinguishing character or personality of an individual human. It's a relationship established by psychological identification. The court case before Judge Rachlyn in Portland is similar to the one before Judge Hightower in San Diego. It's a case of mistaken identity. Arthur told Judge Hightower his name was Arthur Cheshire and the police had mistaken him for his twin brother, Martin. That is what Judge Rachlyn is facing now, only in reverse. In California, I interviewed Arthur in an effort to discover the truth. I looked for misstatements, lies, falsehoods, to see whether his insistence on being Arthur was a charade to avoid justice. Ultimately, I believed him—and told the court that, in my opinion, he was telling the truth—he was Arthur Cheshire. Here, if I am appointed by Judge Rachlyn to psychologically evaluate Arthur's claim to be Martin Cheshire, I would interview him to discover *falsehood*."

Cynthia sat quietly with her chin cupped in both hands and her elbows on the table. When the room went quiet after Liz's explanation, Brick looked at her and motioned to her by raising his hands in the air and calling her name.

"Cynthia?"

"Well, I'm in agreement with Dr. Socorro; this would put her in an awful position. Essentially, she saved a man from a wrongful charge in San Diego. Now she's being asked to reverse herself by telling the court he's lying when before she said he was telling the truth. But she and I have had some good talks about identity. I'm not a medical doctor. She is, and she knows ten times what I know about identity. So maybe I'm completely off base here, but I was wondering if maybe this isn't a case of dissociative identity disorder."

The room went quiet again. Brick looked down at his notepad and scribbled something. Lee got up, walked to the whiteboard, and switched it on. Liz smiled as though one of her students in medical rotation had just made a diagnosis she'd missed.

"I mean, you know, it's not my place to diagnose mental illness, but the DSM now prefers the term DID over the old name, 'Multiple Personality Disorder.' It's a personality disorder characterized by the presence of two or more distinct and complex identities. That's about all I can say. I never was involved in a case like that in school."

Liz beamed like a proud mother whose daughter just won a beauty contest.

"Well, guys and gals, there you have it. I think Cynthia might have Arthur Cheshire figured out in a way that he could never recognize himself. In DID analysis, psychiatrists look for personality states, each of which become dominant and controls behavior. That behavior is to the exclusion of the quote 'others.' By 'others' I mean other personality states. DID patients suffer from disruption in the integrated functions of consciousness, memory, and identity."

Abe looked back and forth from Liz to Cynthia as though he was a bobble-head.

"Jeeze Louise, you guys are saying we have like that movie *Sybil*? I saw that movie when I was a little kid. Scared the crap out of me."

Liz smiled at Abe.

"No, Abe, this is not like *Sybil*. You're remembering the seventies movie hit. It was a big hit and actually started a psychiatric phenomenon. It was first a book and then a movie. But it was a charade. The author was a fraud. The movie people bought it as the 'true story' of a woman who suffered from multiple personality disorder. But years later, she exposed herself, by admitting most of the story was based on a lie. Sybil was made up. The question it raises now is whether Arthur is making his story up, or does he actually believe it? If so, he could be suffering from dissociative identity disorder."

Lee had been making notes on the electric whiteboard. Now she drew a large circle at the bottom of the board and wrote.

"Is Arthur a fraud? Does he suffer from DID? Could he be both? A fraud who believes he is his brother and kills to keep his brother alive in his mind?"

"No, Lee," Liz said, looking down at her lab book for a second. "I've got a note here in my notes from two years ago that might describe what Mr. Cheshire is all about today. He is Arthur when he believes he is. He is Martin when he needs to be. I tried to mix those two realities for the judge in California—when I believed him when he insisted he was Arthur. My note says he believes he is himself by whatever name he wants: *My Brother, Myself*. That's what he is, himself *and* his brother. Two in one.

CUMBERLAND
COUNTY JAIL

Slo, the only detention officer who could talk to Arthur without being spit on, saw him leaning up against the sunny side of the wall that surrounded the yard.

"Top of the morning to you my man, Arthur. Watch ya up to today? Thinking of vaulting over the wall like a seagull headed for open sea?"

For a minute Arthur ignored him, then grinning, he said, "Your name's Slo, right? What kinda name is Slo? Are you from Slovakia?"

"No, my man. Never heard of Slovakia. They call me that name because I'm slow about doing any work. Other men, they fast. Me, I'm slo as molasses in summer. But it keeps me out of eating too much cuz I'm always at the back of the line. Know what I mean?"

"So Slo, you've taken me to court once and to the doctors two times. Do you get paid extra to talk to me? Seems the other detentions don't want my conversations."

"That's because you're on the needle train. You're bad luck to be around."

"Needle train? I'm not on drugs, Slo. And I only have one tattoo; I hate needles."

"The needle train takes you to the strap-down table where they punch the needle of death into you. Dudes are saying you killed three little boys with a short-barrel gun to the head. They right?"

"Slo, I like talking to you but not about other people, namely my brother. Besides, Maine does not have the death penalty, nor does Massachusetts or Vermont, or New Hampshire. That's all I want to say about it."

"You right about those states. But the FBI nabbed you and the feds are gonna try you. You're up for a federal death penalty case. They aim to stick you with a federal needle."

Arthur moved closer to Slo. Too close for the watchers from the tower on the corner. He heard a three-second tap from the yard siren.

"Prisoner 97081, back away from Slo right now or we'll drop you with a thirty-aught-six where you stand!"

Slo turned half around and jumped three feet back from Arthur. Two guards wearing flak jackets but not carrying guns rushed out from the east-side door. But there was no hit-the-deck warning from the loudspeaker.

Waving off the guards, Slo hollered, "Hold on, this man ain't challenging or bothering me none! I just told him something bad and he's hard of hearing, that's all. No need to cuff him or drag him downstairs."

They stopped fifteen feet away. When they turned and went back to the deck watch porch, Slo said, "Holy shit, my man. You ain't got the sense of a turd in a slop bucket. Don't ever get close to a detention officer like me. You coudda got us both in trouble moving toward me all hostile like. So, tell me straight, how come they charging you with triple death? What's your story, my man?"

Arthur could feel sweat sliding down from his armpits and heard that faint rumble in his stomach whenever someone talked about death.

"I only killed someone once in an accident that would never have happened if I'd listened to my brother. Now my life belongs to him, not the f bee eye or that lady judge wearing her black robe like she was in charge of a death temple. I told them, all of them, I never killed anyone, but I didn't mention my brother. Know how I know he didn't murder one, two, or even three guys? You really want to know?"

"Yeah, my man, spill those beans on me. How you so sure of that?"

"Because he told me so. But the problem is sometimes we tell lies to each other. Every goddamned day. Sometimes we did things and then switched places. We called it *Hide and Be*. I'm here in this jail because maybe he did something bad and it's my turn, you know? My turn to be and let him hide. All I know for sure is I myself never killed anyone except for my brother. Maybe he did and didn't tell me. Maybe it's my turn to take the blame. Fumbucked, you know?"

US DISTRICT COURT
PORTLAND, MAINE

Three days after Eppy moved for *habeas corpus* relief, Judge Juliana Rachlyn issued an order.

> The Court has received a motion for *habeas* relief filed by counsel for the defendant Arthur Cheshire, as identified in the indictment, arrest, booking, charging, and detention pertinent documents. No response need be filed by the government. Petitioner Cheshire demands the Sheriff of Cumberland County be commanded to produce Martin Cheshire. (1) The Court *sua sponte* grants the demand for *habeas* relief and orders said Sheriff of Cumberland County to bring Petitioner Cheshire on a day and time not yet formulated to this court. (2) The Court reminds Petitioner's counsel and the Office of the US Attorney that questions of law, procedural process and jurisdiction will be resolved by the Court forthwith. (3) The Court grants relief sought by Defendant Cheshire to be identified as "the Petitioner." (4) This

Court's order granting the issuance of the Writ is a civil matter and not amenable to federal statutory assessment for unresolved factual disputes, such as identity and nomenclature. (5) If the Petitioner's true identity is factually disputed, all criminal charges and process against him are temporarily abated, save and except for his current detention in the Cumberland County Jail, which shall remain in place pending further orders of this Court. (6) Counsel for both parties to this civil proceeding are directed to file advisory briefs within ten days hence on competency issues related to the Petitioner's assertion of mistaken identity.

The court's order came to counsel via email. It astounded both sides. US Assistant Attorney Letica Persuanoli immediately forwarded the order to her boss, US Attorney Stanford M. Crane, and to the Portland FBI office, other lawyers in her office, the investigatory and security staff, and to all members of the FREST FBI team in Quantico.

Mr. Crane responded by walking across the hall from his office to hers with a grin on his face.

Norm Washington read the email repeatedly as though his eyes were lying to his brain.

Brick Cato read it too quickly, focusing on the fifth item in the order: the abatement of criminal charges pending resolution of identity issues.

Within an hour of receipt, this novel court order was read, reread, and passed on to dozens of federal officers in Maine, California, Virginia, and Washington, DC. It's fair to say this order was *sui generis*: one of a kind.

Stanford Crane looked the epitome of a presidential nominee who had mustered at least half of the US Senate to confirm him as a typical United States Attorney. He was tall, white, lean, well-dressed, and walked with the confident stride of a man in charge about to make sure everyone knew he was the man in charge.

"So, Letty, you've sparked a nerve in Judge Rachlyn, haven't you?"

"Stan, I have indeed, but her message is not just about this serial murder case, is it? I think she's signaling the defense more than us. Over the five years she's been on the bench, I've noticed an increase in her level of patience, a growing level of irritation with the PD's office, and a spirit of individuality known only to Article III judges. I sent it to you first since I know you have something of a shared history, am I right about that?"

"Shared might be a bit strong. She was a white-collar crime defense lawyer when I was a First Circuit law clerk some twenty odd years ago. We dated twice, once blind and the second time with eyes wide open. The first time was more fun. And we served on the state bar ethics committee for three or four years. She's smart and ambitious."

Letty nodded, "I hear she's on the hunt for an upgrade to the First Circuit seat that will open up as soon as a certain unnamed judge takes senior status. Know who I'm talking about?"

"Yes, and yes. She's got a good shot. Honestly, I think this *sua sponte* decision might be an arrow in her quiver for that shot."

"How so?"

"Well, Letty, think about it this way. Writs of certiorari or mandamus are the stuff of federal appeals every day. Writs of *habeas corpus* are rarely granted at the trial court level; they push them upstairs by denying them out of hand, knowing the appellate team will accept jurisdiction, sit on the case for a few years, and then bounce it back down for retrial, either in state or federal court. But here, in a case full of thorny issues and little precedent, Judge Rachlyn has taken a dive deep into appellate law and issues of first impression."

Letty sipped her cold coffee, picked up the order for the tenth time and waved it at her boss.

"Stan, this order isn't just thorny, it reminds me of something my favorite scribe, E.B. White said, 'Be obscure clearly.'"

"What in the world does that mean? How can you be clearly obscure?"

"I think Judge Rachlyn knows Mr. Tutt is trying to hide the ball by pitching it as identity, when he knows bloody well the issue isn't who is on trial; it's whether the man on trial is competent to stand trial. He framed his petition in terms of mistaken identity, but his defense is to shield whoever is on trial from going to trial based on lack of competence."

"Letty, give me your side of that same paradox. Do you know which twin is on trial?"

"Yes, I do. It's the twin who blew holes in the skulls of three young men who dissed their twin brothers on their birthdays. It's the twin who left his own hair follicles at the crime scene to ensure the survivor twin wasn't a suspect. He's the twin the FBI investigated, and we indicted."

"What's his name?"

"Cheshire."

"You're playing with me, Letty. What's his full name?"

"I don't know. We indicted Martin based on the FBI's investigation. They arrested the man they investigated based on picture identification, fingerprint confirmation, and partial DNA sequencing. But proving identity in court may be more difficult than we thought when we got the first docket call. My guess is we have solid admissible evidence. The defense has a weak theory based on limited DNA sequencing. There is more DNA work to do, and it will likely show the man in jail is the same man who left hair follicles at three different crime scenes. But even so, that's not what scares me."

"What does scare you?"

"That the man in jail is the killer but he does not know who he is. He's lived two lives at the same time for twenty-nine years by sometimes identifying as someone else and then reverting to his own identity at will. But it might not be his will—it might be his brother's will. And to make the case absolutely nuts, we might never prove which one died in the boat accident, leaving the survivor to face trial as a serial killer."

QUANTICO, VIRGINIA

Brick got the order later than he should have. He'd worked 10/7 on the case for nearly two months. The need for a little adventure, which is what he called fishing, called out to him. He answered the call by loading his kayak on top his F-150 and his tent, tackle box, and sleeping bag in the bed. He drove south down to Port Royal and his favorite spot on the Rapphannock River for a two-night camp. By the time he got back to the office, judge's order had been on his office computer for a full day, with no one paying attention. He pushed it out to the team, and they lit up his screen.

Lee said, "Please translate legalese to civilian."

Liz said, "Wow, this judge reminds me of Judge Hightower. What does she mean by a writ not being 'amenable' to federal statutory assessment? Don't courts wait for the litigants to respond to motions? This seems rushed to me. And I'm totally confused by the judge's ruling that 'all criminal charges are temporarily abated.' For how long? And why abated? I was thinking about going home; may I?"

Abe said, "Lady judges rule differently. They give you bad news nicely. What the blank is going on?"

Cynthia, given to analyzing everything, said, "While most of this thing escapes my right brain, my left brain wants to know what she is hiding by the way she writes. Left brain thinking is more analytical and orderly, you know, like logic, sequencing, and linear thinking. I have to tell my left brain to shut up sometimes. Is this one of those times? Are we meeting about this, and can Lee do an electric whiteboard for us? I'd like to see a diagram of what Judge Rachlyn is ordering and what someone with a right legal brain is going to do about it."

Brick called for a 11:30 meeting with bagged sandwiches from the Marine mess hall. Lee told everyone she'd set up the Whiteboard in advance. Abe said he'd go get the sandwiches. Liz said she'd bring a copy of the DSM, a dart board, and some ibuprofin for the neck pain the order was giving her.

When they settled in at their usual spots, they saw Lee's electric Whiteboard already clustered with circles, boxes, arrows, and words. But the surprise was a brand new, shiny *Vibe Smartboard 51.*

Lee said, "This baby is an interactive digital Whiteboard. It is collaborative as all get out and comes with built-in speakers. You can actually talk to it."

It came with plastic styluses, multiple buttons, and was longer, wider, and cleaner than the old one. She had placed boxes in the four corners, a sizeable oblong box in the center, two large circles on top of the center oblong box, and three smaller circles below the oblong box, and on the left bottom a triangle shaped dotted object with three names in it. As they watched, Lee used the stylus to insert words or names in the boxes, circles, and objects. The top corners were named Arthur and Martin. The top circles were named Identity and Competence. The oblong box screamed HABEUS CORPUS in large cap red font. The lower circles under the oblong were named Alice, Rosie, and Marcella. The lower left of the whiteboard's three smaller boxes identified the serial killer's victims Emil Estancia, Caleb

Lawrence, and Harrington Schwartz. The lower right bottom of the Whiteboard had a ragged shaped anchor with what looked like a chain dragging along the bottom of the landscape-shaped Whiteboard.

Brick seemed a little surprised and maybe a tad annoyed.

"Lee, I see you've been busy and have put names in boxes and circles, but thankfully not yet drawn arrows from one to the other. But let's not get ahead of ourselves. I want to give everyone my sense of what the US attorney in Maine is going to want from us down here."

Lee nodded obligingly, put the stylus back on its little rack, and took her seat. Brick nodded back.

"All of you saw this order before I did and likely have given it more thought. But I have talked to Norm in Portland, and I'd like to start with his view, let's call it the local view. He thinks the public defender's office has no real defense to offer, which explains why they filed this uncommon writ in the first place. He thinks they are trying to shift the focus away from serial murder and toward psychology—that is, toward mental or cognitive deficits as a defense not to the crime but *to the trial* of the crime. He thinks the mistaken identity issue is just a smoke screen for the real defense, which is to avoid going to trial because the defendant cannot communicate with his lawyers and his lawyers do not know for sure exactly who their client is. As he put it, Martin is dead to everyone except Arthur. Now, I think the place where we ought to start is with the identity issue. We should make a list of all of the admissible evidence on that issue. Lee, can we hold off on your main Whiteboard for a few minutes and use it to chart identity evidence?"

Lee left her chair, took three steps to the Whiteboard, and punched the right buttons to reveal a new blank Whiteboard. She used the stylus to identify the page—*Evidence Proving Arthur Is Arthur.*

Brick nodded to Abe. Abe opened his manila folder, lifted a yellow pad out, and read from it.

"Let's start with fingerprints. I'll just read from my list, Lee, if you can put them on the white thing. Okay, fingerprints, DNA hair follicles, eyewitness testimony, mug shots in two states, prior testimony in the identity hearing down in San Diego, Arthur's admission that Martin was dead in multiple 302s and interviews, his polygraph in San Diego, signatures for his apartment lease, temporary California's driver's license, school records in Portland, signatures on his bank records, licenses, notes back to AmHull and the bookkeeper there—Alice something or other, can't remember her name—testimony by the girlfriend Marcella something or other from south of the Mexican border, as I recall, two credit cards with signed bank applications, the PO box in San Diego he set up after moving there, reluctantly he said, two hospital sign-ins at the ER in Portland when he ran into a street light and when he drove his motorcycle off the pier into the ocean when he was nineteen, and more than I found, but am sure exists. We need a handwriting expert. We got lots of things he can compare to current writings by him. He's Arthur alright, and we got the goods on him."

Lee had stayed with Abe and now had a list of twenty-two items to put on the evidence list when the hearing came up.

"Okay," Lee said. "Brick, should I start building a Whiteboard discussion piece now?"

Brick, still seeming reluctant to drill down to that level, asked if anyone else had something to offer before the Whiteboard exercise. Cynthia motioned by pointing at herself.

"Yes, Cynthia, give it to us."

"Well, you guys, you know I barely mentioned DID at our last meeting. But I read the lady judge's order, as Abe calls her, and sure enough the last bullet point, number six, says the lawyers should file briefs on, how did she put it, oh here it is, she said, 'file advisory briefs on competency issues related to the Petitioner's assertion of mistaken identity.' So, both sides will chime in. I'm thinking Mr. Tutt, who represents the Petitioner might bring up the possibility of his client suffering from DID, which sure would go to the issue of mistaken identity."

Abe tapped his ballpoint on his coffee cup. "Well, that takes the cake alright. Cyn, I'm not up to date on this DID stuff, but could you give me a hint about how it might be used in this case?"

"Sure, Abe. Imagine Mr. Tutt sitting in his law office right now and he's reading the same order. Maybe he knows about DID from some other case or maybe his cousin had it. Who knows? But if he knows the basics, he might put one foot in front of the other and think about it this way. His client insists he is Martin, who we think is dead, and not Arthur, who we know is alive. But what if Arthur is alive *but* suffers from DID *and* has an alter! I know Liz could explain this better, but my limited research tells me DID is characterized by alternating between multiple identities. Get it? *Alter-nating* between identities. That's why they call it an *alter.* DID people feel like someone in their head is trying to take control. Male patients don't like it at all. They deny their symptoms and their trauma and can get really violent. That's what I read."

Liz gave Cynthia a little hand clapping and a big smile.

"Cynthia, you capsulized DID succinctly. It's a complex mental disorder, but your description of alternating identities is pretty close. So, everyone, can I have the floor for a minute? You all know I spent weeks interviewing Arthur Cheshire in my clinic in the San Diego courthouse in his first criminal case. There the central issue was identity. The hearing was the first of its kind, at least on the federal bench on the West Coast. The central issue there was the opposite of the one here. In California, Arthur had to prove he was Arthur in order to avoid trial as Martin. There, the authorities thought they arrested Martin in Maine, extradited him to California for the murder of his twin brother, but lost on the identity issue. I offered the court my opinion that Arthur was in fact who he said he was. The judge agreed and dismissed all charges. I'm belaboring that case here because it is the mirror opposite of what seems to be happening in Portland, Maine. In both medical and legal terms, the case before the court has gone 180 degrees upside down."

The room went quiet. Liz sipped from her water bottle, reached for a tissue in her purse and turned away to blow her nose. Then, sounding a little breathless, she continued.

"Sorry, folks, for the dissertation on the facts of a case that is not on our plate. If it's okay, let me switch gears into classroom mode and talk about dissociative identity disorder in medical terms. This book I'm holding up for you is the latest clinical statement defining DID. It's the DSM-5 300.14. I hate to bore you but let me read the official diagnostic protocol. 'The key element in this diagnosis is the presence of at least two distinct and separate personalities within an individual. Although multiple personalities, alters, exist within a single person, only *one* is manifested at a time. Each alter has its own memories, behaviors, and life preferences. At least two of these identities take control of a person's conduct at any given time. Lastly, it is critical that the observed disturbances are not a consequence of substance abuse, or a general medical condition.'"

Liz stopped reading, lifted her water bottle to her lips, and drained it. Brick took over.

"Liz, thanks for shining a bright light on a dark subject. I have a little something to add from the legal side. I followed your lead and brought a copy of an article I found last night on how some defendants have tried to gerrymander their trials by using this DID thing as a legal defense to a crime they committed. I'll just read the opening paragraph. 'Persons with dissociative identity disorder often present in the criminal justice system rather than the mental health system and perplex experts in both professions. DID is a controversial diagnosis with important medicolegal implications. Defendants have claimed that they committed serious crimes, including rape or murder, while they were in a dissociated state. Asserting that their alter personality committed the bad act, defendants have pleaded not guilty by reason of insanity. In such instances, forensic experts are asked to assess the defendant for DID and provide testimony in court. This article reviews historical and theoretical perspectives on DID, presents cases that illustrate the legal implications and controversies of raising an insanity defense based on multiple personalities, and examines the role of forensic experts asked to comment on DID with the goal of assisting clinicians in the medicolegal assessment of DID in relation to crimes.' Now, folks that's a mouthful. I've sent the article to Norm up in Portland. He'll get it to lead counsel on this case, Letica Persuanoli."

Cynthia's eyes looked almost crossed, and her conflict was obvious.

"Way to go, Brick! This is like a trial by experts. Where was that article published and can I have a copy for my files?"

Lee asked, "Brick, do you think FREST should pursue this DID thing any further, or can we assume the DOJ will take over from here?"

"Well, frankly, this is above our pay grade, except for our borrowed in-house expert, Dr. Lisabeth Socorro. I expect the prosecutor's office in Portland will want to talk to her."

Brick was right. The FREST meeting was interrupted by a double-buzz phone call to Brick. He excused himself and walked out into the hall to take the call. Two minutes later, he came back in looking like Schrödinger's cat.

"Well Liz, it's holy pretzel time for you. You're going to need a heavier winter coat. They want you back in Portland today. You'll get to coach the team up there just like you've done down here for us. The DOJ is arranging travel and TDY transfer from the Federal Bureau of Prisons on the left coast to Department of Justice on the right coast."

PORTLAND, MAINE

Dr. Socorro took her seat on the Marine Corps Beechcraft C-12 Huron from Quantico to Portland as the only female, the only civilian, and the only identified doctor on the flight. Fortunately, no one got sick even though the flight bounced like a beach ball popping off the surface of a ten-foot wave. She landed at the Portland Marine base barely able to make it to the ladies' room in the terminal.

An elderly Uber driver took her to the DOJ building on Middle Street in time for the AHOD meeting called by US Assistant Attorney Persuanoli. Liz was escorted to the room by a uniformed guard, as though she was an honored guest.

"Ah, Dr. Socorro," Letty announced, "you made it almost on time. We've been chatting about you as you Ubered in from the Marine base. How was your flight?"

"If you like beach volleyball and you're the ball, then you'd say it was a great flight. Otherwise, it felt like a roller coaster with a maniac at the controls."

"Come up here, sit by me, and I'll introduce you to the team we hope you'll join. God knows we need psychiatric help to unwind the neurons, grey matter, and pretense we are facing in an already mind-boggling criminal case. At the far end of the table sits the head of the DOJ in Maine, Mr. Stanford Crane. Next to him, please meet our honored guest from Washington, DC, Mr. Gonzales, on loan from JMD, that's DOJ lingo for our Justice Management Division. Next to your seat is Dr. Chance Honoliptz, a psychology professor from Bowdoin College, up Brunswick way. We are somewhat hastily gathered because most of us are ill equipped to fathom the defense in *US v. Arthur Cheshire*. You, we're told, have the perfect experience to help us. You know Arthur Cheshire well, right?"

"Thanks, Letty, it's nice to see you again. I can't say my experience with Arthur Cheshire was perfect, but I spent a good deal of time with him one on one, in a consulting role rather than as a treating physician. I was appointed by a federal judge who faced a novel identity issue somewhat similar to the one you all are facing."

"You're quite welcome, doctor. I assume you are not constrained by a physician-patient privilege with Arthur Cheshire, right?"

"Right, he didn't select me to be an expert on his behalf or to treat his condition. The court appointment was acceptable to both sides of the case. As I recall, I was the only witness in the case although several other people had been interviewed by the FBI. I could be wrong on that of course because I didn't attend the hearings, I only appeared once for my testimony."

"Why did Judge Hightower ask you to consult on the case?"

"I can only guess, but his law clerk said it was because the defendant denied the identity they had assigned to him here in Portland when he was arrested. Portland said he was definitely Martin, and that he embezzled money from his employer AmHull Insurance. But he insisted he was Arthur and that his brother Martin was dead—he had a long explanation about a fishing boat accident on a river near Portland. I forget the name . . ."

Letty helped, "Does the Dramiscotta River sound familiar?"

"Yes, that was it. I shouldn't have forgotten it. Wasn't he arrested near there on the serial murder cases?"

"He was, on Jones Point, just a few yards from the fishing camp he owned with his twin brother. That segues nicely into my most important question for you. Can you identify the man you interviewed in San Diego as the same man who is in jail here in Portland facing serial murder charges? I know you worked with FREST on that investigation. Is he the same man?"

"I don't know. Based on what I learned in Quantico I think the man on trial here is Arthur Cheshire—the man I talked at length with a year ago. But that opinion is largely based on what I've been told about the current efforts to identify him with photos, fingerprints, forensic DNA evidence, polygraphs, and handwriting comparisons. And to complicate everything, there is a possible explanation that is very troubling, at least from a medical diagnostic perspective."

"What is that possible explanation?"

"It's possible that Arthur Cheshire suffers from Dissociative Identify Disorder and the murders were committed by his alter. And he is both himself and his alter."

CUMBERLAND COUNTY
SHERIFF'S OFFICE

The Cumberland County Sheriff's Office was founded in 1760, sixty years before Maine became a state. It does double duty— arresting *and* jailing criminal suspects. While it's hardly educational, it could fairly be described as a sprawling campus. A dozen buildings house deputies, detainees, drunks, and deviants. The ones in brown uniforms are deputies. Everyone else is of a lesser status. They claim to have a "a state-of-the-art incarceration facility, and the latest technology in law enforcement support equipment."

Eppy Tutt slogged his way through the parking lot, sidewalks, steps, turnstiles, metal detectors, millimeter wave machines, and backscatter x-ray, all intended to safeguard staff and keep prisoners at bay. He was led through three sets of steel barred doors to one of four legal discussion rooms where his client patiently waited for his arrival.

"Good morning, Mr. Cheshire, sorry I'm a little late, but there was a bit of a crowd out front waiting to get it in."

"Yeah, there's a bit of a crowd inside hoping to get out. I'm one of them. You bringing good news on my case?"

"I have what I hope will be a good start for us. You'll remember our phone call last week when I told you I had filed a petition for a writ of *habeas corpus* and . . ."

"You betcha. I told one of the jailhouse lawyers in my block and he told me it was Roman Latin about bringing a body to court or something like that."

"Yes, it translates to something like that. I'm happy to say the judge granted my petition. She has ordered the warden, who is actually the Sheriff of Cumberland County, to bring you to her courtroom. It will be a civil hearing rather than a criminal proceeding—the difference is very important so let's start there . . ."

"Hold on, Mr. Tutt, is it okay from now on if I just call you Mr. Tutt, as though your first name was a secret, like you call me Mr. Cheshire as though you forgot my first name? Can we settle on that?"

"Yes, that's fine with me. In fact, that's one of the main reasons I filed the writ. You see . . ."

"I see? What do you mean when you say that? What I see is bars, steel doors, and hardly any sunlight. What in hell is a *writ*? You said it on the phone, and I wrote it down. My jailhouse lawyer three cells to my right said it was a fancy way of saying order, like *order in the court*. I don't mean to argue with you, it's just that words are getting harder and harder for me to understand. My younger brother, Arthur, was better at words that I am."

"A writ is an order. Courts issue writs that are intended to force some legal action. In your case the judge has ordered a hearing and she ordered the sheriff to bring you from this jail to her courtroom to participate in the hearing. If you don't mind, let me go over the basics with you and then let's talk about what might happen if the hearing goes our way. Okay?"

"Yeah, but can you tell me the time, right now?"

"It's five after eleven."

"Okay, they don't let you keep your wristwatch in here and there's no clock I can see from my cell. Lunch is at noon sharp, and if you ain't in line by noon you don't get lunch."

"I'll let you know when it's ten to twelve, is that enough time for lunch?"

"Yeah, Mr. Tutt. Slo told me he'd hang around in the hall. He said it smells better over here because they mop the floors. They only mop on Sunday mornings in my block."

"Right. So, Mr. Cheshire, I filed the petition for a writ because if granted, it results in a civil hearing instead of a criminal hearing. The big difference is that in a civil hearing all the strict rules in criminal count are not applied. But the even bigger difference is that the relief that could be granted will work in your favor. The core issue will be whether you are who you say you are—Martin Cheshire—or are you actually Arthur Cheshire?"

"I already said that; I'm Martin."

"Yes, the judge knows your position and I have made it clear that I represent you. You were arrested based on a grand jury indictment against Arthur Cheshire, but they arrested you believing you are Arthur. So, this is a case of mistaken identity. Do you have any memory of your brother Arthur telling you he had a similar identity hearing in San Diego, California?"

"Arthur was always telling me stuff but that was before we got split up. You know AmHull did that, right? They split us up and we gamed them. We did. We did. I told you about that last time, remember?"

"Yes, I do. You called the game Hide and Be. Now, the judge here has granted my petition and has ordered a hearing. I have her order right here, and I made a copy for you to take to your cell. Here's the part we need to talk about today. In part five of her order, Judge Rachlyn says, quote, to the extent that the Petitioner's true identity is factually disputed, all criminal charges and process against him are temporarily abated . . ."

"Hey, wait up. Does 'temporarily abated' mean I can get out of jail? I mean how can they keep me here if I'm abated? That means stopped, right?"

"Her order is a temporary hold on the criminal case while she conducts a civil hearing. You will have to stay here until that civil case is adjudicated. She also ordered that both sides file written briefs on the competency issues tied to our claim of mistaken identity. Now . . ."

"Hold on Mr. Tutt. Did you say competency, like I'm a retard or something?"

"No, nothing like that. But our position is that you are not Arthur Cheshire; they are mistaking you for your brother. It's actually what I hoped the judge would do. It permits me to argue that the identity question calls for a psychological evaluation of why you believe you are Martin in the face of the government's evidence that you are Arthur."

"What evidence?"

"Well, for example, when you were arrested you were driving a truck titled in both names, but the arrest records here in Portland match up with the records in San Diego. There, Arthur was on trial for killing his brother, but he told the court that his brother, Martin, was dead. He died of a . . ."

"No, wait, that was just part of our game, you know, Hide and Be. Martin didn't die. He didn't. He didn't. I'm him, I told you that over and over!"

"Did you tell the judge in San Diego about the fishing boat accident?"

"I never told the judge anything. I only told the psychiatrist. She was something, Mr. Tutt, I mean something. She believed me when I told her everything."

"Was her name Dr. Elisbeth Socorro?"

"Yeah, I think so."

"Did you tell her your name was Arthur?"

"Yeah, probably. I mean, I was really Martin, but I said I was Arthur because he was in trouble out there and because it was my turn. You know, *my* turn!"

"Well, you were very convincing. She wrote a detailed report and gave it to the judge in that case. The judge accepted her opinion that you were Arthur."

"Yes, maybe, but she really knew I was Martin. I tried to show her my tattoo, but she didn't want to see me undressed at all, even my shoes and socks. She was something; I remember her."

"Your tattoo? I read your intake report here and it mentions one tattoo, on your left leg."

"They got it wrong. It's on my ankle, not my leg, and it's so small people might miss it. But it proves I'm Martin."

"How does it do that?"

"Here, let me show you. That's alright, isn't it? I just have to take my left shoe off and pull my sock down."

He pushed his steel chair back, and Eppy moved to the side of the table. His client pushed off his jail-style slipper, peeled down his sock, and pointed to the small tattoo about the size of a quarter below the heel bone. It looked like a tiny rock or fossil. It was blue, black, and had a tiny drawing in the middle, no bigger than the nail of his baby toe. Eppy knelt down and asked his client what the red thing was in the middle of the tattoo.

"That's my initial—it's a capital M—for Martin."

QUANTICO, VIRGINIA, FREST HEADQUARTERS

Because the arrest of Arthur in Portland concluded one part of FREST's focus—identifying the Unsub—the team started dealing with other less important parts of the assignment. Lee knocked on Brick's door and got a cherry read-the-sign-come-on-in from Brick pretending to be a high-pitched rapper. The plaque screwed onto his door read, *"Come On In—I'm Already Disturbed."*

"Hey, Brick, how you doing? And how was the weekend at Hilton Head? Good fishing?"

"Fishing was okay, lots of lines, sharp hooks, and fish much smarter than me. But I finished John Grisham's latest caper and started Stephen King's new non-horror novel. I'm rested and not bested. What's up, Lee?"

"Well, maybe something odd. Just following up on closing out our search for the Unsub, since he's now in the hoosegow in Maine. Last Thursday, before you left, I asked Nala and Jamal to work up an Excel spreadsheet that might show us connections on the tap-and-trace phone calls we got warrants for—Alice,

Rosie, and Marcella. All three should have been happy to help us locate Arthur Cheshire but all of them bolted like doves hearing a shotgun fifty yards away. You posed the 'why' question to the team and none of us had a clue. But Nala and Jamal are analysts for a reason; they would be useless in the field. Guns and bad weather scare them. But they are inquisitive and always think in granular circles. They think as a team sharing thoughts across their cubicle like soccer goals against average, looking for chinks in the defense armor. They have connected all three women to two bank accounts, one in New Hampshire and the other in Panama City, and a man named Maldonado Munoz. He's a surprise."

"Maldonado Munoz, that's a new name, right?"

"New to us, but not to Marcella Munoz, Arthur Cheshire's girlfriend in San Diego. Here's the Excel spread sheet. Can you see the links there?"

Brick spread the landscape spreadsheet out on his desk and ran his forefinger down and across.

'Well, that *is* odd. Looks like every time Alice called Marcella, it generated a flash call to Maldonado. There are, what, five or six calls in a week?"

"Yes, but what's even more interesting is the calls that all three girls made to a bank in Panama City. It's the bank where Alice opened an account while Arthur was still at AmHull. Nala and Jamal checked and found out that the bank is on a watch list for money launderers. And the manager has the same name as the man that Marcella Munoz calls each time she hears from Alice. The banker's name is Maldonado Munoz, but he is almost seventy and is a lifelong citizen of Panama. There is another man with that name in San Diego. He's a thirty-one-year-old tattoo artist. He bears looking into for another reason."

"What's that?"

"I talked to Liz this morning. She had just finished a meeting with the US Attorney's Office and seemed excited that she remembered something she forgot to tell us. Arthur Cheshire has a tattoo that may help identify him as Arthur because he got it in San Diego back when he was Arthur and before he pretended to be Martin when you guys arrested him three weeks ago."

"Help us how?"

"Brick, it sounds almost too good to be true. Arthur got a tattoo on his left ankle. It's a little fish or something from the ocean with a tiny red 'M' in the middle."

"Did you say 'M,' as in Martin? Why would Arthur put an 'M' on his tattoo? Was he pretending to be Martin then?"

"No, Liz says it was likely for Marcella, Arthur's girlfriend. Now, remember that Marcella won't cooperate with us. Why? We don't know. But she might if we ask her about the 'M' on Arthur's tattoo."

"And that would help us how?"

"Well, boss," Lee said with a huge grin on her face, "it may turn out that in the Portland case where Arthur claims to be Martin, that tattoo was photographed when he went through the booking and detention process at the county jail there. They always record things like scars, bullet holes, and tattoos to identify bodies in case a prisoner dies in jail, you know, like death by shiv."

"Wow," Brick exclaimed. "I'll get that info to Norm in Portland, toot suite!"

US DISTRICT COURT, PORTLAND, MAINE

The court bailiff made his all-rise announcement. Judge Rachlyn's courtroom went silent as she walked the ten-foot path from her chambers door to the first step up onto her bench.

"Please be seated, ladies and gentlemen," she said, as she sat down, turned her computer screen on, and surveyed the room from the empty jury box on her right up to the empty benches behind the rail and settled on the defense table on her left.

"Mr. Tutt, would you take the podium, please? I have three questions for you."

Eppy Tutt stood, buttoned his suit coat, and stepped over to the podium. "Mr. Tutt," the judge continued, "as you know from my order, I granted your *habeas corpus* petition. The sheriff's office has produced your client, and he's sitting at the defense table. I'm correct about that, right? The man in the dark blue jail suit is your client, right?"

"Yes, Your Honor."

"Alright, here is question number one. What is his full name?"

"Your Honor, my client says his name is Martin Cheshire."

"Mr. Tutt, not to be too fussy here, but my question was to you, not to your client. I'll ask you again," she said as she moved her gaze from the podium to the defense table.

"What is his full name?" she asked, pointing her ballpoint directly at the man in jail blue.

"As far as I know it's Martin Cheshire."

"What is the source of your knowledge? I'm not asking you to reveal any confidential communication from your client. If that is your only source, you need not answer. But if you have some independent source, knowledge, or evidence to confirm your belief, please let me in on that."

"Your Honor, are you asking me for work product, which is also privileged?"

"No, I'm not, but I'm sensitive to your concern for the central issue your *habeas* writ brings to this court. For now, I'm going to assume that your position that your client's name is Martin Cheshire is based on either client confidentiality or work product privilege. If that's correct, you may return to your seat next to your client."

Eppy returned to his seat.

"Now," she said, turning her gaze and her ballpoint pen toward the government's table, "Miss Persuanoli, would you mind taking the podium?"

Letty pushed her chair back, gathered her notebook, and walked to the podium.

"Good morning, Ms. Persuanoli, I have the same questions for you, and since you are not burdened by client confidentiality or work product privileges, I hope you can answer all of them.

"First, who is the man sitting next to Mr. Tutt?"

"That is Arthur Cheshire, Your Honor."

"Are you stating that as fact, or an opinion, Ms. Persuanoli?"

"Both, Your Honor."

"Thank you. Question two, can you prove by a simple preponderance of the evidence that the petitioner in this civil case—that is the *habeas corpus* proceeding—is in fact *not* Martin Cheshire."

"With respect, Your Honor, I do not believe that burden is on the government. Indeed, it could not because we are convinced the defendant under arrest and incarcerated in the Cumberland County jail, and now present in this court, is Arthur Cheshire. Our position is that if the defendant insists he is not Arthur, it is on him to prove that as a fact, not an opinion."

"Question number three, for the government. Is the man seated next to Mr. Tutt at the defense table competent to stand trial in the criminal case filed against Arthur Cheshire?"

"Your Honor, I have no reason to believe he is incompetent. Is that what your mean?"

"No, it isn't. Can you answer the question—is he competent?"

"I don't know."

"Well, neither do I. But the government cannot try someone in a criminal case who is incompetent, can they?"

"No, Your Honor."

"Who has the burden of proving incompetency, you, or the defendant?"

"I think it is Mr. Tutt's burden."

"Is competency a question of fact or a question of law, Ms. Persuanoli?"

"Competency is a question of law."

"Yes, it is," the judge said, turning her gaze to the defense table.

"You need not take the podium, Mr. Tutt, just answer from your table. Do you agree competency is a question for this court to resolve in the civil case arising out of your writ?"

"Yes, I do."

The judge motioned the US assistant attorney back to her seat. When she was settled in her seat, the judge picked up a sheet of paper in front of her and read from it.

She reminded everyone that the *habeas corpus* writ was granted to the petitioner, who clearly identifies himself as Martin Cheshire. Looking directly at Arthur, seated next to Eppy Tutt, she started what all judges do—she announced her findings and her rules.

"Mr. Cheshire, you have the unassailable right to understand these proceedings and assist your lawyer in his defense of the case. But if you cannot understand or cannot assist your lawyer—if you cannot do that—I have the power to declare you legally incompetent. That has nothing to do with guilt or innocence."

Next, she turned her gaze toward the prosecution table. "You know that mentally incompetent people cannot be criminally convicted in this court."

Then, to show everyone in the room that the presumption of innocence applied in this and all courts in America, she turned her gaze from one side of the courtroom to the other and said, "I order the sheriff's deputies to return the petitioner to his cell. He will be held there until I call this back to order. And I want to remind the lawyers on both sides that the criminal charges are in abatement. They will remain abated until we resolve the identity and competency issues at an evidentiary hearing. Are we clear?"

Mr. Tutt and Ms. Persuanoli quickly agreed. "Yes, Your Honor."

The judge laid the typed order on the bench, took a sip of water, cleared her throat, and continued. "The court wishes to ensure that counsel for the government and the petitioner/defendant understand the ground rules for an evidentiary hearing.

Competency to stand trial is legally unrelated to the defendant's mental state at the time of the alleged crimes committed by the petitioner/defendant."

Letty stood and waited to be recognized by the court. The judge nodded in her direction.

"Thank you, Your Honor. The government understands that we will not be resolving the defendant's mental state at the time we assert he committed the crimes charged in the indictment. Am I right, Your Honor?"

"Yes. The issues we'll resolve will be based on current mental status. Both parties are directed to produce witnesses and evidence on competence and the defendant's mental state now and on an ongoing basis. And both sides should also know whether the petitioner/defendant currently suffers from a mental state as his defense to the alleged crimes is not, at this stage, before the court. To be clear, insanity or diminished capacity will be determined as a matter of law at trial, if any be held on the crimes charged in the indictment."

Both lawyers asked the judge about timing. The government wanted four weeks to prepare.

Judge Rachlyn gave the government three weeks. She told Mr. Tutt that he would go first since he had the burden of proof of *identity* while the government has the burden of proof on *competency*.

"Are we clear?" Judge Rachlyn asked, then waited thirty seconds. Neither side responded.

Taking their silence as agreement, she said, "Thank you, counsel. We are adjourned. The hearing date will be settled by the clerk's office, and you'll be notified by email."

The next day, both sides got an email setting the evidentiary hearing five weeks hence. The judge may have been in a hurry, but her docket clerk was not.

SAN DIEGO.
DR. SOCORRO'S OFFICE

Dr. Socorro had been surprised to get the email from Norm Washington's secretary asking her to come to Portland *your soonest* to meet with Agent Washington and Assistant US Attorney Persuanoli regarding her availability to serve as an expert witness for the government in the upcoming evidentiary hearing. She called Mr. Washington's office and got the secretary.

"Good morning, this is Agent Washington's office, Nancy speaking, how may I help you?"

"Good morning, Nancy, this is Dr. Elisbeth Socorro. I just got an email from you about an evidentiary hearing in the Arthur Cheshire case. Is Mr. Washington in?"

"Yes, doctor, he is, but he's upstairs in the US Attorney's office. Would you like me to try and patch you in? I know they are waiting for your call because Norm said to interrupt him if you called."

Nancy did her job.

"Dr. Socorro, this is Norm, great to hear from you so quickly. Are you here in Portland or down in Quantico?"

"I'm at my office in San Diego. I was unsure whether there was anything else I could do in your case against Arthur, so I flew back here day before yesterday. Brick said there might be a hearing, but he didn't think I would be involved."

"Well, a lot has happened in a short time. I'm in Letty Persuanoli's office, let me put you on speaker."

"Hi, Liz, we are definitely going to need you as an expert witness," the US Attorney said.

"Well, I'm confused but I'm happy to help if I can. Why me?"

"Because you spent a month or two interviewing Arthur Cheshire. I talked to my counterpart in San Diego, and they sent me a very large digital file, almost a full gigabyte. We didn't know if you recorded your interviews with him or that the audios were later transcribed. We're not through reading and listening, but I know enough now to think your testimony will be dispositive in our case. By that I mean you can identify him in open court as Arthur Cheshire; you can do that, can't you?"

"Well, yes, I guess. I mean I did spend a lot of time with him. I watched him testify in Judge Hightower's court. I can say that he looks like the man he identified as Arthur Cheshire. But then, he had an identical twin, whom I never saw. From what he and others said, they were mirror images of one another."

"Yes, doctor. They were, but Judge Hightower accepted and made a factual finding on the record that the twin known as Martin Cheshire died in a fishing shack. That's what he called it, a *shack*, in a small town called Rosario in Mexico. We believe that finding was legally sound, and we intend to ask the judge here in Maine to take judicial notice of that fact. We are on a very narrow path here. Our judge in this case has scheduled an evidentiary hearing on two legal questions—legal identity and mental competency to stand trial. The first issue has to be proved by the defendant in custody—he says he is Martin Cheshire, but we believe based on solid evidence that he is Arthur Cheshire.

We know those twin brothers grew up playing a game they called *Hide and Be*. Can you help us, please?”

“Well, Ms. Persuanoli, the twin I assessed for the court here in San Diego convinced me he was Arthur, not Martin. If that helps your case, I can testify, as an expert, that by all appearances and based on what he told me here in California the man on trial is Arthur Cheshire. But that may not be consistent with a scientific, medical assessment. Norm knows what I’m talking about.”

“Norm mentioned some obscure mental condition called disassociation. Is that what you mean?”

“No, it’s dissociative identity disorder, shortened to ‘DID’ in medical and psychiatric circles.”

“Did you diagnose him as having that condition in California?”

“No, that was never an issue. I’m not even sure it’s an *identity* issue. But it would be a competency issue. Isn’t that also something that the Maine judge is going to rule on? Competency?”

“Yes, doctor, you’re right. And competency is our part of the hearing. The defendant has to prove who he is. But the government has to prove that the man we believe to be Arthur Cheshire is competent to stand trial. The defense lawyer has the burden to prove his client is Martin Cheshire to avoid trial as Arthur. We would call you as our witness on that issue—identity. We would not expect you to testify on any competency issue because you have not assessed him in those terms, right?”

“Correct, I have not. But I suspect that might be the case here. If I’m right that he suffers from DID, I don’t know if that is admissible in a court of law.”

“Neither do we. But we’re working on that legal issue. Can you come back and serve as an expert witness solely on the identity issue?”

"Sure."

Liz stared at the lab books, notations, research docs, and speculations she'd collected while Arthur was in the jail complex. After a half-day sloughing through the research papers and another three hours flipping through the lab books containing her handwritten notes, she felt numb. It reminded her of something a world-class scientist had warned about treating patients suffering from childhood emotional trauma. Trauma causes wounds. Wounds always come with dark passengers—lies. He meant that traumatic wounds can be soothed with long-term treatment by the lie never goes away.

She'd used different colored sticky notes on her lab pages to remind herself about especially troubling revelations by Arthur Cheshire. The varied colors—dark red, glaring yellow, and purple gave her an emotional rush, remembering how sad, mad, and conflicted Arthur was tap-dancing around their childhood. He described Siamese twins without ever knowing what that meant. There was only one of them, not two.

She remembered his off-balance looks as he alternated looking out her office window at Mission Bay and her. Even with two decades of patient therapy, the reality of dealing with emotional trauma, childhood abuse, and false or misplaced beliefs remained as daunting as it was twenty-four years ago. She'd learned in psychiatric rounds in many hospitals the secret that hides deep inside the psyche of emotional wound trauma—the lie. It was a medical reality all psychiatrists had to keep from their patients because the lie would make the wound flare, open a blistered memory, and ultimately make the patient's terror real.

She could remember how much Arthur believed in two diametrically opposed truths—one—that Martin was alive if he was. And two—that Martin would be actually alive but for his failure to just drive the goddamned boat! Had he done that, there would never have been a body in the river, or one under the floorboards in Maine, or stuffed into a box of dry ice in Mexico. The truth was impossible for Arthur to believe. So, he didn't. And he had no way of knowing that once he tells himself the lie, it becomes a fungus, releasing invisible toxic spores on his body, his life, and the lives of everyone he comes in contact with.

She stuffed the papers back into the file boxes, blew her nose, and dialed Brick's number in Quantico, Virginia.

"Hi Brick, it's Liz. Did I catch you at a good time?"

"Sure, Lee's here in my office and we're mulling over some odd things. I'll put us on speaker, and you can update both of us."

When the speaker light came on, Lee said, "Hey Liz. How's the beach out there in always-sunny California? Can you see the surf from your office window?"

"Sadly, no. Our office is in downtown San Diego. It's on the Pacific but protected by a bay and a peninsula owned by the US Navy. On the other side of the bay is Coronado Island. It's surf-less except for occasional squalls that jump the peninsula and gives us a four-inch surf. But I'm glad you're in Brick's office. I want to catch you guys up on a call I had yesterday with Letty up there in Maine. She sort of talked me into being a witness in the *habeas corpus* hearing that's coming up in the Cheshire case. Do either of you have any concerns or advice about that?"

Brick pointed to himself, signaling Lee that he'd answer for the team. "Sort of talked you into it. What's that mean? Is it something you don't want to do?"

"No, I don't mind doing it as long as it doesn't interfere with the serial murder cases. To be honest, I'm not sure the US Attorney there is connecting all the dots between Martin and Arthur's mind-boggling twinness, the original embezzlement charge of AmHull, the crazy upgraded dollars from $26,000 to over $260,000, and finally the murder charge against Martin, thinking he killed Arthur. I mean it's so intertwined it must look like a giant ball of colored strings getting tied and untied by a whirlwind between two oceans. Letty only wants me to be part of her presentation on the identity part of the case, which she thinks she is sure to win and is sure I can help because I got to know Arthur so well in my role as an appointed psychiatrist writing a report for the court."

"And as I understand it," Brick said, "she doesn't need you for the second half of that *habeas* hearing—the competency hearing."

"Yes, that's right. I've actually consulted on two *habeas* hearings out here in federal court. One of our US Attorneys here got scolded by a judge for saying in open court that the defendant was playing 'Hocus Pocus with *Habeas Corpus*.' There was a headline in the *San Diego Union Tribune* with that as a headline on page one."

Lee laughed. "Hey, that's catchy. Maybe our case back here could be called, 'Hide One Twin and Be the Other.' I'm still trying to sort out first names since the first case has reversed the sequence in the second case."

Brick took over, as he always did when his team joked about Subs and Unsubs.

"Liz, what's your call on the identity hearing? Is it possible the judge could believe Arthur Cheshire's baloney? I mean, we all know the man we arrested here is Arthur. That's confirmed by fingerprints, which don't lie, and from photos, which can be obscure but not entirely deceptive. It's also put to bed by sequencing DNA, which proves the man in the Cumberland jail is Arthur, not Martin."

"Well, yes, that's what Letty thinks too. But that finding was based largely on the identity issue, which was the only issue before the court here in California. That's not true for Portland. There are two issues up there—identity *and* competency. I've been tossing and turning on that. Establishing his identity as Arthur could backfire."

"Backfire? Not sure judges do that."

"Well guys, I brought this up at a FREST meeting, remember? What if whichever twin killed those other twins in New England doesn't realize for sure who he is? If, and it's a mighty big IF, Arthur is now reeling back and forth with dissociative identity disorder, then the murders might have been the product of an alter, not the primary identity. I'm getting the feeling he has DID and has an alter that takes over from time to time—especially in emotionally fraught times. It's medically possible that the alter personality could be homicidal and the dominant personality totally unaware of losing control. Remember, the dominant personality has no memory, no actual knowing, of acts by an alter."

Brick had an immediate negative response. "Well, Norm Washington is not too worried about that. He's a lawyer and he thinks the legal precedent is on our side—dissociative identity disorder is not a defense to a criminal felony, especially a murder charge."

"Right, he told me that too," Liz said. "But nobody's thinking about what Mr. Tutt might be hinting at. Maybe he's got an expert on DID who will say Arthur meets the diagnostic criteria for DID but he has no intention of using it as defense in the criminal case."

Brick inhaled loudly and tapped his right forefinger on the side of his head.

"Okay, then what? Why call an expert, introduce the possibility Arthur is a DID guy, and then not use it in the case? What's that get him?"

"Well, follow the dots, Brick. Dot one—Mr. Tutt loses the first round when the judge finds the defendant is Arthur. Dot two—Mr. Tutt wins the second round when the judge decides Arthur is not competent to stand trial. Dot three—Arthur gets out of jail and is institutionalized in a secure mental facility, getting DID therapy and avoiding courtrooms for what, ever? Maybe?"

"Oh, Christ all mighty," Lee said. "Liz, what's the psychological odds here? How hard is it to find a medical expert that might say Arthur is DID?"

"I don't know. I haven't examined him myself or tried to establish a diagnostic profile. But I told the team that I was worried he might have dissociative identity disorder, remember?"

Lee pressed, "How could the defense find an expert who had not seen the patient, not done a psychiatric work-up, and had not done the great job you did?"

Liz knew they could not see her. This was only a tele call, not a Zoom session. She was glad.

"Well, any qualified psychiatrist who had access to my full file from San Diego could develop a second-hand diagnosis based on my work-up. Probably not a full diagnosis, but enough to convince a worried judge managing a triple murder case that where's there's smoke there's fire. That cliché works in medicine and law as well as it does in firefighting. I can imagine a judge calling a halt to the case if there's a professional opinion that DID is a disqualifying condition, meaning the patient is incompetent to stand trial. Norm doesn't think DID could be a defense in a murder trial. But I want you guys to know, and I'll remind Letty of this, from a medical standpoint, identity is not the biggest problem for the prosecution in this case."

"What's the biggest problem?" Brick asked in a muffled voice.

The telephone line went silent for at least thirty seconds. Brick and Lee could hear what sounded like heaving breathing on the line from San Diego. "Here's the elephant in the courtroom," Liz said slowly. "What if Mr. Tutt persuades the judge that he has the right to cross-examine me during the identity phase? What if I get locked into hypothetical questions about whether

I considered DID as a possible mental illness in the context of the three serial murder cases we were working on?"

"What would you say, Liz? Remember you're a witness for the prosecution."

"Well, I would be called to the witness stand by the prosecutor. But I'm really a court witness, not a prosecution witness. My role in this case, as in all court appointments, is to be honest with the court. What bothers me is dot number three on my list. The more I read up on DID, and the deeper I get into reviewing my notes and the report I wrote for Judge Hightower, the closer I get to a *second-hand* diagnosis. I think Arthur is afflicted with dissociative identity disorder—he thinks he is Martin when Arthur is threatened. To put it another way, Arthur has an alter personality state—Martin."

Lee pushed back into the conversation.

"Liz, you said you had three dots—Arthur's identity, Arthur's competence, and possibly Arthur's institutionalization for DID treatment. Is there a fourth dot? Seems to me that it's possible that Arthur has DID, Martin is an alternative personality state for Arthur, but there is no evidence about the serial killer's mental state at the time the crimes were permitted. Isn't that a fourth dot?"

"Yes, I think so. The fourth dot is memory. In a clearcut dissociative case the dominant personality state has no memory of what his alternative personality did. If the defendant in a case is in his dominant personality state, he cannot know what he cannot remember. So, how could he—the dominant personality—have formed criminal intent to murder someone?"

Brick interrupted. "Hold up, Liz, and you too, Lee, is there a fifth dot we have not talked about? It's just occurring to me because of this conversation—dot number five might be the mysterious connections between Alice, Rosie, and Marcella! We were working on that when we got the tip about the Unsub in

Maine. We didn't finish figuring out why people who ought to be helping us find Arthur went deaf and dumb on us. We got no help from Alice Singworth, Rosie Andersen, or Marcella Munoz. Why not? And this dot also includes the mystery phone calls between them and somebody in Panama City—a bank number if I remember correctly. The embezzlement at AmHull Insurance was thought to be $26,000 by Martin. But later it ramped up to $269,000 somehow. And that was *after* Martin died in the fishing boat accident. How could the amount of embezzled money go up after his death? And is it possible another AmHull Insurance employee was involved—how about Alice? Abe was doing the trap-and-trace and found calls between the three girls and a Panama bank. Was that one of those banks where rich Americans open accounts to hide ill-gotten gains? I remember Abe saying that all of that is probably tied to Arthur and Martin."

Lee reminded them that her whiteboard assessment got close but never was expanded to test the Panama connections and the huge increase in embezzled money. "Brick, do you want me to update the Whiteboard?"

"Yes, today if possible." Brick said. "Liz, we'll keep you in the loop. But for now, let me tell you something new in the case. Abe kept on that track and found out that Alice Singworth had opened a new AmHull account in Manchester, New Hampshire. It was a branch office of the one Martin opened. Same big bank, simply different branch. Abe managed to persuade the bank manager to give us a little info without a warrant. Alice made deposits over a six-month period of time—approximately $270,000."

Liz could not quite see how that related to her part. "I didn't know about that, but it doesn't seem relevant to Arthur's mental health."

Brick responded. "No, probably not. But it is part of the track leading to Arthur's arrest that when Alice closed the New

Hampshire account, she had the money wired to a Panama bank she opened down there."

Lee added, "And Liz, Abe also talked to a travel agency in Portland that arranged a trip to Panama, airlines, and hotel reservations for Alice and two other women. The agent balked when Abe pressed for names of the other women. Then Abe did his 'do you really want a warrant' gambit and it worked. The other travelers were Rosie in Boston, and Marcella in San Diego. We think they were all in on the heist."

US DISTRICT COURT, PORTLAND, MAINE

As it turned out, it took almost seven weeks before the evidentiary hearing was held in Judge Rachlyn's court. As predicted, the judge directed Mr. Tutt to present his evidence proving his client was Martin Cheshire. The only witness he called was the petitioner himself. And he did that only after making a statement in open court.

"Your Honor, for the record, I ask this honorable court to confirm our chambers discussion. Any testimony by my client will not be treated as a waiver of his Fifth Amendment privilege against self-incrimination. I will question my client and refer to him as Mr. Cheshire. He says his first name is Martin. He is here today testifying on his own behalf in a case where Arthur Cheshire is named as the defendant. His testimony is conditioned on the court's ruling in chambers that his testimony today will not be introduced in the criminal proceeding under abatement. His testimony is not a waiver of his due process rights under the Fourth Amendment."

Judge Rachlyn picked up another sheet of paper from her desk and read it into the record.

"Mr. Tutt, Ms. Persuanoli, the record will reflect the extensive chambers discussion we had on the record this morning about any testimony the petitioner offers in this evidentiary hearing on the issue of his identity. His testimony is not a waiver of any constitutional rights under the fourth or fifth amendments to the constitution. This ruling is not contested by the government. The government may cross examine the petitioner on identity issues, but the petitioner's answers are not a waiver of his constitutional rights. I would ask the government's counsel to speak on this open court record to that issue."

"The government agrees, Your Honor. The petitioner's testimony in this proceeding regarding identity is not a waiver of his Fourth or Fifth Amendment rights and privileges. But as noted in chambers, any testimony the defendant offers on the competency issue also before this court may be a waiver of his Fifth Amendment right to remain silent."

"Yes, Ms. Persuanoli, you made that clear in chambers. There is no ruling. We will revisit waiver when and if the petitioner chooses to testify in the competence hearing which will follow this identity hearing. Now, are the parties ready to proceed? Mr. Tutt, since you have the burden of proof on identity, you may call your first witness."

Looking surprised, Eppy leaned forward and up at the bench before speaking.

"Your Honor, I'm ready to make our opening statement, I was just assuming that . . ."

"Mr. Tutt, I know your position on this issue, and I've read your petition and heard you in chambers. I don't need an opening statement. Call your first witness."

"Yes, Your Honor, the petitioner will take the stand."

Arthur got up, gave his lawyer a tight smile, glared at the prosecutor's table, and ignored the judge as he sauntered to the witness stand. Once seated, the bailiff asked him to raise his right hand

and place his left on the bible to take the oath. The bailiff began the customary notice to a court witness, but Arthur crossed his arms across his chest and kept his glaze on the prosecution table.

"I don't have to touch a book to tell the truth. I'm here to identify myself, not to swear oaths to God or anyone else. I'm Martin Cheshire."

Judge Rachlyn intervened.

"Mr. Cheshire, is it your intention to tell the truth when you answer questions from either your lawyer, the prosecutor, or myself in this case?"

"Yes."

Turning away from the witness, the judge said in a measured tone, "The record will reflect the witness has confirmed his testimony will be truthful. He identifies himself as Martin Cheshire. The record will also reflect the charges before the court are docketed as against a man identified by the prosecution as Arthur Cheshire. So, the issues are joined. Proceed, Mr. Tutt."

"Mr. Cheshire. You've just identified yourself as Martin. Who is Arthur Cheshire?"

"He's my brother."

"Is he alive?"

"My brother Arthur, you mean? You asking about the boating accident on the Dramiscotta?"

Letty rose in objection. "Your Honor, move to strike the answer as unresponsive. We're here to establish the identity of a man we believe is alive and well and indeed sitting on the witness stand before you and . . ."

Judge Rachlyn, while typing on her benchtop computer, said, "Objection denied. Motion to strike witness testimony denied. Continue, Mr. Tutt."

Eppy said, "Mr. Cheshire, I won't be asking you questions not pertinent to today's hearing. All I asked was whether your brother Arthur is alive. You can say yes or no, okay?"

"My brother is alive to me. But maybe not to the lady next to you. She wants to prosecute him, but she can't. I know that."

"When you say Arthur is alive to you but not to the prosecutor, what do you mean?"

Letty objected. "Your Honor, the question lacks foundation, calls for speculation, and is immaterial to any question before this court."

"Sustained," said judge, turning again to her computer keyboard.

"Mr. Cheshire," Eppy said, "when did you last talk to Arthur?"

"In person, you mean?"

"Well, either in person or by phone, and please do not say what was said, just tell the court the date you last talked to Arthur."

"I don't remember the exact date, but one time when we were in our boat, and we hit a big rock and . . ."

"Hold on, Mr. Cheshire. We won't be going over those details. Just confirm for the court that you have not talked to Arthur since the day of your boating accident."

"I'm confused. You said when we talked over in the jail that I could say what my brother told me. And I told you I talk to him every goddamned day, in jail even. I talked to him this morning before Slo brought me here from the county lock-up."

Eppy held up his hand, palm forward, to his client on the stand, and turned to face the judge.

"Your Honor, I would ask the court's indulgence here. Ultimately, the record will show a reliance between the petitioner and a man he insists is his brother, Arthur. The question before the court is who is the man on the witness stand. I urge the court to give that man the opportunity to identify himself, but I vow to the court that it might not be possible without allowing him to identify himself precisely and truthfully in relationship to his brother. May I proceed?"

Judge Rachlyn turned to the prosecutor's table. "Ms. Persuanoli, I suggest we allow the petitioner to speak his mind as he testifies about himself and his brother. I will allow some latitude here because this is a civil matter—the question is identity. But I will give you wide latitude to object after the fact. By that I mean I will entertain a motion to strike the testimony as immaterial and unduly prejudicial if that is your position at the end of the direct examination. And I will give the government a full and fair opportunity to cross-examine when petitioner's counsel completes his direct."

Without waiting for a response from the government, the judge told Eppy to continue.

Eppy closed his notebook, leaned forward from the podium, and asked the broadest question he could think of.

"Mr. Cheshire, the court wants to know who you are. Her Honor knows that you were arrested on a warrant naming Arthur Cheshire as a defendant in three murder cases. So, if the only way you can identify yourself to the judge is to explain your relationship with your brother, please tell the judge what you mean when you say you talked to him, to Arthur, this morning while you were in a jail cell. We all know there are no phones in jail cells. So how did you talk to Arthur this morning?"

The witness had scanned the room but didn't settle on anyone. Now, he wheezed in a large breath and seemed to point his left ear out into the room from his left side to his right side. His chest continued to rise and fall as he telescoped the large wood paneled courtroom. When he got to the defense table on the right side of the room, he seemed to settle on the two people seated behind the prosecutor's table. Dr. Socorro sat in one and Agent Norm Washington in the other. From the witness stand, the petitioner moved his head slightly back and forth between Dr. Socorro and Agent Washington. The glare on his face softened when he focused on Dr. Socorro. He lifted his right arm as though it were mildly painful and gave a delicate wave with his right hand cupped toward her.

"Okay," he said, turning his focus back on his lawyer. "Me and my brother were at our best when we were in the same room together with no one else around. We could talk without words and without making sounds. We talked through our eyes, even when they were shut. Get that? Shut and not even moving. And then this one time, the one I started talking about a little while ago, we were fishing. So here goes.

"The river. I'm driving the boat and I'm alive. My brother might have died. It was probably like black sky and cold ocean water, in the river, you know. We were in the estuary. The water in the bottom of the boat was greasy, mixed gas, salt water, rainwater. Fluids. Maybe piss too. Empty beer cans floating. The bait box overturned. Fish flopping out of the fish tank. Then the toolbox popped open. We both screamed. Seems like I wet myself. My brother could have just pulled the anchor, and let the tide do its work. We were drowning and our minds were the same. The boat rocking side to side and felt good. Really good. Helped with my shaking. Muck, bilge water, Arthur's blood. All pooling. So, I just looked upriver. Funny thing about that blood. His blood. I'd seen blood before, several times. It was always black, never red. But now, the blood from Arthur's head was red, at first, as it slowly seeped out, then turned black when it hit the bilge in the bottom of the boat. He had blood all over that too. It's okay. We always share. Blood. Lives."

Arthur leaned onto the railing separating him from the courtroom. He rested his forearms and cupped his chin in both hands. The courtroom went silent, then faintly, the judge and her bailiff could hear Arthur's sniffling. Then, a minute later, the sniffling became a high-pitched scream. Arthur lifted his head and glared at the prosecution table.

"Why am I yelling? The blood! Not red anymore. Black as coal. I already told you that. And besides, it was a pool, not just spilled blood, but pools of it. No, it did not smell! But the river smells like salt, trees, seabirds, and the damn boat itself. It all smelled except for the blood. I thought the blood meant that he was not dead. Dead men don't bleed. Drowned does not bleed. But if he's not dead, he couldn't have drowned. But, he bled, and bled, and bled, and I could see all that blood, and none of it was mine. You say you want to know my name? But you lie. All of you lie. You want to know who died and who lived. Well, here I am. I am who I say I am. That is how we were born and how we lived. Who's talking on this witness stand? We are. We are telling you what happened, and you think it's our game. Hide and Be. The game. Yeah, maybe. You see, I thought maybe I was him and we were playing the game again, but I forgot who was who. So, Arthur died. Not his fault. But I know he's alive because I'm alive. I took care of his booty. She was bamber."

Eppy, at the podium, clicked his ballpoint pen and slid it into his shirt pocket. Taking in a deep breath, he paused and then parsed his next question as slowly and deliberately as he could. "Mr. Cheshire, is your name Martin or Arthur?"

The man on the witness stand looked perplexed as he shifted in his seat. He tucked at his shirt cuffs and slid first one hand and then the other along the sides of his head. Finally, when the pause in the courtroom seemed to overtake him, he looked directly at the judge for the first time. Moving his body back and forth toward the podium while keeping his head aimed at the judge, he spoke to her, not his lawyer.

"That lawyer is a nice man. He told me to tell the truth and no hiding and being in court, you know? We had to be one another sometimes. But we were telling the truth to each other. So here is Cheshire truth to the court. Yes. Yes, my name is Martin *and* Arthur. We can be named any way we have to. Right, Judge?"

He stood up in the witness box, cleared his throat, and took a handkerchief from his rear pocket. He blew his nose and said, "Judge, can I go now? Can Slo take me back? I'm getting sick, again."

Judge Rachlyn said, "The court will be in recess. The bailiff and the sheriff's deputy will escort the petitioner to the holding tank on the third floor. I'll see counsel in chambers."

With that, she stepped down from the bench and walked briskly to her chambers door as the audience hurried to rise.

With the judge out of sight and the petitioner removed from the courtroom, all three reporters sitting in the first row of seats behind the rail got up and quickly gathered their cell phones and clicked shots at the lawyers, FBI agents, and the so-far unidentified woman who'd been sitting behind the prosecution table. The two men wore open-neck collared shirts, light-weight fleece jackets, and athletic shoes. The woman showed better taste with a knee-length skirt, knee-high black leather boots, and a camera bag with flowers and animal rescuer decals. She walked quickly to the other side of the room and approached Liz.

"Hi," she said with an engaging smile. "I'm Celeste Nomkin with the AP. Are you a government lawyer on loan from somewhere? I cover the courthouse beat here and I don't remember seeing you in court or at a legal press conference."

Liz had learned the hard way in San Diego to be wary of reporters but always tried to be polite and cheerful.

"No," she said, "I'm a federal employee in California, just on TDY here for a few weeks."

"TDY? " the AP reporter asked.

"Temporary duty. It's kind of like a borrowed servant deal. I work in San Diego full time."

"Really? How lucky. I love San Diego, well at least I love Coronado. I went to high school there; dad was in the Marine

Corps. Did one year at San Diego State College. Can I ask you what your role is in this case?"

"I'm just a consultant for the DOJ, on loan sort of from the federal court out there to this one here."

"Consulting on what? I mean, I suspect you can't tell me much, but are you law enforcement, like Norm the guy you're sitting next to?"

"So, you know Norm?"

"Sure, he's a sweetheart on Friday nights at the Fish Bucket House, but all business when he's FBI, you know."

"Celeste, I can't talk about this case, because I'm going to be a witness for the government."

"Okay, I respect that. But could you tell me when you expect to take the stand? I've got a feeling I ought to be here for that."

"Have you looked at the court docket on this case, Celeste?"

"No, but I have talked to Eppy, he's another sweetheart and when he thinks it helps his client, he lets me have copies of non-sealed court documents. So, I've read his petition for *habeas corpus*. Great stuff! I'm very interested in this case because it could turn out to be a barn burner when the serial murder cases get going. Well, I guess I should say *if* they get going."

"Okay, my part will be short. I'm just a witness on the identity part of the *habeas* relief petition."

"So, can I guess at something? My guess is you are an expert on fingerprinting or DNA sequencing, something like that."

"Sorry, Celeste, but I really can't talk about my testimony although I can say psychiatrists have no business talking about fingerprints."

"Holy bananas! You're a psychiatrist? A real MD psychiatrist?"

Liz didn't have to answer. She was rescued by Norm.

"Hey, Celeste, I see you're nosing about again digging for that Pulitzer Prize. When this case's all done, I'll buy you a cool one at the Fish Bucket, but meanwhile, I have to rescue Dr. Socorro from your grasp. Give her a break, she's not a Nor Easterner."

Letty and Eppy waited in the judge's ante room where her secretary loomed large. Ms. Springstead was well known to the legal and law enforcement community. She weighed in at something over 250 pounds and had the whitest teeth you could ever imagine. She frowned more often than she smiled but was always polite as she guarded her boss's accessibility like a Marine Gunnery Sargent. Her oversized desk-model telephone buzzed, and a blue light lit up.

"Okay, counsel, the judge is ready, you may go in."

Judge Rachlyn's chambers were, as befits a decades-old courthouse, expansive and inviting. The eleven-foot ceiling was papered and glowed from two small chandeliers at either end of the thirty-foot expanse for door to double windows behind the judge's polished oak desk. They were topped by half-moon arcs of brick and stone. She was blond, wore faux minks, and was stylish in a New England sort of way—nothing ostentatious but clearly noticeable. She had a charm bracelet that clinked when she waved her right hand, motioning them forward after Ms. Springstead opened the door to her chambers.

"Come in, gentlemen, take off your coats if you like. We're going to be here awhile, I think. I've asked my reporter to make a record of this chambers session because I can feel motions coming on from both sides. Let's start with the petitioner's counsel. Mr. Tutt, do you have additional witnesses to present on identity issues?"

"No, Your Honor. I have two witnesses on standby, but given the strength of my client's testimony, I think they would be repetitive. We'll stand on the evidence from the petitioner. I think he stated his identity rather well, even if it did tend to wander off course a time or two."

"And what say you, Letty? You have the right to cross-examine the petitioner. I've secured Mr. Cheshire on the third-floor lock-up. After we conclude this chambers meeting, I can have him brought back up."

Letty had opened her three-ringer binder on her lap and looked back at it for a moment. "Your Honor, as you know, I'm rarely at a loss for words, but I have to say I'm unsure the court needs any further testimony, on cross-examination, from the petitioner. I think he admitted he was Arthur Cheshire, albeit in a hopscotch sort of way."

"Hopscotch? Is that a metaphor for what we all heard?"

"Precisely, Your Honor," Eppy said.

Letty followed up like a power forward, snatching a rebound and swirling for the dunk right at the buzzer.

"Your Honor, I think that's a perfect metaphor for Mr. Cheshire's testimony. He played a game with us as sidewalk spectators. He jumped from one brother to the other, always jumping back and forth and leaving everyone alongside the sidewalk wondering which was which. At the end of his monologue about himself and his brother, he said, quote, 'So here is Cheshire truth to the court. Yes. Yes, my name is Martin *and* Arthur. We can be named any way we have to, right Judge?' Unquote. Under oath, he said his name was Martin and Arthur, both, not separately. He admits his name is Martin. And he insists his other name is Arthur. Well, he cannot have it both ways."

The judge leaned forward. "Go on."

"He cannot claim to be Martin for one purpose and claim to be Arthur for some other purpose. The law does not allow parties to define identity as dual. I'm ready to put the government's response on the stand by calling three experts—a psychiatrist, a handwriting expert, and a detention officer—who will say that the petitioner admits to being Arthur Cheshire in conversations within the last week in the Cumberland County Jail complex."

Judge Rachlyn's office chair was a large old-fashioned leather desk chair that rocked backward, forward, and sideways with the slightest movement. She leaned back into the soft leather and looked at the lawyers.

"Well, Mr. Tutt and Ms. Persuanoli, the metaphor that comes to my mind as I listen to Mr. Cheshire is Humpty Dumpty falling off a wall. And this court can't put him back together again. I think we were witnesses to a life none of us could possibly understand. We were, willingly or not, transported into another person's world, I kept thinking as I listened to him answer questions with questions and pose answers to names, identities, and reality as though we all understood what he was trying to tell us. He related childhood experiences not with sentences so much as with his emotional energy that oozed and spurted out onto the witness box. Just as both of you did, I took notes. But mine are typed on my bench computer. Let me read from my typed notes just a small part of what he said, under oath, on the stand."

> . . . the river smells, salt, trees, seabirds, and the damn boat itself . . . smelled . . . blood . . . blood meant he wasn't dead . . . Dead men don't bleed . . . if he's not dead, he couldn't have drowned. But, he bled, and bled . . . could see all that blood . . . none of it was mine . . . You say you want to know my name . . . you lie . . . All of you lie . . . who died . . . who lived. Well, here I am. I am who I say I am.

Judge Rachlyn turned away from her computer screen, got up from her desk, and stepped over to the seven-foot-tall bookshelf. Reaching to a shelf two feet above her, she removed two large books and returned to her chair. She thumbed through the first for a minute, found what she was looking for, and read out loud to the lawyers.

> IDENTIFICATION: A mental mechanism of the unconscious by which (1) the ego attaches to or transfers to itself qualities or properties belonging to other persons or objects; or (2) the ego transfers to one person the representation it holds of another person or of itself.

Then with a wave of her hand for the lawyers to be patient, she found a page in the second book and read a section from it aloud.

> IDENTIFICATION: Proof of identity; the proving that a person, subject, or article before the court is the very same that he or it is alleged, charged or reputed to be; as where a witness recognizes that the person at the bar is the same person whom he saw committing the crime, et cetera, et cetera.

"So, Mr. Tutt," Judge Rachlyn said, "you have the burden of proof of identity on this civil *habeas* hearing. Which definition do you think the court should adopt in this case?"

"Honestly, Judge, I think the second definition probably comes from a legal dictionary. But the first rings true to me for this particular case. May I ask you where that first definition comes from?"

"Yes, you may, Mr. Tutt. It is on page 722 in *Dorland's Illustrated Medical Dictionary*. The second is from page 880 of my copy of *Black's Law Dictionary*. So, Ms. Persuanoli, which of the two best fits this case from the government's point of view?"

"Your Honor, as fond as I am of the English language, I have to say the second definition is apropos this hearing. Whether civil or criminal, the test here is evidence. Mr. Cheshire's testimony, however illogical and beside the point his ramblings were, must be tested under the law of evidence. Under evidentiary rules, identification is measured by the standard of *sameness*. The test of sameness is whether a subject or a person before the court is the same as what it, he, or she is charged as. Here the petitioner was investigated, indicted, charged, and arrested as Arthur Cheshire. We will prove that by offering in-person testimony. We will call a handwriting expert, a fingerprint expert, the arresting FBI agent, and a federal officer employed by the US Bureau of Prisons who has personal knowledge of the petitioner and can identify him as Arthur Cheshire. This particular witness spent a good deal of time with the man on the stand in a federal court case in San Diego, California. Her name is Dr. Elisbeth Socorro, a court psychiatrist from Arthur Cheshire's first case in California. I'm confident her testimony will resolve all doubt, even though we do not have the burden of proof on identity. And, Your Honor, due to demands on her job in California, we will call her first and follow with the other three identification witnesses."

Everyone rose, as directed by the bailiff, when Judge Rachlyn's chambers door opened, and she took her short walk to the bench. Once seated, she clicked on her computer, arranged her bench book in front of her, and nodded to the courtroom.

"Thank you, ladies and gentlemen, the record will reflect we are still in the identity phase of petitioner's writ of *habeas corpus*. The petitioner is present in court with his lawyer, Mr. Tutt. Ms. Persuanoli is present for the government. Mr. Tutt, do you have additional witnesses to call on the identity issue?"

"No, Your Honor."

"Ms. Persuanoli, I believe you have four witnesses on the identity issue, correct?"

"Yes, Your Honor. Our first witness is a psychiatrist who evaluated the petitioner in a separate proceeding in California. Our handwriting expert will say the petitioner's handwriting is consistent with samples of Arthur Cheshire's handwriting.

We have an expert on fingerprints who will say the petitioner's fingerprints at booking here in Maine are identical to the fingerprints Arthur Cheshire gave when he was booked into the federal court in San Diego. A detention officer will testify about a tattoo on the petitioner's left angle which was also at issue in California. With the court's permission, we call Dr. Lisabeth Socorro to the stand."

Liz stood, smoothed her skirt down, reached beside her chair for the black nylon shoulder bag, and walked to the witness stand where the bailiff stood ready to take her oath. With that out of the way, she took the stand, opened her bag, and arrayed two manila folders on the desktop.

The prosecutor asked routine preliminary questions about employment, education, qualifications to testify, experience with the court case in California before Judge Hightower, and whether she had personal knowledge with respect to the identity issue before the court. Then, Letty began her direct examination.

"Thank you, doctor. Please look at the man seated at the defense table to my right, the man in the dark grey suit, starched white shirt, and stripped orange and black tie. Do you know this man?"

"Yes. Not personally, but I was here in court on this case for the last two days and am aware he is the lawyer for the man charged in this case—his name is Ephraim Tutt."

"Quite right, he is counsel for the petitioner. Seated next to Mr. Tutt is the petitioner in this case. Are you aware that man is charged in this case under the name Arthur Cheshire? By 'charged' I mean the docket says his name is Arthur Cheshire, the grand jury's indictment is against a man named Arthur Cheshire . . ."

Eppy rose, "Objection, leading."

"Sustained."

"Yes, Dr. Socorro, let me rephrase. Can you identify, by name, the man seated next to Mr. Tutt, in the gray shirt, without a tie."

"Yes, I can."

"What is his name?"

Eppy rose and objected, then waiving his hand toward the prosecutor's table, said, "Sorry, never mind."

Liz looked at the court for guidance. Judge Rachlyn nodded back to her.

"His name is Arthur Cheshire."

"Dr. Socorro, on a scale of ten to one, how confident are you about his name, and for the record, I mean the man seated next to Mr. Tutt at the defense table. Are you sure he is Arthur Cheshire?"

"I am. I'd say ten."

"Thank you. The court is aware of your participation in a federal case two years ago. That case was originally filed against a man named Martin Cheshire. The petitioner in this case was the defendant in that case. What was your role in the case out there?"

"I was appointed by the court to conduct a psychiatric assessment of the defendant in that case, and I testified in the identity phase of that case based on my written assessment and personal knowledge of his identity."

"Have you interviewed or conducted any professional assessment of the petitioner in this case, which would be in any way analogous to the work you did in the California case?"

"No, I have not. I read the charging documents in this case, but that's all, other than talk to the prosecutor in her office. There is no psychiatric work-up here in this record. That said, I was present in court and watched the petitioner testify before this court. That experience alone proves to me that the man charged in California, the man I spent three months interviewing and testing, is the same man that testified here in court yesterday. His name there was Arthur Cheshire. He's charged here as Arthur Cheshire. I know him to be the same man."

"Thank you, doctor. Now, let me ask you some general questions about identity, self-identification, and false identity. First, can you define from a medical perspective what *identity* means?"

"Ms. Persuanoli, I can try. Perhaps the best place to start is with a medical perspective inherent in one of our formal documents called the *Diagnostic and Statistical Manual*. It defines central diagnostic criteria for personality disorders. Identity diffusion is a borderline personality organization. But individual humans have only limited self-rating inventory, by which we identify by name, relationship, or awareness. We do that differently in adolescence than we do in early teens, and in adulthood. It is a complex dimension, varying from identity *integration* to identity *diffusion*. The medical/scientific community evaluates psychometric properties to arrive at a judgment about whether a patient has a borderline personality disorder, or a healthy recognition of identity at various stages of life. I could give you a simple analogy if that's permitted in court."

"Yes, please, doctor," Letty said.

"Okay, when we are very young, two or three, we identify by what we're called. When we become speaking and thinking little children, we respond to how we are called. But traumatic experiences can either confuse or alter how we identify to others—family members or outsiders. Some children at an early age identify one way to family members but recoil at identification by other children or unfamiliar adults. By way of oversimplification, I can say that we are who other people think we are, in terms of names, identities, and recognition. At first, we accept our identities as defined by someone else. In time we identify that way because we like how we're identified. But for some, with borderline personality disorders, childhood trauma, or even adult trauma, we withdraw and identify as *who we say we are*."

"Thank you, doctor. Now let me move forward from childhood to adulthood. Even if an adult person has a borderline personality disorder, does that mean the patient is no longer the same person he or she was as a child?"

Liz inhaled deeply and paused for a few seconds before answering.

"It's unfortunately not that simple. The outside world treats us as who we were at birth, in childhood and adulthood, as the same person, even if we change our names, or no longer believe we are who we used to be. But that does not mean someone who suffers from an emotional traumatic wound will act the same way in terms of personality and rationality as they did as children or teenagers. Time benefits some identities and wounds others. Consequently, personal identity becomes debatable."

Letty looked a little perplexed. She squared her shoulders at the podium and leaned forward over the podium for her next question. "Debatable? I take your psychiatric thesis as stated, doctor, but in terms of simple identification in a court proceeding, isn't identity a straightforward process of identifying a person by name, and personal history, simply a fact-finding process?"

Liz nodded slowly and said, "I take what you say as a given reality, in or outside court. But our identities to the outside world may be factual and still wrong when it comes to crime and victimization."

"Yes, of course, doctor, but let me put it this way. This hearing is limited to identity, not crime or victimization. Let me ask you the identity question in a different context. By whatever name he chooses, and without trying to tie him to one name or another, is the man seated next to Mr. Tutt the same man you examined in your California office? Is he the same man you saw in court in San Diego?:

"Yes, he is the same man."

"Thank you, Doctor Socorro. Your Honor, I have no further questions."

Judge Rachlyn turned her gaze from the witness box to the defense table.

"You may cross-examine, Mr. Tutt."

"Good afternoon, Dr. Socorro. In your testimony today, you mentioned the *Diagnostic and Statistical Manual*. Have you consulted that manual to diagnose Mr. Cheshire?"

"No, not in this case. I have not diagnosed him at all. I did a clinical assessment for the court in San Diego, but not a full diagnosis."

"I see. I assume you did not use the diagnostic criteria for personality disorders in preparing for your testimony in this case, right?"

"Right."

"You made no attempt to establish an identity disorder for Mr. Cheshire, right?"

"Yes, that's right."

"And you do not know whether he has a borderline personality order, do you?"

"No, I do not."

"And in mental health terms, you've not been asked to assess him for veracity in any way, have you?"

"I have not."

"You told Ms. Persuanoli that we humans have limited self-rating inventory when it comes to how we identify ourselves, establish awareness of who we are, or explain our relationships with others, right?"

"Yes, but of course there is more to identity than self-identity."

"Ah yes, I take your point, doctor. That's especially true in adolescence, isn't it?"

"Correct."

"And that's why, on direct examination, you said identity is a 'complex dimension, varying from identity integration to identity diffusion.' Am I quoting your correctly, doctor?"

"Yes, you are."

"So, with that foundation, tell us whether Mr. Cheshire is likely varying from identity integration to identity diffusion, based solely on what your heard from him on the witness stand this morning."

That got Letty out of her chair.

"Objection, Your Honor. Beyond the scope, immaterial, and lacks foundation."

"Your objection on foundation is overruled. You laid the foundation on direct. Identity is the issue here, and whether it's diffused or integrated seems obviously material. You may answer the question, Doctor Socorro."

"Alright, but it's a bit more complicated, Mr. Tutt. I'm not talking about legality or sociology, but psychologically. *Identity* is a mental state. When that state is disturbed, it is viewed as a central construct in psychoanalytic and psycho-dynamic assessments. Identity is, clinically speaking, a *unity of being*. To test that in a patient, psychiatrists try to develop a healthy identity development for disturbed patients. We address psychodynamic as well as social-cognitive and empiri-cal approaches."

"Precisely, doctor. And you did not have the opportunity in California to assist Mr. Cheshire in understanding the dynamics of identity integration or identity diffusion, did you?"

"No."

"Thank you, doctor. Now, the term 'identity diffusion' refers to a part of the process of a person figuring out who they are. That process starts in adolescence when a person has not yet fully realized their social identity or defined their personality traits, is that fair, doctor?"

"Quite fair, Mr. Tutt, and if I can add something here, adolescents pay almost no attention to *who* they are. They are whoever raises them thinks they are. In fact, they actively avoid self-identity questions. They develop identity as they grow, make choices, and enter into commitments."

"Would you agree, doctor, that identity disorder, as opposed to identity diffusion, is a common affliction in this country?"

"Objection, Your Honor," Liz said loudly. "This entire line of questioning is irrelevant to the narrow question of identity in this phase of *habeas corpus*, Your Honor."

"Overruled. You elicited the front part of identity and your witness mentioned assessments on how identity can be acquired or mistaken. But I will only allow testimony as it relates to the petitioner, not the general population. Mr. Tutt, please rephrase your question accordingly."

"Yes, Your Honor. Doctor Socorro, did you hear in Mr. Cheshire's testimony or in Ms. Persuanoli's questions, any suggestions, or characterizations that Mr. Cheshire displayed an identity disorder, either in California or here in Maine?"

Doctor Socorro looked at the prosecutor's table for guidance. Letty nodded her head in response.

"Yes, Mr. Tutt. Mr. Cheshire displays in this court the same ambiguity about who he is as he did in my office over a year ago. He clearly is unsure about his identity. He is who he says he is at any given moment. If he says he's Arthur, that's what he believes. If he says a few minutes later that he's Martin, that's what he believes. He's being truthful with whoever questions him. He may believe he is Arthur on Monday and Martin on Tuesday. If I say he is Arthur and he denies it, he may be telling the truth. He's the same person, but he may change personification from time to time. One of the hallmarks of some mental orders is a blurred sense of identity, which Mr. Cheshire presented here on the witness stand."

Eppy turned to the bench.

"Your Honor, may I suggest a short recess to discuss this matter in chambers?"

"No, you may not, Mr. Tutt. This proceeding is civil in nature, not criminal. Your client is at your table. The prosecutor has a government official at her table. They are, in both equity and law, obligatory participants in due process. Discussions will be conducted in open court, especially so that Mr. Cheshire, and Mr. Washington, the government official, may hear what you have to say and how the prosecutor responds. So, make your case here and I'll call on Ms. Persuanoli to respond."

"Thank you, Your Honor. If I may, please allow me to place on the record my position as counsel for the petitioner. Mr. Cheshire displayed in this court emotional wounds deep in his psyche and his memory. My limited research into his emotional wounds, as displayed in court, in jail, and at the scene of his arrest augers for a professional assessment by someone with the training, experience, knowledge, and intellectual capacity displayed in this court by Dr. Socorro. Young children do not have the experience or maturity to understand what they are seeing and experiencing, and this can lead to dysfunctional rather than healthy coping mechanisms. Of course, I am not qualified to define or present Mr. Cheshire's brain function or his belief structure. But we have, on the stand today, a witness, Dr. Socorro, who has spent a great deal of time with the petitioner, but not as a treating physician, only as a consulting expert appointed by a court. I move for a temporary recess in this *habeas* proceeding and ask the court to appoint Dr. Socorro to re-engage with Mr. Cheshire for the purpose of advising this court on his current mental function, the extent to which he may be afflicted by a DMS diagnosis known as dissociative identity disorder or DID for short. If he is afflicted by DID, she can advise the court and the parties as to whether he himself knows, from one day to the next, whether he is Arthur or Martin Cheshire."

"Thank you, Mr. Tutt. We are in the identity phase of this case. The court's goal in separating this identity phase from the next phase, competency, was two-fold. First to separate the civil aspects of *habeas corpus*, identifying the defendant before the court from the criminal aspects of *habeas corpus*, qualifying or disqualifying the defendant as competent to stand trial on the indictment handed up to this court by a duly empaneled grand jury. And second, to ensure the defendant's constitutional rights under the Fourth and Fifth Amendments to the US Constitution. In particular, the court was and is still unwilling to make any orders that might infringe on the petitioner's right to remain silent. He has testified here in the civil case. He has not waived his self-incrimination privilege. I cannot order him to speak, in consultation with Dr. Socorro, because that might violate his Fifth Amendment rights. I cannot order her to seek evidence from him, which might violate his Fourth Amendment rights regarding forced evidence. And to add to the legal complications your motion brings to bear, we must first resolve the identity issue before approaching the competency issue. Otherwise, the court would be conflating issues. We can't have that, can we? For those reasons, your motion to temporarily suspend this proceeding is denied. However, I should advise counsel that I am prepared to decide the issue of identity, as a matter of law based on the evidence thus far admitted. Ms. Persuanoli, what say you?"

"Your Honor," Letty began, leaving her table to stand at the podium, "the government has additional documentary evidence which is stipulated by Mr. Ephraim in evidence. That evidence strongly suggests, via fingerprint identification, DNA evidence, handwriting confirmation, and photos of a tattoo on Mr. Cheshire, his attempt to evade his true identity. So, we don't need to call those additional witnesses. We rest this phase of our evidence, the identity phase."

"All right," Judge Rachlyn said. "Based on the briefs filed, testimony offered, and written evidence stipulated in, I find the petitioner's legal identity is Arthur Cheshire. He is not Martin

Cheshire, as he stated to arresting officers, detention officers, and others. That matter is now resolved. I am not prepared to commence the second issue—competency—without expert testimony. Ms. Persuanoli, you have the burden of proving that Arthur Cheshire is component to stand criminal trial. How much time do you need to need?"

"Your Honor, that will depend on the availability of experts. My expert here, Dr. Socorro, would seem to be the logical choice since she already knows much of the relevant history, the defendant Arthur Cheshire, and the charges against him here. If the court were to appoint her as the court's expert, to advise the court independently of the positions taken by either side, that would accommodate the interests of justice, as well as that of the government."

Judge Rachlyn focused on Mr. Tutt.

"What say you, Mr. Tutt? Are you in agreement that Dr. Socorro would be in the best position to independently advise the court on the question of Arthur Cheshire's competency to stand trial?"

"Yes, Your Honor, we agree, but I need to confirm that with my client in private."

"Fine, I'll have him brought up here and you can talk to him in private in one of our conference rooms on this floor. In the interests of brevity, let me ask Dr. Socorro whether she's willing to undertake a court assignment on his competency to stand trial. Dr. Socorro, can you assist the court on this issue?"

Liz rose, but as she stood up her three-ring binder dropped to the floor. Something snapped and a sheaf of papers spilled out onto the polished oak floorboards.

"I'm so sorry, Judge. That was clumsy on my part. I am willing to assist the court but would have to ask my office in San Diego for a brief extension of my absence there. And I would need the cooperation of the sheriff's office here to transport Mr.

Cheshire to a private office, preferably on a secured floor here in the courthouse. I would want to conduct some tests on Mr. Cheshire. I don't perform psychometric or other tests on patients if there are questions about his or her competency to make medical decisions. Perhaps Mr. Tutt could be engaged at that level since I don't believe Mr. Cheshire has any living relatives. There will likely be other issues that can be resolved by the court."

The judge asked counsel if there were any objections to Dr. Socorro's role as a court consultant or Mr. Tutt's ability to confer regarding Mr. Cheshire's competency to make medical decisions. There were none. She suggested Mr. Tutt might secure a POA and asked Dr. Socorro to notify Ms. Springstead of permission granted by her office in San Diego. She asked if either party had anything to add to the record. Neither did. Then she said the magic words.

"We are adjourned subject to call by the clerk of court."

Her brisk stride from the bench was upped today. She looked like a woman running from a bad date; not running exactly, but definitely not turning around to say goodbye.

Slo, the detention officer assigned to transport Mr. Cheshire, delivered his prisoner in fresh jail clothes to the fourth floor in the federal building, fifteen minutes before his order sheet required. He'd kept the cuffs on until a young woman came to the detention room and told him to take his prisoner to 4212, a conference room at the end of the hall. Once there, Dr. Socorro asked him to take the cuffs off the prisoner. Slo said he was told not to do that unless he stayed in the room. He insisted. After a thirty-second stare down with Dr. Socorro, Slo took the cuffs off. There were only two chairs in the room. He stood with his back to the door. Dr. Socorro folded her arms across her chest and closed the lab book on the table in front of her. Two minutes passed before Slo turned, left the room, and settled in the stiff-back chair next to the door out in the hallway.

"Good afternoon, Mr. Cheshire, I'm so glad to reconnect with you here in Portland. Did Mr. Tutt explain what I've been asked to do here?"

"No."

"Okay. Do you remember me from our talks back in San Diego last year?"

"No."

"Well, I remember you. And I saw you in court last week. You testified first, then I testified. Do you remember that?"

"Sure, and besides, Arthur remembered you. He remembered your white coat and that time you took it off. He remembers good."

"You told the judge last week your first name was Martin; do you remember saying that?"

"Arthur told me to say that."

"When did he tell you that?"

"When I woke up."

"Was that the day you and I both testified?"

"No."

"Okay, when did he tell you that?"

"I just told you. This morning when I woke up."

"You remember lots of things, don't you?"

"Some things. Arthur's better."

"Do you talk often to Arthur?"

"Never."

"But you just said you talked to him this morning."

"No, I listen when he talks. He talks good. He remembers good. He told me you were bamber."

"Bamber? I'm sorry but I don't know that word."

"It's our word, nobody else's."

"What does it mean?"

"I don't tell our words, but it's not bad or anything. He likes you especially when you take your white coat off, you know?"

"All right, so bear with me here. Mr. Tutt is your power of attorney now and he gave me permission to ask questions and to tell the judge what you say to me. You understand that, don't you?"

"He says you are going to help us."

"Now, I want you to pay close attention to me. I want you to look at me, just like Arthur would want you to pay attention. Just listen to my words and fold your hands together like you were in church. Can you do that for me?"

"Yes, like this?" he asked, moving his arms closer in, and cupping his hands on the table with his palms and fingers touching but his thumbs askance.

"I want you to take a deep breath when I ask you a question. Then let your breath parse out before you answer. Did you love your brother more than anything else in the world?"

"I am his brother."

"What is your brother's name?"

"Arthur."

"But the jail people say you are Arthur, right? That's what Slo, your detention officer, says, right?"

"Yes, but I already told them he never did anything wrong, so why is he in jail?"

"Is he in jail or are you in jail?"

"We are."

"You and Arthur?

"Yes, we don't turn on one another. We share our birthdays. Not like them."

"Like whom?"

"Them!"

"All right, do you remember last week in court when I told the judge I thought you were Arthur? Do you remember that?"

"Maybe, or maybe Arthur told me. Slo says they think I'm Arthur pretending to be Martin. That's what he says."

"What do you say to Slo when he says that?"

"I don't talk to him very much. Arthur does, I think."

"Arthur talks to Slo, is that what you said?"

"You don't listen to us, do you? We keep telling you who we are and stuff."

"Have you ever hurt someone, really hurt them?"

"I want Slo to come get me. My head hurts."

"Sure, but let me ask you one more question. When you're locked across town in a jail cell, how does Arthur talk to you? I mean, it's not on the telephone, is it?"

"I told you we don't talk. He does. I listen. Used to be different. Not now."

"How do you know when he wants to talk to you?"

"He just talks. Every time I listen. Every goddamned time."

"Sort of comes and goes, is that it?"

"We used to play a game; he told you that, right? Hide and Be. He told you about that, right?"

"He did. Out there in California."

"So, when the strap comes out, I'd be him even though I didn't do anything. Didn't do anything."

"We're talking about Arthur, aren't we? When you talk about the strap, you mean you would pretend to be Arthur and he'd get the strap. Is that right?"

"Sometimes. But he took it for me, too, sometimes."

"Do you remember being arrested a few weeks ago near your fishing camp up at Jones Point on the Dramiscotta?"

"He told me about that. He did too! Don't you say he didn't, cuz he did!"

"All right, now you're saying Arthur told you about the arrest. When did he tell you about it?"

"Don't remember. Don't remember. Ask him. He remembers good. Do you remember I told you he remembers good! It's my turn."

"Alright, Mr. Cheshire, you can loosen your hands now. Don't cup them together on the table. I want you to push your chair back and then stand up, just like I'm going to do."

Dr. Socorro pushed her chair back, placed her hands on the desk, and stood up. But Arthur didn't move. He laid his hands flat on the table and didn't push his chair back. She clapped her hands together twice. He looked up at her with a blank stare and then, slowly like it was painful, pushed away from the desk and looked around the room from one side to the other and then back again.

"Where's Slo?" he asked.

"He's outside in the hall, but he can hear us, I think. Should I call him for you?"

"Yeah, yeah, I need an aspirin. He has a little bottle of 'em in his pants pocket."

She turned and opened the door. Slo got up and looked around her at his prisoner.

"He's hurting upstairs in his brain, ain't he?"

"Yes, that's what he told me. You carry aspirin for him, right? He'd like one now, please."

"He only gets two a day. He already had two after his breakfast. But you're a doctor, right? So, I can give him one on your say-so, I guess."

"Yes, I say so. And you can take him back to the jail. I want to see him every day for the next three days, here in this office, at the same time. Can you schedule that for him?"

"No," Slo said. "I ain't the scheduler. Transport does that, you gotta go through them. You got their number, right?"

Liz spent the afternoon at the Maine Medical Center. She was impressed with the ease of entry into the large teaching hospital for the Tufts University School of Medicine. It was a Level I Trauma Center, one of only three in Northern New

England. More important, they had an excellent medical library, staffed by a white-haired woman in her sixties who personified medical and scientific research. She eagerly helped Liz refresh on the latest data and published work on DID.

She spent the afternoon reading a fascinating paper released in July 2016 by the *Harvard Review of Psychiatry*. She spent three hours reading, digesting, and indexing eleven other research papers before returning to the July 2016 abstract. The friendly librarian made copies of all twelve publications. But as was her lifelong habit, she made notes in her lab book to organize her thoughts for the report she would give to Judge Rachlyn.

1. DID = Complex. Posttraumatic. Widely accepted and treatable developmental disorder.
2. If not targeted in treatment, will not resolve.
3. Vigorous dissemination of knowledge base warranted.
4. DID patients benefit from psychotherapy.
5. Essential to addresses trauma and dissociation in accordance with expert consensus guidelines.
6. Scientific scholars and treating psychiatrists found documentation of early signs of dissociation in childhood records of more than six men imprisoned for murder—all assessed and diagnosed with DID in reputable research studies—All men were unaware of having DID.
7. Signs and symptoms of early dissociation included in imprisoned men include hearing voices (100%), having vivid imaginary companions (100%), amnesia (50%), and trance states (34%).
8. Evidence of severe childhood abuse detailed in medical, school, police, and child welfare records in 58%–100% of DID cases. Studies indicate that dissociative symptoms plus history of severe childhood trauma are present years before DID is suspected or diagnosed.

9. Research confirms approximately 1% of general US population suffers from DID, mostly undertreated and underrecognized.
10. Science based, evidence based, fact-based conclusion = DID is a legitimate and distinct psychiatric disorder recognized worldwide. Can be reliably identified in multiple settings. Trauma-based disorder—generally responds well to treatment consistent with DID treatment guidelines.

Liz gathered her copies of the research studies and her notes before asking the librarian whether there was data on the relationship between DID patients and criminal justice studies. Understandably, the medical librarian gave her a quizzical look.

"Goodness no," she said. "We take in shooting victims and shooters. We treat bank officers and bank robbers. But we don't have any books or research papers on crimes and medicine. Try the law library at the University of Maine, it's not far from here—over on Deering Avenue, I think. Of course, I've never been there, law and science don't mix well, ya know."

Liz spent the rest of the afternoon in a law library that dwarfed the hospital's library. It seemed to support row after row of shelving dedicated to law, legal education, and lawyering. After scanning shelved volumes for a few minutes on her own, she made the right choice. To know about law, ask a law librarian. The young man at the front desk turned out to be every bit as helpful as was the hospital librarian. He showed her to a computer in a small carrel, used his credentials card to fire it up, and quickly found a list of papers, including law review articles on using medicine and science in defense of criminal charges.

She spent a half-hour tabbing her way through articles and case abstracts that vaguely discussed medical defenses in criminal cases. None made sense to her, much less were helpful in connecting DID as a medical diagnosis with criminal charges.

As she was thinking about powering down the computer, the young librarian came to the carrel.

"Hey, guess what?" he said, smiling. "I found a case for you. I printed it out. The cite is *Orndorff v. Commonwealth*. It came down in 2010 from the Supreme Court of Virginia. It seems on point, although I really didn't understand what you're looking for. Anyhow, this one's about a woman who killed her husband and tried to defend the murder case because she had that thing you told me about, you know, dissociated identity disease."

Liz smiled thinking maybe the man was on the right path. Disorder? Disease? Is one legal and the other not? The facts were interesting. The couple had been married for ten years before it unraveled. There was evidence confirming her state of mind. She told her mother-in-law she "would see him dead before he left her for another woman." That turned out to be the case. Murder won out over divorce. The jury found her guilty.

The case didn't seem to help or harm the medical assessment she was trying to make. But the defense had put on some evidence that the defendant's mental state deteriorated in jail. The trial judge doubted that she could properly participate in the sentencing phase of the trial and ordered a competency evaluation. That resulted in a finding she was not competent and was committed to a state hospital for eight months.

Liz got very excited when she read that while in hospital, the poor woman was found to have an increasing number of *alter personalities*, who manifested themselves to various doctors and nurses in the hospital. She was diagnosed with DID. But other doctors consulted by the prosecution disagreed. Eventually, a jury found her competent. She went to prison.

Courts rarely accepted the medical notion that a criminal act was committed by a *destructive alter* of a defendant who was the dominant personality. Her research confirmed there was currently no consensus within the legal system as to the extent to which individuals with DID can or should be held responsible for their actions.

Liz knew she would have no influence on whether Judge Rachlyn accepted or rejected DID as a defense to murder charges. And she knew it was not her job to make that case. As she understood her mandate, it was to advise the court on competency grounds. Perhaps her advice would be good news for Mr. Tutt and bad news for Ms. Persuanoli. She decided not to contact either and focus on writing a coherent report for the judge. She thought competency was a medical issue, and the legal consequences of that were not on her plate.

She spent the next three days in thirty-minute meetings with Arthur in her temp office. He continued to duck and dodge but in a way that convinced her that neither of them, could clearly, no-doubt-about-it identify him as a single, dominant personality. At the end of their fourth consultation, she told him she'd be writing a report over the weekend for the court. He didn't seem to care, one way or the other.

She felt conflicted by the assignment. In the medical world, competency was simple. Patients were often confused or unable to make a coherent decision about medical treatment or understand medical advice. She had treated patients with mental disabilities that made it nearly impossible for them to make reasonable decisions about their own diagnosis or appropriate treatment. Still, in medicine the underlying premise is that all patients make reasoned decisions unless they clearly show they could not. Psychiatrists tested patients ability to assess capacity. If in doubt, they fell back on advance directives, surrogate decision making, guardianship, and implied consent. She believed the defendant she had spent five consecutive days with was Arthur Cheshire, but she was equally confident that he was unsure who he was. He presented clear DID markers.

She typed her fanciful title and centered it on the first draft page of her report.

Arthur Cheshire Is Who He Says He Is—From
One Day to Another

As she read it on her computer, it hit her that competency is not a medical issue in the sense that medical skills, treatment, or medical judgment is. She switched from Word to a browser and searched the word, "competence." In a matter of minutes, she discovered that competence is far more important in the legal world she had thought.

Lawyers and legal scholars used analogy and language choices to move from plain garden-variety competence to legal competence. The latter, she learned, is twofold. First, can a person make and communicate a decision to consent to either legal advice or medical treatment? The browser offered a variety of sites to evaluate competence. It is central, said one website, to determining consent and reflects the law's concern with individual autonomy. A person's decision about medical treatment must be respected when that person is competent to make that decision. Conversely, if a person is not competent to give informed consent, it is necessary to employ an alternative decision-making process, such as the use of a proxy, to determine whether treatment should be provided.

After skimming through the complexities of legal competence online, she called Lee, remembering that Lee was an FBI agent, but also a lawyer. Lee told her that lawyers assessed the client's competence to make legal decisions and assist in their own defense easily. They assumed competence and never treated clients as incompetent merely because they acted or spoke in ways that were out of step with their families or their community expectations.

Liz often used two tests for mental status: the *Mini-Mental Status Examination* and the *MacArthur Competence Assessment Test*. During her next to last visit with Arthur, she tried the MacArthur test to no avail. It was an assessment tool designed to test a patient's capacity to make treatment decisions. Since she wasn't treating him, the tool was useless.

On her last visit with the defendant, she used the *Mini-Mental State Examination*, sometimes called the *Folstein* test. It measures cognitive impairment. It worked on Arthur. A side benefit of the test measures severity and progression of cognitive impairment. Arthur was off the charts. While it wasn't a diagnosis, it capsulized Arthur's belief system. He was precisely what he thought he was—Arthur sometimes, Martin sometimes, and seemingly transferable without thought or motive.

Lee had told her that American common law presumed adults were competent and minors incompetent. Since Arthur often acted like and talked like a child, both presumptions seemed applicable. Competence was assumed if an adult understood his surroundings and could explain what and who he was. Arthur could do neither, without reference to his brother. For Liz, this meant that Arthur must be incompetent because he had no understanding of who he was unless his brother told him who he was. And that varied depending on which brother he believed he was at any given moment.

The other issue she built into her report was Arthur's obvious inability to communicate with her, or on the witness stand in court, not to mention with Slo or likely with his own lawyer. She discovered on legal research sites, like Lexis-Nexis Advance, that criminal defendants can be declared incompetent to stand trial solely because they lacked the ability to communicate a decision, make one with assurance, or understand what their lawyers said. In one famous case, a criminal defendant with "locked-in" syndrome was found incompetent because of his apparent lack of ability to interact with the outside world. Arthur was not that far off center, but he was more than one bubble off plumb.

Lee had sent her a short list of legal cases where judges argued there should be a greater level of competence required of people when they make high-risk decisions. Others stated that greater competence is not required but rather admissible and reliable evidence of competence. There is the legal danger that requiring greater evidence in high-risk cases may discriminate against people who make unusual decisions, as only they will be subjected to greater scrutiny. That's problematic in most courts, at least in urban communities. Rural courts seemed more prone to accept competence rather than prolong cases.

At the end of her research slog through the legal world, she found a quote that resonated with her role as a psychiatrist reporting to a judge on what she now knew was more legal than medical. In the famous Sirhan B. Sirhan trial in Los Angles in the late sixties, the prosecutor said, "I think the law became an ass the day it let psychiatrists get their hands on the law."

Her four-page report was succinct and to the point. The final paragraph was as definitive as it was ominous.

Defining competence is both a legal challenge and a psychiatric conundrum. Its existence in this case depends largely on assessing whether the defendant has sufficient present ability to consult with his lawyer, Mr. Tutt, with a reasonable degree of rational understanding. From a mental health perspective, his competence depends on whether he has a factual understanding of the proceedings against him. Based on five consultation sessions, I do not believe he understands who he is except in the context of his unique mental and historical relationship with his identical twin brother. I am fearful that his fixation on living as, protecting, and communicating with his deceased brother is evidence of a severe case of *dissociative identify disorder* as defined in the widely recognized standard under the *Diagnostic and Statistical Manual of Mental Disorders* (DSM-5TR). I cannot diagnose the defendant as having DID, but I cannot rule it out without a prolonged period of study, evaluation, and treatment. DID is treatable. I also believe his brother is dead. If so, the legal question is, whether Arthur or his alter is treated, no one will know whether he committed the murders or his alter personality did. One or the other is innocent of premeditated murder.

Dr. Socorro hand-delivered her report in a sealed envelope to Judge Rachlyn's chambers on a Friday morning. Judge Rachlyn read it, digitized it, and sent it via email to the lawyers. Then, she ordered a status hearing for the following Friday. That gave the parties ample time to absorb the shock. As she read the report a second time, slower this time, she spilled a half-cup of coffee on her desk. Then she buzzed her secretary and asked her to summon her law clerks toot suite. Everyone in her chambers knew what that meant—bad news.

"Come in, come in," she said as they stood in the open doorway. "I need you to drop what you're doing and help me fathom this four-page chainsaw it might indefinitely delay trial in three serial murder cases."

As they grabbed chairs at the six-person conference table, she took her seat at the head.

"I don't know whether God has intervened, or the Devil has filed an amicus brief, but I need your legal skills and maybe psychiatric inclinations. You can read the report after I tell you what just happened."

Judge Rachlyn spent five minutes explaining DID, legal competency, and the derailment of an important criminal case that had come off the rails and seemed headed into a swirl of either brilliance, madness, or maybe parricide.

"Parricide? Not sure what that is, Judge. It means killing a parent, right?"

"Yes, but it also applies to close relatives, like monozygotic twins in an environment where the death of one of them went unrecorded, uninvestigated, and probably accidental. To turn it into a total legal conundrum, it's unclear which twin died and whether the other knows about it. The consequences may have led to a bizarre mental illness known as DID, or dissociative identity disorder. So, log onto LexisNexis or WestLaw and let me know what you find. Oh, and read Dr. Socorro's report and let's talk Monday morning. Okay? I'm sending it to counsel and will schedule a status hearing week after next."

Letty Persuanoli reacted in a way no one could have predicted. She read Dr. Socorro's report as factually accurate, legally sound, and supportive of both sides. She asked her secretary to send the report to the full team, schedule a quick meeting, and then schedule a thirty-minute telephone call to Mr. Tutt.

The team gathered in the same conference room they'd been in a few weeks earlier. Stanford Crane, US Attorney for Maine, Ray Gonzales, on loan from JMD, and Dr. Chance Honoliptz, a psychology professor from Bowdoin College, met over coffee and donuts to hear her assessment of what was being called the DID Defense.

"Well, this report is riddled with wild-ass guesses, don't you think?" Letty's boss said.

"No, Stan," Letty said. "I agree with her. If you'd been with us in Judge Rachlyn's courtroom three weeks ago, you would have been shaking your head just like all of us were. The defendant was so unbalanced that I'm surprised he didn't froth at the mouth as he snapped at whoever asked him a question about his brother. It got so weird that I thought he was the twin whose body was found in a fishing shack in Mexico—Martin Cheshire. Remember, we first charged the man we now believe is Arthur Cheshire under the name Martin Cheshire. Then we switched to the live twin, Arthur, and charged him with a crime that we later discovered was committed by Martin before he died. Then we arrested Arthur here in Portland, up by Jones Point, and he said he was Martin. The family game was to play Hide and Seek, only they called it Hide and Be. Dr. Socorro is the only person who could affirmatively and correctly identify the defendant as Arthur Cheshire, not Martin Chershire as he now claims to be. She did that to the complete satisfaction of the court, who was so impressed, she asked her to take it one step further, to assess Arthur's competence to stand trial. Now we have a written, thoughtful, well-researched report that confirms what we all thought at the evidentiary hearing. The defendant is Arthur and, in the vernacular, he's crazy as a hoot owl. He doesn't know who he is. He is most likely a victim, excuse me, a patient afflicted with that rare but well documented disorder they call DID."

"So, Letty," Stanford Crane said, "what's your plan from here, declare victory and stay prosecution?"

"Exactly, boss. The victory is identifying the defendant. The consequence is, because we're sure he committed three murders, that he will be off the street, in a secure facility, wearing a strait jacket. That's not going to sit well with the victim's families, but even so, there's some solace we can give them. We caught the guy that did the crime. He's locked up, not in prison, but still locked up."

"Well," Dr. Honoliptz, interrupted, "I have to say I was underwhelmed by a four-page report that, based on four thirty-minute interviews, comes to a conclusion that the defendant is afflicted with a disorder that is not only difficult to make, but that is still widely mistrusted in mental health circles."

"Thanks, doctor. But unless I'm completely off base here, I think you would have come to the same conclusion if you had the extended knowledge Dr. Socorro has. She met Arthur a year ago in a different court setting in California. She was appointed by that judge to do the same thing our judge here in Maine did—identify the defendant by name. That experience led to the FBI's use of her as a consultant looking for a serial killer here in New England. Again, she identified Arthur Cheshire as what the FBI calls an Unsub. Then to cap it all off, she is ordered by a federal judge to take the next giant step: opine on competency to stand trial. She finds he's incompetent, based on a mental disorder that is treatable. You wanna know why I take that as good news?"

"Good news? You think it's good news?"

"I do. We're barely at the charging stage in this case. But for Dr. Socorro's involvement, we'd be working up a very complicated pre-trial in three cases for a few years. Then, when some smart defense lawyer got inside, he or she would do what Eppy Tutt did, call for a competency work up. Maybe after a trial, upending the whole thing! So yes, her report is good because it will be tested. Probably in a federal institution. By psychiatrists who know the ground—competency—better than Dr. Socorro does. If she's right and his disorder is treatable, then, however long that takes, we can move forward to trial. The victims will get their day in court, justice will be served, and the risk of mistrial or appellate relief is gone. Call me idealistic, but I think ensuring competency is a good thing, for both sides of this case."

The parties arrived early to court for the nine o'clock hearing on Friday. The optics were obviously different. Earlier hearings in *US v. Arthur Cheshire* had not attracted any media attention, the benches were nearly vacant behind the rail, and there was no sense of heightened drama of any kind. But this Friday-morning hearing looked like a media circus ten minutes before the judge got there.

Photography of any kind is not allowed in federal court rooms, so the dozens of media reps in the room stowed their cameras and audio recorders. Print reporters and court groupies filled almost all ten rows of hardwood benches. The unexpected attention was generated by a leak to the local AP staff, who leaked it to the print media. It didn't go viral, but social media outlets poked CNN. Tweets soon followed: ***Serial killer claims dissociative identity disorder***; ***Three faces of Eve in three serial murder cases***; ***Portland court considers twin brother suspect as killer of other twin brothers on their twin birthdays!***

The chairs inside the rail behind the prosecution table were filled by stern-faced FBI agents. The chairs behind the defense table were filled by investigators and backup counsel from the Federal Public Defender's Office. But there were no crime victims in sight. The room bustled when Slo came in, arm linked with Arthur Cheshire who sported Cumberland County Jail grey pants and top-buttoned shirt. Noticeably, he had shaved all the hair off his head. He smiled at the crowd as Slo frog-walked him to the defense table and turned him over to Eppy Tutt.

"Be seated, please," Judge Rachlyn said as she took the bench, clicked on her computer, and arranged her three-ring binder on her desk.

Looking up and past the empty podium, she said, "And good morning to our media press and other visitors. I'll remind you that cameras and recording devices cannot be used and that rustling about and talking is disruptive. Now, for the benefit of counsel and Mr. Cheshire, let the record reflect that this hearing is limited to a brief discussion of next steps that both parties think appropriate given the report filed by Dr. Elisbeth Socorro, whom the record will reflect is present in court. Now,

I have questions for both parties. Ms. Persuanoli, I'll start with you. Do you accept the factual findings in Dr. Socorro's report?"

Letty stood, walked to the podium, held onto it on both sides, inhaled, and locked eyes with the judge.

"May it please the court, Your Honor. The government has carefully reviewed Dr. Socorro's report and shared it internally. We accept Dr. Socorro's basic position, but would reserve judgment on next steps, pending what defense counsel has to say on the matter. As we read it, Dr. Socorro is confident that the defendant, Arthur Cheshire, suffers from a mental illness, which may or may not be DID, as defined in the *Diagnostic and Statistical Manual of Mental Disorders*. We accept that Dr. Socorro did not diagnose Mr. Cheshire as a DID patient, and we agree and accept her finding that, to quote her, Mr. Cheshire 'does not understand who he is except in the context of his unique mental and historical relationship with his identical twin brother.' We agree that DID needs to be ruled in or out by the medical community before we will be able to try him. But we have grave doubt about Dr. Socorro's suggestion that DID might be a defense in a criminal trial for pending first-degree murder cases. With respect, Your Honor, there is no question before you, as also suggested by Dr. Socorro, that Arthur Cheshire may not have been the dominant personality, but rather an *alternative personality* state. Now, Your Honor, the government moves the court to reject the expert's suggestion in this regard, and . . ."

Holding her hand up, Judge Rachlyn said, "Motion denied. But please continue, Ms. Persuanoli."

"Yes, Your Honor. I should not have said 'I move.' I should have said it is not up to medical consultants to suggest a diagnosis. Dr. Socorro is a highly regarded physician and has proved to be a valuable resource to this court. However, it is not her function to define legal competence to stand trial. Both sides are acutely aware of the conundrum we face; does Mr. Arthur

Cheshire *have enough present* ability to consult with his lawyer and assist in his defense? I've talked to Dr. Socorro. She said she does not believe he understands who he is except in the context of his unique mental and historical relationship with his identical twin brother. She found him fixated on living as, protecting, and communicating with his deceased brother. That led her to opine that he is severely impaired. He has, she believes, a dissociative identity disorder. But she also said she could neither diagnose him nor rule it out without a prolonged period of study, evaluation, and treatment. She told the court that DID is *treatable*. The government agrees. But we do not agree that he presented to this court as a personality state on the witness stand or as an alternative personality state, called an 'alter.'"

Turning to the defense table, Judge Rachlyn asked Mr. Tutt to take the podium. "Mr. Tutt, I find that your client is incompetent to stand trial. I will abate the criminal cases pending diagnosis and treatment of your client to restore him to legal competency. Now, I do not want you to tell us anything that might invade your client's right to confidentiality regarding communications with counsel, but can you say whether your client will agree to abating the criminal case and commencing a psychiatric assessment and treatment? Of course, he will remain in custody because the criminal charges are not dropped. They would just be abated pending medical status."

Eppy Tutt stood up, took three steps to the podium, and faced the bench. "Your Honor, I will talk to my client about abatement and medical treatment. But as the court knows, I am constrained to some extent by the fact that the government, the court, and the court's highly qualified expert all agree he is impaired. Our ethical rules apply here. Ethical Rule 1.14 says, and I quote, 'When a client's capacity to make adequately considered decisions in connection with a representation is diminished by mental impairment, the lawyer shall, as far as possible, maintain a normal client-lawyer relationship with the client,' end quote. I will talk to my client today, as soon as this hearing is adjourned. And I will promptly advise the court concerning Dr. Socorro's evaluation, the government's position, and the Court's ruling. But on the record, I should also note that communicating with my client is challenged by who he thinks he is. As the record reflects, sometimes he's Arthur and other times he's Martin. I think our ethical rules allow me to treat him as a client without assuming which twin brother he thinks he is. That's what the rule means when it says I should maintain a normal client-lawyer relationship."

"Thank you, Mr. Tutt, and you too, Ms. Persuanoli. The court's findings and rulings will be restated in a written order by the close of business today. Court is adjourned."

As the lawyers packed their brief cases, two reporters approached the defendant from behind the court railing. The short one had the loudest voice.

"Mr. Cheshire, how do feel about yourself now that the murder cases have been abated? And are you Arthur or are you Martin Cheshire?

Arthur turned toward the man holding up a cell phone camera in his direction.

"I don't want to talk to you."

"Okay, that's okay. Hey, Mr. Tutt, what do you feel about winning this case, at least so far? How long will it take for the defendant to get over whatever thing he has about his identity? Is that even a defense—multiple personality disorder?"

Eppy smiled but did not answer the reporter's question. Seconds later, Slo came back into the pit of the courtroom and put Arthur's handcuffs back on. The short reporter thumbed his iPhone and hustled out of the courtroom like a bird dog on the hunt.

Back at the Cumberland County Jail, Eppy asked to see Slo at the front desk. They'd come to an agreement about trying to schedule the defendant for legal consultation. All Slo wanted was a carton of cigarettes a week to make sure the prisoner would be more or less instantly produced in one of the legal consult rooms. Eppy agreed but told Slo a carton a week was too much smoking. Slo said he didn't smoke. He sold cigs in the chow hall to needy prisoners and gave cigs free to staff schedulers.

By the time he passed the two metal detectors between the sidewalk and the legal consult room, Slo was already there with his prisoner in tow. Both were smiling.

"Good morning, Arthur, and good morning to you too, Slo. It's going to be a cool day in the bay, they say."

"Can't see the bay," Arthur said. "When can I go see the bay, Eppy? That's what Slo told me to call you, Eppy. He says the suits all call you that. What's it mean, Eppy?"

Eppy arranged his papers on the steel-topped table, his clickable ballpoint pen, and his yellow legal pad close at hand. Forcing a smile at his client's clenched-jaw look, he answered the question.

"Arthur, Eppy is short for Ephraim, my first name. My folks called me that, and somehow it stuck with me. Actually, I like it better than my birth name because it makes people laugh. But we have serious things to talk about now, Arthur. The judge has ruled in your favor. All the criminal charges against you are going to be legally abated. And . . ."

"What's abated?" Arthur asked, moving his lower jar from side to side as though it were a tic.

"Abated, in law, means that the court has halted your case from going forward for the time being. Instead of facing trial and continued incarceration here in jail, you are going to be transferred to a hospital, a special hospital . . ."

"What for?" Arthur asked as he leaned back in the straight back chair and rocked back and forth like it was a rocking chair.

"Well, Arthur, the judge has decided that you are not competent to stand trial and cannot assist me in defending you. So, under the US Constitution and the laws of Maine you cannot be prosecuted until you have been returned to full competency and can assist your lawyer on the charges against you. Do you understand that?"

"You talking about me or Arthur?"

"Yes, Arthur, I'm talking about you. Let me explain. The judge also found as a matter of law that your true identity is Arthur Cheshire, but that due to a mental impairment, you are unsure of your own identity, even though it's been proved in court by fingerprints and witness identification. You remember being in court last week, when Dr. Socorro, the lady psychiatrist . . . ?"

"Yeah, I remember her from San Diego, and she took off her white coat once. I remember that."

"Arthur, that's wonderful that you remember that far back. Now let me . . ."

"I remember it because Arthur told me all about it, just yesterday, I think, or maybe another day. Are you saying I don't remember or that we both are going to be in a hospital, what exactly?"

"No, Arthur, I mean that you will be treated in the hospital by doctors to help you. You will be in therapy and there are medications that can help you think more clearly and understand things . . ."

"Like what? What things?"

"Well, I'm glad you asked. Here's one thing. At different times, you've identified yourself as Arthur and Martin. For example, when your case in San Diego started, the FBI and the US attorney said you were Martin Cheshire, but you insisted you were Arthur, and . . ."

"Hide and Be, Eppy. Hide and Be. But it was for real, not just our game, you know. I was Arthur and the judge said so and . . ."

Eppy quit taking notes and smiled.

"That's absolutely right, Arthur. The court out there in California identified you as Arthur and so did the judge here in Maine. You are Arthur Cheshire. But when they arrested you up at Jones Point, you said you were Martin. And at times you say things like Arthur talked to you in your jail cell, or other places. There is a mental disorder that afflicts people. It's called dissociative identity disorder. Do you remember the testimony in court about that last week?

"Yeah. I remember. They were saying I was nuts, right? They think Arthur and I are fooling everybody with our Hide and Be game, don't they? That's why they are after me for what he did."

"Arthur, when you say *he*, you mean your twin brother, don't you?"

Arthur asked if he could have one of those cigarettes that I had given to Slo. Eppy told him he should ask Slo. Then he repeated his last question.

Arthur said, "Hey, Eppy man, you're my lawyer, no matter who you think I am, right? I have this jail uniform on, I live in a jail cell here—well, not here—but over there by the bay in the Cumberland Jail. You and everybody else get confused about us. You can't tell which one of us is talking, can you? Well, just you listen for one last time. We are who we say we are."

PORTLAND, MAINE, INTERNATIONAL JETPORT

Brick was waiting in his rental car while Liz checked out of her room at the Hilton Garden Inn. They drove to the airport making small talk about the continuous rain in Portland and the lack of it in San Diego. She had a three-hour wait due to a last-minute weather delay on takeoffs. So, she offered to buy him a beer inside the terminal at the Portland International Jetport.

The waitress brought a bottle of Bud Light to him and a latte to her. Brick knew Liz had something serious on her mind, but she seemed reluctant to talk about whatever it was. After talking about left coast politics and right coast rigidity, she tapped her plastic spoon on the table.

"Brick, you are a perfect gentleman, and I only wish there was more time for us. Do you know what I'm talking about?"

"Liz, I've been living alone for more than ten years. My wife died. Your husband died. But somehow, we managed to work for three months together without getting personal. Is that the way you want to leave it? Just the facts, Ma'am? Nothing personal?"

Liz leaned back in the plastic chair and nodded slowly. Then, she pointed to the bottle of Bud Light in front of him.

"Brick, you're Bud Light and I'm espresso tall. We love different oceans and enjoy different climes. But I've seen your dedication to your job. I know you're a patient man who likes to fish. I'm impatient and like to read. We live in complicated worlds which neither would give up, right? How about this? Let's give ourselves a few months. I'll call you. How does that sound?"

"Liz, you know I'm twenty years older than you. So, letting my line swirl on top of the river for a few months sounds just fine to me. I know there's something else you have on your mind, don't you?"

"Brick, you've talked to all three families now, haven't you?"

"Yeah, I thought that's the least I could do. They seemed almost relieved to know that there won't be a trial for the man that murdered their sons. They were so glad we caught him but dreaded a trial. They want justice but you know New Englanders, they are private and keep things to themselves."

"Would you say, Brick, that New Englanders are *just* people, I mean in terms of criminal justice? Do they want the death penalty for Arthur Cheshire? Do they understand how sick he is and how unable he is to identify himself, much less his dead twin brother?"

"Well, I used the last hearing transcript to explain to the families what was going on now—you know, the competency hearing and the judge's decision to abate the trials until Mr. Cheshire is legally competent to stand trial."

"That was a good idea on your part, Brick. But what I'm wondering is whether the families know anything about *restorative justice*. Do you? Is that something you've had any experience with?"

"All I know about that is from a seminar I attended years ago. It was sort of a cultural movement, wasn't it?"

"No, it's a policy movement that approaches criminal justice very differently than the stark reality of crime, conviction, and punishment. You know how it works better than most. You investigate, identify, and arrest. Then the government prosecutes, and the judicial system holds trials. Then, if convicted, the defendants are sentenced to prison and sometimes death. But, under restorative justice principles, the goal is to treat the process differently. It connects convicted felons with families and crime victims. Collectively, they approach justice from a restorative view rather than just punishment. The criminal and his victim share their experience. Hopefully, if it works as intended, they focus on what the offender can do to repair the harm from the offense. Sometimes, the convicted criminal pays money to the victim's family. There are apologies. The long-term goal of restorative justice is to prevent the offender from causing future harm."

"Well, Liz, that's all well and good, but prison does that, doesn't it?"

"Yes, if the prisoner is doing life, it does. But restorative justice aims further out than a prison term. It is a justice reform movement. Honestly, I don't think it is useful in murder cases, but it seems to have caught hold in open-minded places like California. There the conversation is about moving away from a purely punitive criminal legal system and closer to healing and well-being. It's seeking a restorative path forward."

Brick shifted in his chair uncomfortably but nodded his head.

"I'm core FBI, but we all know doing time in prison doesn't modify criminal behavior. It does not cut down on repeat offenders. Most convicted criminals are not interested in healing or well-being. And crime victims want harsh punitive measures, not hand holding."

"Yes, you're defining America's criminal justice system to a T. But in some states, the restorative justice project is making a difference. In fact, it's happening now, here in Maine. I looked it up last night on Google. And I printed something from their website at the business center in the hotel. Let me read it to you."

Liz opened her briefcase and took out a yellow piece of copy paper and started reading.

> Restorative Justice Project Maine (RJP Maine) was founded in 2005 to offer responses to crime and wrong-doing that are grounded in restorative principles. Our Mission: to promote a justice that is community-based, repairs harm, and creates safety and wellbeing for all. RJP Maine is a nonprofit organization that promotes fundamental change in communities, schools, and institutions, and the justice system. Our responses to crime and wrongdoing seek renewal and safety for the community, support and healing for victims, and accountability and reintegration of the offender.

"So, Liz," Brick said, "are you saying that Arthur Cheshire ought to meet with the families and together they could support one another and bring healing? Really?"

"No, not at all, Brick. What I'm saying is that Arthur Cheshire is himself a wounded, deeply troubled man. He lost his twin brother. He thinks he killed him. And I suspect no one will ever know whether Arthur knew what he did back when he and Martin had that terrible boating accident on the Dramiscotta River. But I think that traumatic event might be the explanation for what happened. Those boys could not live without one another. Their defense against the world was a game they called Hide and Be. If one did something wrong, the other took the blame. They played it in early childhood. They played it as teenagers, and they played it in their mid-twenties. And, I think, they played it here, without realizing it was no longer a game. It became the terrible reality psychiatrists now call dissociative identify disorder."

"Liz, you're probably right. We all saw him in court. He is not right in the brain. He really doesn't know who he is. But what's that got to do with criminal justice?"

"It has everything to do with criminal justice. You cannot try a man who cannot assist in his own defense and who believes, even if it is based on a mental disorder, he didn't do it. In this case, a sentient human being killed three innocent young men in three different states. New Hampshire, Massachusetts, and Vermont. By states I mean, of course, *political* states. Now, turn your mind to *personality* states. If a man is afflicted with DID, he moves in and out of mental states. We call them the dominant personality state and an alternative state. Or, in therapy sessions we shorten it to the *person* and his *alter*."

Brick took the last sip of his beer and checked his watch.

"Okay, Liz, but the US Attorney said the DID defense in a homicide case has been constantly rejected by the courts. Where are you going with this? We both believe Arthur Cheshire committed all three murders. Even if he has DID, it's no defense."

"You're right and so is Letty. But just assume for a moment that Arthur committed those three murders while in his alternative state of mind—assume in that state he was his brother, Martin. In that state he no longer has to face his brother's death because he *is* his brother, Martin. That's no defense in court but it is a product of his mental illness. His therapist in the state mental hospital will work with him to understand his trauma and a possible resolution of it. If therapy works, he might be able to accept the true fact—his brother died in a horrible accident, and he was not the cause of the accident. It's possible he could, with medication, live untroubled by moving from one dominant personality state to an alternative state. The crime is not forgiven but the consequence is treatment, not imprisonment. That's an example of restorative justice, at least for Arthur. He's restored to mental health."

Brick checked his watch again.

"You've got thirty-two minutes to get to the gate but it's only about fifty feet from here. So, tell me how restorative justice might help the crime victims."

"I don't know because I don't know them. But all three families had identical twins and would surely understand the bond, the brotherhood, and the sameness that comes from twinness. They might want Arthur punished if they thought he was mentally fit. But if they accept his DID diagnosis and think about the trauma that Arthur and Martin faced as children, they might see the awful reality of what emotional trauma wounding can lead to. In this case, Martin's actual death was Arthur's psychological death. So, he became his brother and punished other twins who didn't seem to need their twins in young adulthood. Remember, he only killed on the twin's birthdays and then only because the twins didn't celebrate the day together. He could never celebrate his birthday with his own twin, so he punished those who could but chose not to. Does that make any sense?"

"Yes, in a rational way. But murder and the death penalty are not rational—they are irrational products of an evil mind, or at least a diseased one. I'll say this. I've seen hundreds of criminals that were mentally unfit. And in a few cases, the criminal harmed those he loved. So, both needed justice and both needed healing. It took a few years for me to absorb that knot in the criminal justice system. I know justice is not just for victims."

"So," Liz said softly, "what about *Justice for All?* Shouldn't it include the perpetrator as well as the victim? You've helped me balance the scales a little. Therapeutically, the ultimate penalty is their just reward. But for wounded killers, maybe life in prison is their just due. Restorative justice is a balancing act. We all need rehabbing once in a while. Cops, robbers, bankers, murderers, and doctors—we all must pay for what we do wrong and get paid when we do it right. If that works for Arthur and the three families who lost their twins, I'm all for it."

The End

ABOUT THE AUTHOR

I am a retiring lawyer, a working author, and a preserving blogger. I was a full-time trial lawyer for thirty-two years in a large Phoenix firm. I was a part-time law professor for the last twenty-nine years. As of summer, 2023, I am writing, publishing, and blogging full time. My first book was a textbook published by the Arizona State Bar Association. My first novel was published by the University of New Mexico Press. I've written ten novels and eight nonfiction titles as of July 2023.

From the day I entered law school, I've been reading cases, statutory law and writing about legal conundrums and flaws in our criminal and civil justice systems. I've always read novels, nonfiction, and historical fiction by great authors who were never corrupted by the staid habits of trial lawyers. I write long-form, interspersed with the occasional blog, op-ed, or essay. One of the unexpected benefits of reading the law is learning how to write about it. Somewhere along the trajectory from a baby lawyer to a senior one, I became intoxicated with blending nonfiction with fiction in books, rather than legal documents. After spending thirty years in courtrooms trying cases, I started writing about them. That led to writing novels while borrowing from famous historical settings and lesser-known characters. My courtroom days were chock full of ideas, notions, and hopes about ultimately becoming an author. I organized and memorized critical information for judges, juries, and clients. Now I use that experience to write vivid fiction and immersive nonfiction. I moved away from trial practice to teaching law students how to use creative writing techniques to tell their client's stories, in short form.

F. Scott Fitzgerald said, "All good writing is swimming under water and holding your breath." The same could be said of my transition from trying cases to writing crime fiction. I've been holding my breath for twenty years waiting for galley proofs and book reviews. Anais Nin spoke for all of us when she said, "We write to taste life twice."

My first novel, *The Gallup 14*, won a coveted starred review from *Publishers Weekly*. I won a Spur Award from *Western Writers of America* in 2004 for my first nonfiction book ("*Miranda, The Story of America's Right to Remain Silent*"). I won the 2010 Arizona Book of the Year Award, The Glyph Award, and a Southwest Publishing Top Twenty award in 2010, for "*Innocent Until Interrogated—The Story of the Buddhist Temple Massacre*." My third nonfiction title ("*Anatomy of a Confession—The Debra Milke Case*") was highly acclaimed. My nonfiction title "*CALL HIM MAC—Ernest W. McFarland—The Arizona Years*" was widely and favorably reviewed. My latest nonfiction crime book, "*Nobody Did Anything Wrong But Me*, was published by *Twelve Tables Press*, one of America's most distinguished publisher of law books about important legal issues. No New York Times bestsellers, yet.

www.ingramcontent.com/pod-product-compliance
Lightning Source LLC
Chambersburg PA
CBHW061654190726
48289CB00006B/1875